THE AMERICAN COUNTESS

Linda Bennett Pennell

Black Rose Writing | Texas

First printing

ISBN: 978-1-68513-323-8
PUBLISHED BY BLACK ROSE WRITING
www.blackrosewriting.com

Printed in the United States of America
Suggested Retail Price (SRP) $23.95

The American Countess is printed in Sagona Book

*As a planet-friendly publisher, Black Rose Writing does its best to eliminate unnecessary waste to reduce paper usage and energy costs, while never compromising the reading experience. As a result, the final word count vs. page count may not meet common expectations.

THE AMERICAN COUNTESS

CHAPTER 1

York, England
August 1913

Lady Kilnsey, the former India Elisabeth Petra de Vries Ledbetter of The Falls, Pisgah, North Carolina and Washington Square, New York City, stepped onto Deangate's cobblestones and closed the shop door, setting its little bell tinkling. Placing a hand over her eyes, she looked toward York Minster. Its spires beckoned her to a place of peace and grace. Having just committed enormous sums for bathroom, kitchen, and central heating fittings for the entire castle, a moment's quiet reflection seemed in order.

She glanced at Althea, her lady's maid and friend, the only other American residing in Kilnsey Castle. "I fear these renovations may be far messier than getting the electricity installed. Two years later and the housemaids are still wiping plaster dust from odd corners." Pointing toward the Minster, she continued, "Come. I want to light a candle in memory of Papa and for a little good luck for the renovations."

Althea grinned and gave India "The Look" complete with raised brows. "When His Lordship sees the bill, you may need it."

They were still several blocks from the cathedral when a roar arising from the end of the street caught India's attention. Her eyes narrowed and her mouth became a thin line. Mounted policemen accompanied by others on foot waded into a crowd, the outer rings of which were comprised of men with raised fists, some of them holding rocks or fruit. It was impossible to see what lay at the center of the commotion, but India had her suspicions.

She grabbed Althea's arm. "Come on. I bet my bottom dollar they're harassing our suffragists again." Instead of turning away from the disturbance, she plunged toward it.

Althea yanked her arm from India's grasp. "Oh no you don't. We can't get involved in that. His Lordship and the Dowager would be furious."

India's expression hardened. "I'm going to do what I can. Stay here if you must." India winced inwardly at her tone. Mistress and servant was not the true nature of their relationship.

Althea grimaced, shook her head, but fell into step. India glanced from the corner of her eye. Althea was clearly irritated. Perhaps a reminder was in order.

"When he proposed, Charlie promised not to interfere with my interests." India cast a mischievous grin at Althea. "Furthermore, my mother-in-law needs a little shaking up. She's too set in her ways."

"So, just when are you planning on telling them about your donations and afternoons working in the office of the York Suffragists' Union?"

"When I'm good and ready and not a minute before. A few pounds here and there and an occasional afternoon hardly warrant mentioning. Besides, what they don't know won't hurt them."

As they approached the crowd, India hiked her skirt and stepped up onto the base of a streetlamp for a better view.

What she saw set her pulse racing. Women, whose only crime was asking for what should have been theirs long ago, were being taunted, threatened, and assaulted by the public. Their placards had been snatched from their hands and were being trampled beneath the boots of a crowd of cretins. This simply would not do.

Jumping down from the lamppost, India marched into the gang of men surrounding the women. Jostling increased and objects began to fly.

She tapped a mounted policeman's booted leg and shouted, "What is the meaning of this? Who are these women harming that they should be treated thus? I demand you disperse this crowd immediately."

The policeman's face turned as red as the rotten tomatoes splattered on some of the protesters. He tightened his mount's reins and leaned down with his nose inches from India's face. "Madam, unless you want to be arrested along with these other women, you will leave the area at once. We've had enough of these hussies and harlots."

"Of all the nerve. These women are nothing of the sort. They are only asking for what is rightfully ours."

"Oh, you're one of them, are you?" He sat upright and motioned to a colleague on the ground. "Hey Tommie, this here one wants to join her sisters. Take her along with the others."

"How dare you threaten me? I have done nothing but ask an honest question and demand that you do your job. Your job is to protect citizens, all of us, but it is a responsibility you seem determined to shirk. You, sir, are as lazy as you are stupid and insolent."

Hands grabbed India's upper arms from behind and propelled her over the cobbles. Lurking out of sight around the opposite corner, the open door of a police van greeted them.

India struggled against the policeman's grip. "Let go of me, you stupid oaf. I am Lady Kilnsey, wife of the fifteenth Earl of Kilnsey."

Before she could say more, the officer lifted her bodily from the ground and shoved her into the already packed vehicle. He slammed the door and frowned at her through the bars. "I don't give a tinker's damn if you're the bloody Queen of Sheba. You're going to the nick along with the rest of these blighters. No decent woman would be seen with such rabble."

India glared down at her captor. "My husband will hear of this. Y'all are gonna be in big trouble." India covered her mouth with her hand. Had she really just said y'all and gonna, vestiges of a childhood spent in America's Appalachian Mountains?

The officer snorted then tugged the brim of his helmet, turned, and strolled back toward the now dispersing crowd.

Within the van, women of all ages and classes, some covered with the detritus of rotten fruit, others bleeding, huddled together on rough wooden benches. India squeezed into the spot made for her.

The women, all strangers, watched India with interest as though she might be some rare specimen pinned to a board in a science laboratory. India nodded in the direction of no one in particular, but the acknowledgement was not returned.

Finally, the woman directly opposite bestirred herself. "You are not English, are you?" Her enunciation and vowels revealed she was of the gentry or perhaps a well-educated middle-class matron.

India shook her head. "Not originally. Before my marriage, my home was in North Carolina. That's in the southern United States. I lived in the mountains. They are exquisite and sometimes I miss them very much." Her words tumbled to a halt. Babbling, a habit she thought she had shed, had returned full force. Her nerves must be wound tighter than she wanted to admit.

"I see." The woman eyed India in speculation. "One of these American heiresses come to save our poor old British aristocracy from ruin, I suppose?"

India's lips thinned. She had no patience for the direction this conversation was taking. She leaned back against the wall and ignored her inquisitor. Within moments, the sound of reins slapping horses' backsides followed by the rumble of the van's wheels brought her upright again.

Gripping the door's iron bars, she searched the road and sidewalks. Word must be gotten to Charlie. She found Althea at the forefront of a small crowd following the van.

"Go straight to the solicitor's office. Tell him to come to the police station at once."

The last thing she saw before the van rounded a corner was Althea's horror-stricken face, her head bobbing up and down in frantic agreement.

CHAPTER 2

Charlie, the English schoolboy patches across his cheeks rosier than usual, glared at India through the gaol cell bars. An older gentleman in morning dress and powered wig stood at Charlie's elbow, glancing nervously at his pocket watch.

"My Lord, I am assisting in a case before the court within the hour and cannot delay further. All the necessary forms have been completed to release Her Ladyship into your custody."

Glancing at India, Charlie's lips thinned as the crease between his eyes deepened. To the solicitor he said, "Thank you, Mitchell. It was most kind of you to see to the maid's lodging and passage home this morning. You will, of course, be reimbursed." Charlie eyed India again with a disgruntled expression. The solicitor cleared his throat, and Charlie returned his attention to the matter at hand. "Is there any way to keep this out of the papers and out of court?"

Mitchell nodded. "I will endeavor to that end. I cannot promise, but a liberal application of . . . ahem . . . cash in the right places is certain to make headway. I believe Your Lordship has friends who are in positions to help, as well. With luck, this unfortunate occurrence need not be made public." He bowed slightly. "Now, I really must be away. My clerk will be available should you need further assistance today."

Charlie turned back to India, crossed his arms over his chest, and frowned. "When I said I would indulge your interests, getting yourself thrown into gaol was not exactly what I had in mind. Do you have any idea how much it will take to keep your little escapade from public knowledge?"

Although she should probably feel at least a little guilty for the trouble she had caused, fury flamed in India. The heat it created crawled upward until her face burned. He spoke to her like she was a contrary child in need of correction. He knew she was interested in the suffragist movement long before he proposed. She would be damned if he would keep her from expressing her rights to free speech and assembly. They were guaranteed by the U.S. Constitution, but then cold reality washed over her. She was now a British subject. Rights on both sides of the Atlantic were guaranteed to men, but less so for women, especially women married to British peers. That knowledge did nothing to dampen the fire raging through her veins.

"If you see speaking out against injustice as an inconvenience, you married the wrong woman. You weren't there. You didn't see what those men were doing to women whose only fault is asking for what should be ours. We pay the same taxes as men; we deserve to vote just as men do."

"While your arguments may be persuasive, they in no way mitigate the potential damage caused by the current situation. Perhaps your time in York gaol has opened your eyes to the consequences of barging in where you shouldn't."

India squinted and hissed, "My night in gaol could have been avoided had you bestirred yourself sooner."

"That is untrue and unfair. You will recall you insisted you would stay in York if your errands kept you past teatime. I was settling into bed by the time I received Mitchell's telegram bearing the glad tidings. Setting out in the auto would have put me in York little sooner than getting some sleep and taking the first express train of the day. As it is, I left for the depot before dawn." Keys rattling drew the attention of both. Charlie stepped aside. "Ah, release is at hand. Thank you, Sergeant. My solicitor will be available to you should you need to contact me further." The gaoler tugged on the cell door, which creaked back on its hinges. Looking at India, Charlie held out his arm. "Shall we?"

She seethed as she placed her hand in the crook of his elbow. He was being his most supercilious, condescending self. Thank goodness this was not his norm. In their almost two years of marriage, he had proven loving, kind, and sensible. Maybe her actions had led to an unintentional violation of propriety, but all she had done was ask questions. It seemed those who disagreed with the status quo were to be silenced at every turn. Between the working poor and the status of women, tradition and conservative policy had well over half the population in a stranglehold. Women must have the vote. If it meant she picked up some dirt in the process, well, just too damned bad.

An icy silence ensued until they were settled in a first-class compartment. India felt Charlie's body relax as the train chugged away from the platform. Sensing his eyes on her, she glanced at him from beneath her lashes, trying to gauge his mood. His expression was solemn, but not particularly angry.

When he realized she was watching him, humor softened his eyes and mouth. "While I'm not amused by your arrest, observing your interaction with the policeman might have been entertaining. I understand you gave him quite the tongue lashing. Was it calling him stupid, lazy, or insolent that got you arrested, I wonder? Probably stupid."

He chuckled and kissed her temple. "By-the-by, I agree with your assessment. His governor will receive a letter from our solicitors demanding an apology. Did I mention the York Commissioner of Police went to school with my father?"

The tension of the last twelve hours boiled over, sending India into a fit of uncontrolled laughter, followed by a shuddering tempest of tears. Charlie held her until the storm wore itself out. "Feel better?"

India nodded. "I'm sorry I've embarrassed you. Do you think it will affect attendance at the fête? I do so want my first foray into charitable work to be a success."

"Mitchell will see that any hint is stamped out, but should he for some reason fail, I suspect news of your escapade will attract more rather than fewer attendees." Charlie ran his fingers along India's cheek. "Have I mentioned how wonderful you have been with Mama and how much I love you for it? Letting her remain in charge throughout last year has made giving up the reins far easier on everyone. She commented just the other day that she felt the castle and its obligations to the community will be in steady, competent hands. She'll be ready to move to the Dower House by the end of summer. Mama has grown to love you, you know."

"And I her. She took an ignorant American girl under her wing and is teaching me how to be a British countess. I will depend on her advice and support for a very long time. I only hope I deserve her trust. Is it necessary for her to move?"

"Realistically, she doesn't need to, but I'm not sure what Mama will say. She is devoted to a tradition which dictates the castle must not have two countesses in residence."

"But I love having her in the house. The castle is big. Surely we can find an apartment for her that will be far enough removed from the master suite."

"We'll see. She may wish the smaller, cozier confines of the Dower House. In the end, it must be her decision."

"Does she know about my night in gaol?"

"Ainsworth, good man, saw no need to alert the household when Mitchell's telegram arrived. He brought it to me alone. I made my excuses before breakfast, saying I had urgent business with the bank in York regarding funds for the renovations. As I did indeed go to the bank before going to the gaol, it was not a complete falsehood. I think we must tell Mama the truth, however. It will not do for her to hear of it from another source."

Dread at the thought of confessing her misadventure to the Dowager Lady Kilnsey churned in India's midsection. The meager amount of unseasoned, tasteless gruel she had choked down at 6:00 a.m. now threatened to make a reappearance. Making matters worse, her head had begun to throb. The night in gaol had taken a toll. India leaned against the seat back and closed her eyes.

***

The trip home was blessedly uneventful. The train's gentle rocking and the care with which Barton drove the Rolls allowed India to sleep for most of her journey. She arrived in the castle courtyard more refreshed than she had a right to expect given her previous night's accommodations.

Ainsworth greeted them in the Great Hall. "The Dowager Countess has held luncheon for your return. May I tell Cook we are ready to serve?"

India's stomach rolled at the mention of food, but she had to eat something or feel weak and depleted until teatime. "What has she prepared?"

"I believe a light chicken consommé with summer herbs followed by poached salmon and a lettuce and tomato salad."

"Please give Cook my apologies and tell her I will have only the soup with dry toast. Send my maid to our suite. Give us fifteen minutes and then you may serve."

"Very good, My Lady."

India hurried to her washroom, where Althea had already laid out a fresh summer frock and bathing items. The maid looked up from the washbasin with a smile.

"Thank goodness you're home. Mr. Mitchell assured me all would be well, but I've been a wreck waiting to see you in the flesh." Althea placed her fists on her hips and ran an evaluative gaze over India. "You look completely exhausted. Did you sleep at all last night?"

"Not really. When luncheon is over, I'm going to come back here for a good rest. Please see that I'm not disturbed."

After a speedy wash and change of clothes, India rushed to the dining room where Charlie and his mother waited. India took her seat with less grace than she would have liked, a little out of breath from racing through the castle hallways. Ainsworth nodded to the footman, and the soup was ladled. India took a sip, which went down better than expected. Cook was a treasure. The broth was light with no little islands of fat floating among the snipped herbs. Thinly sliced toast was a perfect shade of light brown. The combination settled nicely, giving India a much-needed energy boost.

When she refused the salmon, accepting only a small portion of salad, the Dowager raised a brow. "I see you are eating very little. Surely, you are not concerned about your weight. If anything, you are a tad too thin."

The perfect opening. Better now than later. India placed her salad fork on the edge of her plate and gave Mama, as she now thought of her mother-in-law, a weak smile. "I did not sleep well and awoke with a headache and unsettled stomach. After luncheon, I'm going to rest in our suite. Work on the fête begins in earnest tomorrow and I want to be fit and ready. Yesterday was exhausting, and I had a rather bad night."

Mama ran true to form when she asked, "To what do you attribute your nocturnal distress? I hope you are not ill."

"No, illness is not the issue. You see, I'm afraid I got myself into a bit of trouble and . . . and . . . well, I spent the night in York gaol." India paused, waiting for a gasp, a cry, a shout, anything to show her revelation had registered. The Dowager remained calm and stoic, as though she already had some inkling of what had happened in York. With no response from mother-in-law or husband, India rushed on. "It was a complete misunderstanding that has been cleared up. Mr. Mitchell assures us there will be no publicity. It will be kept out of the papers. No one will know." The spate of words depleted India, leaving her exhausted and teary.

The Dowager's posture became even more correct than her norm, while a brittle expression filled her eyes. "And pray, what form did this misunderstanding take?"

For the next few minutes, India explained the suffragists' plight at the hands of the York constabulary and her part in attempting to intervene. Charlie, damn him, sat silently, watching her babble with an amused look on his face. He clearly had no intention of helping. The tale's retelling did nothing to improve India's disposition. As her explanation ground to its end, her tone matched the level of her temper. "You must see that it was the policemen and the crowd of hooligans who were in the wrong. Those women were peacefully asking for what should be ours by right." Her fist hitting the table rattled the china and bounced the sterling.

Mama placed her fork on the side of her plate, made a bridge of her fingers, and studied India in silence for a full fifteen seconds. Whatever she sought, she seemed satisfied. "My son believes me as hidebound as an old Tory bishop. In most things that is true, but I have lived long enough to recognize how women suffer under a system which expects us to sit quietly by as our fathers and husbands do as they please. There was a time not long ago when our children did not even belong to their mothers. Insufferable. Your passion does you credit. That said, you must exercise it with caution and where it will be of greatest benefit. Charging pell-mell into a situation that is already out of control does no one any good, as I hope you now see." Dumbstruck by her mother-in-law's attitude, India could only nod. The Dowager acknowledged India's agreement with a tight smile. "Good. In future, I suggest you offer your support for these women in a more discreet manner."

Luncheon ended in companionable small talk between Charlie and his mother. India did not really pay attention to their conversation. Instead, she mulled her mother-in-law's injunction. Other than monetary support, what form her discreet involvement in the York suffragists' work would take she could not yet see.

***

The day of the fête arrived with cloudless skies and temperatures predicted to increase rapidly as the day progressed. India had asked to be awakened just after dawn. She learned early on that married ladies were not expected to appear at the breakfast table, but she rarely took advantage of the option. This morning would be different. She would breakfast in bed and then a have quick wash. There was still much to oversee in preparation for the onslaught of guests.

After a maid placed the breakfast tray over her knees, India removed the plate covers, preparing to gobble down a substantial meal, including the grilled tomatoes and mushrooms she had come to love. The aromas rising from the tray were not as enticing as usual. A twinge in her midsection should have been a warning, but she ignored it and speared a forkful of scrambled eggs. Before she even swallowed the first bite, she gagged and dashed for the night commode, threw back the lid, and emptied the contents of her stomach, mostly bile, into the porcelain receptacle. These episodes were becoming a trial. They began with her sojourn in York gaol. Whatever she picked up there had better pass and fast. She did not have time to be ill with the entire county expected to turn up in her garden in a few hours. The church roof depended upon a successful event.

Movement behind her made India jump. The toilet lid slipped from her grasp and slammed shut with a bang. She wiped her mouth with a hand towel and turned around. Althea stopped a few paces away, cocked her head, and studied India.

"You're sick again, I see. When are you going to bring in a doctor? This has gone on too long. What if you have dysentery? It kills even the young and sturdy. It killed just about as many soldiers as bullets did during The War Between the States."

"Let me get this fête over with and I'll send for the doctor at Kilnsey or maybe go to a physician in York. For the time being, do not mention these episodes to His Lordship or my mother-in-law. I will not have them see me as ill and weak."

Althea shook her head. "Instead of growing milder, that stubborn streak of yours seems to be getting worse. Be careful it does not lead you into real trouble."

CHAPTER 3

Althea gathered India's soiled nightgown and towels and dumped them into the wicker laundry basket by the washstand. She hoisted the basket to her hip, stopping for a moment at the window to look down at her mistress heading across the lawn just beyond the Chinese boxwood garden, no doubt attending to last-minute fête details. The tents and attractions set up were arranged around a central path leading to the food marquee. Housemaids, footmen, and local volunteers carried trays and boxes of supplies or bent over tables arranging displays. All was well in hand. There couldn't possibly be anything left for India to do, yet there she was scurrying about like doom would be upon them if she didn't touch every item in the jumble sale and adjust every tablecloth in the food marquee. Although Mrs. Wilson had been perfectly capable of doing the job, each detail of the fête had been strategically planned by India herself, much to Althea's consternation.

A rueful smile lifted one corner of Althea's mouth as she remembered the aggrieved expression on the housekeeper's face when it became clear who was in charge of the planning. Althea shook her head. That girl was going to make herself sick if she had not already done so. And there she went, dashing off again, this time toward the tombola.

Althea started toward the door, but the view from the next window caught her attention. A little thrill surged beneath the starched front of her black shirtwaist. There he was being his usual helpful, chivalrous self. A maid had dropped what must be a heavy box, scattering its contents over the lawn, and there was Mr. James picking everything up. He lifted the box but did not return it to the maid's outstretched arms. Instead, he appeared insistent on carrying it to its destination. The maid pointed to a tent at the far end of the grounds and he was off without a backward glance. He was such a nice man. The estate would be lost without him as manager.

Althea leaned against the windowsill and watched until Robbie James disappeared into the tent. Not for the first time, she wondered why such a good-looking, kind, capable man was not married. One of the maids said he was once, but his wife died some years ago. Back home in North Carolina, he would be thought a catch. The girls would have flocked to him like butterflies to nectar. And that nectar would be very sweet indeed.

Althea's jaw clenched. She must stop this infernal daydreaming. It would only lead to unhappiness and heartache. Robbie James would be no more interested in her than he was that maid he had just helped. He could have his pick of the tradesmen's or farmers' daughters in the county. She had even noticed a daughter of the landed gentry eyeing him with interest during the Christmas house party. He had no reason to look at a thirty-year-old American with little formal education who had escaped the drudgery of life as a mountaineer's wife by becoming a maid.

She turned away from the window, catching a glimpse of herself in the cheval mirror near the door. While her figure was shapely and her face might be considered handsome, she had little else to offer a man like Robbie James. Her station was too far beneath his. A gray cloud of resignation chilled her heart and lowered her spirit as she left the master suite headed for the service stairs.

After she left the basket in the laundry, she went to the servants' hall and took her place on the butler's right at the head of the table. Grace had already been said, and serving platters and bowls were being passed. Mr. Ainsworth was strict about the order of precedence, ruling the table with the same firm grip he employed in other areas of the house. Being lady's maid to the countess gave Althea a certain distinction among her fellow servants, a place for which she was eternally grateful.

She accepted a platter of pan-broiled tomatoes, a breakfast dish that had taken some getting used to and spooned a couple onto her plate. She might sorely miss her mother's home-ground, sage-laced sausage patties and stoneground grits slathered with hand churned butter, but she could not go back to that life. Her escape had been a narrow one.

Just yesterday, another letter arrived from her father beseeching her to come home and marry the neighbor who purportedly pined for her more than ever. The neighbor's manifold attractions? A widower with several small children, one hundred acres abutting Daddy's farm, a belly protruding over his belt like a sow ready to give birth, rotten front teeth, and a balding head.

Her sister had written also. That letter contained the truth of her father's request. The neighbor had promised Daddy fifteen acres of prime bottomland if he could convince Althea to come home and get married. Even without her sister's warnings, she would rather become a streetwalker than marry that man. At least as a lady of the evening, she would be able to choose her customers.

Althea glanced at the other end of the table and stifled a chuckle. The housekeeper held court opposite the butler, both engaging their underlings in polite conversation. If these superior folks were privy to her thoughts, they would no doubt faint from shock. They would think her vulgar and they would be correct. She had been common and vulgar until she became determined to get away from the life her mother had known.

By all accounts, Althea's mother had been a beautiful girl, but a hardscrabble life and birthing ten children left her old before her time. Althea had decided an early marriage would doom her to the same fate, so she had refused all suitors. Instead of marrying, she had clawed her way up the social and economic ladder by sheer willpower. She had improved herself through reading any and every book or periodical she could get her hands on. It was how she had learned to style hair and care for fine clothes. It was how she had improved her manner of speech and grammar. She had come far. There was not another daughter of an illiterate mountain dirt farmer who served an English countess. Even so, on days when a touch of loneliness played with her emotions, thoughts of a home and children of her own could make her wistful.

Down the table, two maids started giggling, their eyes darting toward the windows lining the interior wall of the servants' dining hall. A stern look from Mrs. Wilson quieted the pair, but not before the other servants turned to see what drew the girls' attention. Mr. James was in the service passage. He nodded to the group with a quizzical expression, as though he had no idea the effect he had on the female staff. He must be wondering if the giggling was at his expense.

Althea's heart lurched as her eyes darted away from the scene, fearing her thoughts might be a little too evident in her expression. It would never do for anyone to know the dreams she harbored where the man was concerned. She had no desire to be the object of pity or the laughingstock of the servants' hall.

CHAPTER 4

India stood at the far edge of the grounds and surveyed the area where the chief entertainments were set up. The first of the guests had arrived promptly at ten o'clock and were clearly enjoying themselves. For a county made up of vast moors, large farms, and small far-flung villages, the turnout was rather amazing.

India sighed with satisfaction. The fête was a success. People of all classes and social stations played the games, drank the tea, ate the sandwiches, bought items they did not need from the jumble sale, and vied for an opportunity to chat with the new, young, aged only twenty-two, Lady Kilnsey.

India eyed yet another crowd surging toward the tea tent. Given the day's warmth, it had been particularly popular. Perhaps it was time to check on the refreshments supply. As she made her way forward, she caught Mama's eye, who smiled and lifted her hand in a subtle gesture of affirmation.

Charlie's mother seemed pleased with the day. India grinned and ticked off another worry turned success. Sitting in state beneath the shade of a garden tent, Mama greeted her friends and neighbors with subtle nods and engaged them in quiet conversations. She wore a lavender cotton lawn garden dress enhanced with touches of lace and sat upon one of the heavily carved, throne-like chairs from the library. Queen Victoria would not have looked more regal.

India sighed in envy. Mama appeared calm, cool, and to be enjoying the solicitous attention of the Reverend Archibald Howard, in whose church roof's aid the fête was being held. He must be pleased, for he looked more puffed up than usual. An image of Lewis Carroll's Cheshire cat dressed in vicar's garb popped into her head, and she covered her mouth to hide a giggle. With a final glance at Mama and Charlie's ecclesiastical cousin, she rushed on. Try as she might, she could not stop herself dashing from one stall to the next checking all was well.

As she entered the tea tent, Althea stepped into her path, palm outstretched. "You haven't eaten a thing, and it's well past lunchtime. You're going to make yourself sick. Sit down and let me get you some sandwiches."

India ran the back of her hand over her forehead where perspiration had begun gathering. "Just get me a glass of lemonade. I'll be back after a quick trip to the house. It seems they've run out of tickets at the tombola. Isn't it great?"

"You should let somebody else take care of things. What's the good of being a countess if you don't order people around?"

"My papa always said if something is important to do it yourself. The fête's success is important because the church roof is in crisis. We can't have water or snow pouring in on worshipers, now can we?" India glanced toward the serving tables. "It looks like the maids are keeping the food and drink under control. I'll be back in a few minutes. I think I'll be ready for those sandwiches by then."

After downing the lemonade, India headed across the grounds toward the house. Waves of heat swept through her, raising sweat that ran down her cheeks and dripped from her chin. Her feet felt as if they had turned to lead. Although the thought of food made her stomach churn, Althea was probably right. She needed to eat something. A few more steps and her head began spinning, making walking even more difficult. She stopped beside the hoopla tent and grabbed a guy rope. Her vision blurred, then the world disappeared.

***

From out of darkness, whispers and odors floated across India's tangled senses, stirring them partially awake. A strong whiff of ammonia laced with a sweeter scent brought her up from the depths to find Dr. Millhouse sitting beside her bed. She instinctively swatted the bottle of smelling salts away and tried to sit up, but Charlie gathered her in his arms. She melted into the embrace because everything began spinning again.

Mama and Althea hovered at the foot of the bed, their faces anxious, clutching one another's hands. It was such an incongruous sight India would have laughed aloud had she possessed the energy. Instead, she breathed deeply and sat up a little straighter. "Did anyone get more tickets to the tombola?"

Nervous laughter erupted all around her. Still chuckling, Charlie raised her hand to his lips. "Your priorities, while well intentioned, are somewhat misplaced. The fête is doing beautifully without your running around seeing to every detail yourself."

The doctor stirred, taking her wrist between thumb and fingers while he placed a stethoscope on her chest. A satisfied smile lifted the corners of his mouth as he nodded. "Good, good. Heart rate and rhythm have returned to normal." Addressing the others surrounding the bed, he continued, "If you will leave us, I wish to examine Lady Kilnsey."

Charlie did not move. "Surely, I am allowed to remain."

The doctor's white hair flopped over his brow with an emphatic shake of his head. "Young man, your presence would only be an encumbrance. Be gone, the lot of you. I wish to consult with my patient in private."

India suppressed a giggle as she watched her family troop from the room and close the door. Dr. Millhouse was not intimidated by rank or class. He knew his worth to the community and was comfortable with his place in it. If India hadn't felt so weak, she would have shouted a hearty bravo. It was a blessing he had stopped by the fête on his round of house calls.

The old man patted India's hand and said, "Now tell me. Why do you think you fainted?"

After India described the symptoms she had experienced since her sojourn as a guest of the York constabulary, Dr. Millhouse nodded. "I see. I believe a physical examination is in order before I give my final diagnosis. Do you wish your maid to assist you in disrobing?"

Once the exam was concluded, Althea helped India into a nightgown and departed, sending Charlie in to take her place at the bedside.

The doctor smiled. "There is no need for alarm regarding your wife's health. Quite the contrary. You are to be congratulated. Lady Kilnsey is with child. About two months gone, I'd say."

Charlie counted off the months on his fingers. "A baby in May. How wonderful." He placed his arm about India's shoulders and kissed her temple. “What about the illness and fainting? Is that normal?”

“It is indeed. The morning sickness will hopefully pass within the month. It usually does, but failing that, healthy babies are born to women who experience sickness throughout their pregnancies. Fainting is also common.” Turning to India, the doctor picked up her hand and gave it a squeeze. “Now that you know your condition, young lady, you must take better care of yourself. Eat well and get plenty of rest. No more of this running about trying to do everything. You have well-trained staff. Use them.” With emphasis on his last words, he peered at India over the rim of his spectacles until she nodded agreement.

***

As predicted, India’s morning sickness magically disappeared upon entering her second trimester. Instead of feeling nauseated and lethargic most of the time, her skin shone, her hair glowed, and she had more energy than ever. In fact she felt so well, she persuaded Charlie to resume the tradition of the Kilnsey Christmas House Party. She felt optimistic and marvelous. This having a baby business wasn’t going to be so bad after all.

She laid her pen on the blotter, stretched her back, and rolled her shoulders. Addressing invitations had taken a good portion of the morning and she was only halfway through the guest list. Her back ached from bending over her desk. It was set beneath the west-facing parlor windows of their private suite in the corner of the castle’s northwest tower. Despite having banks of windows on two outer walls, the parlor was cozy thanks to the newly installed radiators and the coal fire glowing gently in the corner fireplace. India loved this room. It afforded privacy and unencumbered views out over the formal boxwood garden and moors. Snow now blanketed the vistas in every direction, creating a sense of being cocooned in a castle floating in the clouds. She picked up her pen and resumed her task.

Mama had been forced to abandon the long weekend house party after Charlie's father ruined the family financially, but with central heating and plumbing now in place and plenty of income, there was no reason for further delay in entertaining their friends and neighbors. As India looked over the list of invitees, she reminded herself not to refer to the event as a weekend gathering. Mama decreed the term vulgar and insisted the correct reference was Saturday-to-Monday. That the English wouldn't use ordinary, economical words was sometimes frustrating, but tradition being what it was with her fellow subjects, it usually won out over any nod to practicality.

A shadow dropped over the desk. Charlie leaned down, kissed the top of her head, and placed a solicitous hand on her shoulder as his gaze ran down the list. "You've made good progress, but please don't overtire yourself. Remember Dr. Millhouse's injunction. Your priority must be your health and that of the child. Mama will be happy to help if needed."

India smiled and placed her hand over his, giving it a squeeze. "You and Mama are worrywarts. Since the morning sickness has passed, I feel like I could conquer the world. I have lots of energy. When I was younger, I thought all this social business was a ridiculous waste of time, but I find now I am rather looking forward to being lady of the manor. I have grown quite fond of our friends and neighbors."

Charlie chuckled. "I see you failed to include family among those who have entered your affections."

"What family? I thought all your extended family had gone to their rewards long ago."

His brow arched. "I note you omitted Bumpy from those invited."

India's lips drew into a sneer. "Oh, him. Must we? He is a bore, a philistine, and a cretin. Surely you recall he tried to provoke you into a fight at our wedding?"

"While what you say is true, I fear we must. Until you produce a male child, as detestable as it is, Bumpy is my heir. To snub him would cause undue speculation. Mama would abhor it. You know how she hates gossip. If it will make you feel better, I'll ask Robbie to be Bumpy's keeper while he's here and I will not allow him to come earlier or stay longer than the other guests. Will that do?"

India's sneer straightened into a thin line of resignation. "I suppose it will have to. Now, go away. You have become a distraction with your irritating demands."

Charlie's insistence on inviting his distant cousin, His Grace, Fifth Duke Hawik, Bumpy to his friends and enemies, cast a pall over her delight and anticipation. The man was completely insufferable. He had made nothing but condescendingly rude remarks about Charlie, the Westmorland family, and herself since their first meeting in 1911 at the Shakespeare Memorial Ball. He had tried to lure Charlie into an unseemly display of temper during their wedding reception by disparaging India's heritage with barely veiled references to the scandals that had followed her family since long before her birth. She tapped her pen against her teeth as she considered how best to endure his presence.

Considerable comfort lay in knowing that the loyal and highly competent estate agent, Robbie James, would take Bumpy in hand for the duration of the party. If anyone could keep the blaggard in his place and away from her and

Charlie, it was Robbie. He had served as best man at their wedding and had acted as a surrogate father to Charlie since the previous Lord Kilnsey's death from alcoholism and a dissipated life. No doubt the odious Bumpy would take every opportunity to remind anyone within earshot of the Westmorland and Ledbetter misfortunes and scandals with more of his veiled references. Thank goodness their friends and neighbors would be too polite to inquire into his meaning, but Bumpy was sure to make them wonder. It was his usual pattern of behavior.

Just thinking about him sent her pulse racing. Why, oh why, must one always bend to the dictates and expectations of society? Why did other people's opinions even matter? If she had her way, Bumpy would never darken their door again, but the last thing she wanted to do was upset Mama. On that desire alone hung the damnable Bumpy's invitation.

Disgruntled but resigned, she wrote Lord Hawik's name and address on an envelope.

CHAPTER 5

India stood with her fists on her hips surveying her decorating efforts in the Great Hall, the oldest part of the castle. She pursed her lips in frustration. Things had not come together as she had envisioned. Oh, the Christmas tree was beautiful, filled as it was from top to bottom with handmade ornaments from Germany, ribbons, and strands of electric lights from America. The lights had been a great expense, but India had insisted. She had no intention of burning the house down with candles on a drying tree during her first house party.

The tree's enormous height and impressive girth filled one corner of the room. It needed to be huge or it would be dwarfed by the fireplace large enough for three or four grown men to stand upright and shoulder-to-shoulder beneath its flue. Moreover, the hall's ceiling was three stories above her head.

When she first set eyes on the space, Charlie told her they had not used it in years, but she immediately envisioned garlands of flowers strung between candelabra marching around the entire room. Elegant couples waltzed over the smooth stone floor to strains of Strauss floating down from the gallery set high in the wall opposite the fireplace. In her mind, the hall had appeared both inviting and elegant. At present, it was neither. With dancing planned for the Saturday evening of the house party, India needed the Great Hall to be perfect. She pivoted in a complete circle, eyeing every inch of the space. The candelabra festooned with garlands of greenery and colorful ribbons were lovely, but they were not enough. What more was needed?

India tapped her foot in irritation. This was not the first house party hosted within these walls. Perhaps Mrs. Wilson could advise her. As the castle's longtime housekeeper, she was the true minder of all things Kilnsey.

India passed from the Great Hall into the dining room and paused to survey the work carried out by footmen under the supervision of the redoubtable Ainsworth. He had been employed as butler only days before she set eyes on the castle, but he had already established his authority when she first stepped down from the carriage as a soon-to-be bride. Ainsworth ruled his staff like the kindly but determined autocrat he was. Those who displeased him did not stay long in Kilnsey's employ.

A grin played across her lips as she considered what must have transpired in this room. She could envision him, ruler in hand, going from one place setting to the next measuring the placement of china, sterling, and crystal. The footmen would have stood at attention quaking in fear of a stern reprimand had any item not met muster.

Going to the newly installed electric switch set in the wall beside the door, she pressed the button. The heavy crystal chandelier sprang to life, setting the room's green damask walls, snowy moldings, and mahogany table aglow. It really was a beautiful room. Several generations of earls had taken a cold, medieval stone fortress built to protect Fountains Abbey's Cistercian monks driving their flocks over Mastiles Lane and turned it into a family home.

Satisfied this room, at least, lay in readiness, she let her fingers drift over the glossy backs of dining chairs as she made her way toward the Grand Staircase hall, behind which lay the entrance to the castle's beating heart, the service areas. A series of doors marched along the passageway, starting with the butler's pantry followed by the housekeeper's office, and finally the kitchen and sculleries.

At Mrs. Wilson's door, India knocked and waited to be bidden entry. She found the housekeeper at her desk working on her accounts, a cup of tea cooling at her elbow.

Mrs. Wilson's scratching pen did not stop as she spoke without looking up. "What is it? I'm sure you can see I'm busy."

Mrs. Wilson could intimidate simply by breathing. India had to remind herself she was the boss here and not an errant maid interrupting important duties. She cleared her throat and shifted from one foot to the other. "I'm hoping for your guidance."

Recognizing her mistress's voice, Mrs. Wilson dropped the pen and looked up, her eyes large with surprise. She jumped to her feet. "My Lady, had I known of your need, I would have come to you." She gestured toward wingback chairs beside the fireplace. "Please, sit and tell me how I can be of service."

After India explained her concern, Mrs. Wilson nodded. "I see. Yes, it is indeed an enormous space. Making it inviting has always been an issue. Have you thought of suspending large garlands of greenery from the rafters? It would have a twofold benefit. They would cover more space while providing a noise-softening effect once the room is filled with guests. I'm afraid the Great Hall is something of an echo chamber with no soft surfaces to dull sounds."

"What a wonderful idea, but do we have ladders tall enough to reach that height?"

"Of course we do. Ask Mr. James to organize the project. He helped his father, the head gardener in the Fourteenth Earl's time, with just such a scheme. He will know what to do. Shall I send for him?"

India stood and stretched her shoulders. Her center of gravity was shifting as the baby grew, causing her to ache in places she had not in the past. "Thank you, but no. I'm feeling in need of exercise. The walk to the agent's office will be a good start."

Stepping out into the courtyard, India pulled her coat close and breathed in the crisp December air. The day was glorious. The sun shone in a cloudless sky, its beams setting the castle aglow. The four-story towers, one on each corner of the square, and the three-story sections connecting them bore a thick frosting of snow on their roofs and crenelations. Icicles hung from eaves and windowsills. The combination of sunlight and ice gave the castle the look of a fairytale palace. This was how Kilnsey must have looked in winter when the first earl lived here. If she used her imagination, she could see lords and ladies in thirteenth century garb dashing from their wagons to the castle entrance, their long capes and skirts leaving trails in the snow. In the two years since her marriage, she had grown to love this house and the wild, windswept moors surrounding it.

Across the courtyard, the postern gate swung open and Althea swept through, lugging an enormous basket of boxwood cuttings. The door to the agent's office, set in the original porter's lodge, flew back and Robbie rushed forward. He skidded to a halt in front of Althea with his hands outstretched.

"Please. Let me take that. You should have called for a footman. It's much too heavy for a young lady."

It could have been the cold, but it seemed Althea blushed as she placed her burden in his arms. "Why, thank you, kind sir. While I appreciate the thought, I assure you I'm stronger than I apparently look."

"Of course. I . . . I meant no disrespect. It's just such a heavy . . . I . . . " Robbie stuttered as his words ground to a halt.

India cocked her head in wonder. Robbie, usually the most eloquent and self-assured of men, appeared tongue-tied in her maid's presence. Perhaps she should give the couple time alone. The ladder could wait until later. With the briefest of waves, she called, "I'm going for a quick turn about the garden. When I'm finished exercising the kinks out, I'll send for you, Robbie. The Great Hall needs your expert attention."

***

Althea's heart jumped as her fingers brushed against Mr. James's palms. She had felt an attraction to him from the very moment they met. While she had not been overly blessed with suitors in her thirty years, it seemed he might find her attractive as well. Either that, or he was about the kindest, most solicitous man she had ever met. Unfortunately, she was not sure what to think. At times like this, she could almost convince herself he had feelings for her, but then he would pull back and be aloof in the next moment. The man was a puzzle.

She fell into step beside him, glancing up from beneath her lashes. Yep. He was looking straight ahead, ignoring her completely. His attention seemed glued to the front door.

When they were in the vestibule, he stopped and turned to her. “Where should I take this?”

“To the drawing room, please.”

Without looking back, he headed into the house. She waited for a moment before following. The man could be infuriating while at the same time being so darned kind and gracious. Would she ever totally understand men? Maybe, but probably not Englishmen.

CHAPTER 6

The house party's success exceeded India's expectations. Robbie, good man, had seen to Bumpy and kept him in line with constant attention. The other guests seemed content and happy throughout the weekend. Although her condition prevented her riding, a welcome break in the weather allowed the hunt on Saturday to go forward. India waved the riders away with a heart filled with envy. She even loaned Zara, her Arabian mare brought from The Falls in America as Charlie's wedding gift to her, to one of the ladies whose own horse had thrown a shoe while being unloaded from the horse van. That evening, games, lively conversation, music, and dancing had kept everyone entertained.

With the Sunday farewell dinner now under way, dual emotions circled one another. India scanned the long banquet table, scrutinizing each face. She smiled in satisfaction. Yes, their friends appeared happy and relaxed. They were very fortunate in their cook, Mrs. Bertrand. Her carefully prepared meal was giving as much pleasure as the previous night's activities. She had produced a dinner worthy of royalty, yet comforting in its homey familiarity. After much discussion with Mrs. Wilson and Mama, India settled on a menu of an elegant turbot with hollandaise for the fish course and a roast beef with

Yorkshire pudding and winter vegetables for the remove. The whole was preceded by soup and various delectables and would be followed by a traditional Christmas trifle of jams and candied fruit. By luncheon tomorrow, the house would be empty and feel a little lonely after such a lovely and successful weekend. Shoving the thought aside, she embraced the knowledge of a job well done. Both Charlie and Mama had given her approving glances all evening, making it all the sweeter.

As the footmen removed plates after the final course, the sounds of a chair scraping back and the ring of sterling tapping against crystal drew everyone's attention. To her dismay, Bumpy was on his feet, wine glass held aloft.

He cleared his throat loudly to quell the final murmurs of conversation. With all eyes upon him, he began. "As all gathered are aware, I am our host's heir, at least for the time being. Given Lady Kilnsey's happy condition, I may be sent down the line within a few months. I think I can be forgiven a prayer or two for a girl, but with my luck, the baby is sure to be a boy. Of course, anything can happen..." India held her breath as Lord Hawik allowed his words to die away with a grin. "Oh, don't look so shocked. I certainly do not wish my cousin-in-law ill. I'm simply pointing out a possibility." A mischievous gleam entered his eyes. "But would it really be such a disaster? After all, why should the son of a poorly bred American from a scandal-ridden family inherit one of our oldest and most noble titles?"

Gasps were audible around the table. Seeing the effect his words had on the other diners, Hawik quickly changed course. With a chuckle, he continued, "I have been told my sense of humor often leaves something to be desired, but I digress. Let us raise our glasses to our hosts in thanks for a most pleasant stay. I give you Lord and Lady Kilnsey. Long may they live and love."

The other guests rose as a body and turned toward India and Charlie, but some did not meet their eyes. Everyone was clearly embarrassed by the scene that had just transpired.

When their health had been drunk, Charlie rose from his seat. "Thank you, dear friends, for the good wishes. We cherish your friendship and are delighted you accepted our invitation." He made eye contact with every person at the table save one. When he turned his attention to Hawik, Charlie's face flamed and his fists balled at his sides. "But you, Cousin, you are either drunk beyond reason or you are once again showing yourself to be the villain I have always known you to be. You were a bully when I was a child and an abuser of younger boys at school, even sending one to hospital. As even drunkenness cannot excuse your behavior, you will take your leave now and be gone before everyone rises in the morning."

When Bumpy did not move, Charlie's eyes glittered, and he nodded to the butler. "Ainsworth, Lord Hawik has decided to leave at once rather than wait for the morning train. Please notify his valet to have his bags packed within the quarter hour and Barton to ready the auto. Should there be any failure to comply with my wishes, have our most able-bodied footmen eject His Grace from the house." Charlie returned his attention to his cousin. "Leave this room at once. You are no longer nor will you ever again be welcome at my table or in this house."

Bumpy rose, his eyes darting around the table, and extended his hands palms up as if to ask what he had done to be treated thus. "As you wish, but I fear you err on one point." He pointed to India's belly. "Should the child be a girl, I may one day own this house and all that comes with it. My contacts in the Foreign Office hint war may be on the horizon what with Germany armed to the teeth and Britain matching her dreadnaught for dreadnaught. The Kaiser's thirst for territory seems on the rise and his insecurities about being surrounded by enemies increase daily, or so I am told." He glanced around with a satisfied smile at the shocked faces of the other guests before returning to his theme. Making a temple of his hands, he tapped the index fingers together and cocked his head in an imitation of deep thought. "Of course, one must give the man his due. Britain *is* in league with Russia and France, after all. I suppose one can see the Kaiser's point." His face grew harder and his voice harsher. "Mark me. Sabers are rattling all over the continent. I will be exempt from service due to my weak lungs. But you, dear cousin, will be expected to lead men into battle. War has a way of changing things." With that, Hawik threw his napkin on the table, knocked his chair to the floor, and marched from the room.

An immediate quiet fell over those assembled. The guests glanced at one another from lowered eyes, then one-by-one the men rose. A cry of three cheers came from someone at the far end of the table, followed by three resounding shouts of "hoorah for Kilnsey." When they finished their show of support, India looked at Mama, who nodded.

Rising from her chair, she swallowed hard and placed a hand on the back of her chair. She plastered a smile on her features before her gaze swept the table. "Ladies, I believe coffee is awaiting us in the drawing room. Shall we leave the men to their port and cigars?"

Shaky legs carried her through to a sofa beside the elaborately carved fireplace where logs blazed. For once, the room's beautiful yellow damask walls and intricate moldings did nothing to calm her nerves. Mama sailed past several guests and settled herself beside India. She leaned in and whispered through barely parted lips. "Sit up and smile. Show people you are unfazed. They will respect you for it."

Following Mama's advice, the last evening of the house party ended with more pleasant conversation and bridge games. If the guests thought about the seeds of doubt Bumpy had planted regarding her heritage, they were polite enough not to mention it within her hearing.

When they were finally in bed after the last guest had gone up for the night, Charlie took India in his arms and kissed her deeply. "Have I told you how wonderful you are and how perfect your first house party has been?"

India snuggled against his shoulder, basking in the glow of his praise. "It was a lovely weekend, wasn't it? We should do something nice for the staff. They all worked hard. Perhaps we could give them an extra half day after Boxing Day. What do you think?"

Charlie stretched, then drew her closer and nibbled her ear. "I think you are as kind and thoughtful as you are beautiful. If you want to make the staff a gift of an extra half day, who am I to dissuade you? But do ask Ainsworth and Mrs. Wilson to set up a rota so the house does not grind to a complete halt."

India squirmed around to make herself more comfortable. Finding just the right position was getting harder with each passing week. She rolled onto her side and scooted her back against Charlie's chest. Still not totally right, she squirmed around, shifting her hips and legs. Just when she found the perfect placement, a little twitch deep within her lower abdomen made her brow crease. Perhaps the turbot and Hollandaise had not been the wisest choice at dinner. The last thing she needed was a bout of gas. She shifted again, and the twitch became a tiny thump. Gas didn't act like that. It wasn't gas at all.

She grabbed Charlie's hand and placed it on her belly. There it was again. He leaned up on one elbow. "Are you going to be sick? I thought you were over that."

She giggled and rolled to face him. "No, you silly goose. It's our baby telling me to shift so he or she will be more comfortable."

Charlie's eyes grew wide, and he was quiet for a moment while his hand pressed a little more into her belly. With another twitch, his expression became thoughtful. "It's truly real, isn't it? Until now, the baby has felt like a dream of sorts. Of course, I've noted the changes in your body, but there has been nothing I could feel. Thank you for sharing this moment with me."

India studied her husband's face. His eyes seemed brighter than usual. It had not occurred to her that men could feel such deep emotion for their unborn children. She had assumed they did not really form an attachment to the child until it entered the world. Charlie was a truly wonderful husband and it was clear he would be a good father. He would have his heir and the odious Bumpy would be out of their lives for good. A vision of Charlie holding his son swelled her heart, but only momentarily.

With a shock, an unwelcome thought rocked her musings of a secure future and covered them with a gray mist of apprehension.

Stroking his cheek, she asked, "Will you be terribly disappointed if this baby is a girl? It is a 50-50 chance, you know."

Charlie kissed the tip of her nose. "We will love this child whatever its sex. If it's a girl, we will just have greater incentive to try harder for more babies. And speaking of which..."

India felt his desire through the thin fabric of her gown. The pace of his breathing beckoned her join him in moments of mutual bliss, an invitation she never tired of accepting. As his hands began the now familiar and intoxicating exploration of her body, India's pleasure grew. Her hips rocked in rhythm with his. She wanted him, needed him inside. Her passion was nearing the breaking point until it was suddenly marred by the memory of another unwelcome remark made by His Grace, the contemptible Lord Hawik. If war was coming, as some people believed, would Charlie really be expected to fight? Would he have to leave his newborn child and wife for an uncertain future?

With visions of Charlie in military khaki spinning through her head, she did her best to return to her previous state of euphoria, but the moment was tarnished. She prayed it was not lost for good.

CHAPTER 7

Althea stormed from the house and marched across the courtyard toward the postern gate. She needed exercise and lots of it. A walk on the snow-covered moors might cool her temper, but there was no guarantee her absence would change attitudes beyond the green baize door. The interrogation she had just experienced at the hands of her fellow servants had been intrusive and intolerable. They thought she was privy to the private thoughts and conversations of India and His Lordship and they believed she would gladly divulge all she knew in exchange for their tepid, inconstant friendship. Well, they could go to blazes.

A gust of wind rolled over the crenelations, swept down into the courtyard, and crept beneath her collar. The air stung as though it held ice crystals. With a shiver, she pulled her coat closer, turning the collar up to protect her neck. She should have gone to her room for a shawl and scarf, but she wanted away from the hall before she said things she would regret.

A rueful smile lifted one corner of her mouth. The other servants were right, of course. She had access to her employers' conversations, and India confided in her more like they were sisters than Countess and lady's maid, but she would be damned if she'd violate India's confidence to please a bunch of toffee-nosed English servants.

She snickered. Toffee-nosed, indeed. What a grand description of her colleagues. Not how she would have described them before her years in the castle. Snot-nosed and too big for their britches would have been her choices then. However she chose to describe them, her co-workers liked to pry and gossip. Of particular interest were their employers' reactions to the cousin's pronouncements at dinner the night before.

The Christmas House Party farewell dinner had gone well until that ass Hawik made such a scene. Despite Mr. Ainsworth's admonitions, behind the butler's back the footmen spread the story of how they were ordered to physically eject His Grace from the house if the need arose. Fortunately, it had not come to that, but it was the talk of the servants' hall, nonetheless. Althea shook her head in dismay. Some people's arrogance was beyond understanding.

The sound of a door slamming drifted on the invisible wings of another gust, breaking into Althea's musings and making her jump. Glancing over her shoulder, she saw Mr. James holding a blanket and striding toward her. She didn't know whether to be pleased or irritated. She sought solitude to regain a sense of peace, but that would be impossible if he insisted on joining her. His company was both perplexing and far too stimulating. The urge to run before he reached her side grew with each little whirlwind of snow swirling around her feet. Robbie James both confused and intrigued her.

Her name floated to her. Of course, she could pretend she had not heard him, but he would probably redouble his efforts. He had shown he did not give up easily once he set his course. She had no choice but to turn and acknowledge him or be insufferably rude.

Robbie came to rest beside her. "Miss Henderson. Please allow me." He placed the blanket about her shoulders. "It is much too cold to be out on the moors in just a coat." He stopped and looked unsure. "That is where you are going, isn't it?"

Resigned, she pulled the blanket about her throat. "It is. Thank you."

He opened his mouth but did not speak. After an awkward pause, Althea raised her brows. Red crept onto his cheeks. It could be the cold, but somehow, she didn't think so. Only moments ago, the only color in his handsome face had been wrought by years of exposure to the elements. Even in winter, he kept his tan. Dark eyes and hair could harken to Spanish or Italian ancestry. Whatever his heritage, the bits and pieces combined to create a beautiful whole.

Althea stamped the ground to increase circulation. Standing still in freezing temperatures had become too tedious. If beauty refused to speak, she might as well continue on her way. "I'm going for my walk now. Thank you for the wrap."

"May I . . . would you . . . might I accompany you? That is, unless you prefer solitude, which I should advise against." He nodded toward the sky. "Those clouds are heavy with snow. It would not do to be caught out in unfamiliar territory when it begins to fall. Storms develop rather quickly this time of year." His voice trailed off to a near whisper.

Althea eyed him for a moment. Should she be insulted or flattered? She had lived in Yorkshire long enough to understand its weather. On the other hand, he seemed earnest in his desire to walk with her. The color in his cheeks deepened. She smiled and replied, "I would welcome your company. I have had a rather difficult morning."

Robbie offered his arm onto which Althea placed her hand. Together, they passed through the postern gate and onto the path leading to the moors. He was polite enough not to pry given her overt opening. Another thing in his favor. He was not given to gossip. The rest of the staff discussed their employers like they were reading the latest copy of The Tattler, but Robbie was completely loyal to His Lordship. She felt his eyes on her and glanced up. He looked at her with such sweetness that her heart jumped. If he kept this up, she was in real danger.

He stopped and tilted his head as though considering a matter of great importance. "I hope you will forgive the abrupt nature of what I am going to say, but if I do not speak now, I fear I will lose my courage." He guided her around to face him. Due to the rise in the terrain, she came to rest looking down at him. Creases formed between eyes clouded with uncertainty. "Miss Henderson, I realize a widower with grown children is too old for a young lady such as yourself, but I hold the hope you might consider walking out with me despite the difference in our ages. I find you deadly attractive and have done so from the moment you arrived." When she did not answer, he cleared his throat and gave a shallow bow. "I see. Please forgive my impertinence. May I escort you back to the house?"

Had she dreamed his words? Althea clutched the wrap at her throat and gave herself a mental shake. "No. I mean yes. You misunderstand. Drat, I'm making a mess of this. Yes, you may take me back to the house. No, you are not impertinent. And yes, I would be pleased to walk out with you."

A smile worthy of the Cheshire cat lifted his features. "By Jove, you have made me a very happy man."

CHAPTER 8

India peeked at the mantel clock. Was it really nine a.m.? Althea had let her sleep, bless her. India placed her hand in the indentation where Charlie's body had lain. The sheets were cool to the touch, eliciting an affectionate smile. He would have breakfasted before seven and would be long gone to the Home Farm seeing to the docking of lambs' tails and notching of ears. Even though he no longer needed to participate in the manual labor on the farm, he still lent a hand when the workload was heavy. He enjoyed working the land, and the farmer was grateful for the help. More importantly, the farmer bragged about Charlie to the other tenants, and they respected His Lordship all the more for his willingness to get his hands dirty.

India pushed the bed linens away while she rolled her ankles. Peering over her enormous belly, she could feel her toes, but did not feel like struggling to sit up in order to see them. The last look at them before bed the previous evening revealed plump sausages where her digits should have been. Her energy flagged a little more each day now that she was close to term. She raised her arms above her head and stretched her body to its fullest. It was a mistake. A cramp curled the toes on her left foot. It traveled up over her ankle until it reached her calf, bringing her upright to massage the offending muscle. The doctor had insisted she avoid ingesting salt as much as possible. How a country doctor in a Yorkshire backwater knew the latest in medical science was a mystery, but he insisted new theories indicated salt intake was the culprit in her abnormally swollen ankles and feet. She had unhappily followed his ban, and these blasted cramps were her reward.

With a light tap, Althea peered around the bedroom door. "I've brought a tray. Feel like eating something?"

India nodded, and the tray settled over her knees. Althea removed the lids from the plate, revealing eggs and mushrooms but no bacon, sausages, baked beans or anything else containing even a modicum of sodium. India scooped a bite into her mouth and gagged. "Yuck. Unseasoned food isn't fit to eat."

Althea's forehead creased in "The Look," for which she was well known. "True, but you aren't eating for yourself alone. That baby needs food. You won't have to live without salt much longer, so eat up."

After India choked down as much as she could tolerate, she pushed the tray away and struggled to scoot her unwieldy body to the side of the bed. Breathing hard, she dangled her feet over the edge. Althea helped her to stand and wriggle into the only garment she owned that was actually not torturous. Turning sideways, she looked at herself in the cheval mirror. "I look like a beached whale."

Althea smirked. "When was the last time you saw a whale of any description?"

"Never, but this is how one must look. I'm enormous."

"You are just the size you are supposed to be."

India grimaced. "I guess, but I'm afraid I'll never fit into my clothes again."

"You will. It just takes time after a baby."

"How can you be sure? You haven't ever looked like a cow about to give birth." Being grumpy with Althea was unfair, but India couldn't help herself.

"You forget. I'm the oldest of eleven. My mother always got her figure back and you will, too."

"If you say so." India turned away from the mirror with a grunt. "Lord help. If this baby doesn't come soon, I'll end up with a permanent sway in my spine." Massaging the small of her back, she waddled to the parlor and flopped down on the settee facing the moors.

Picking up the newspaper Charlie had left on the occasional table beside the settee, she scanned the headlines. Nothing but talk of the newest dreadnaught, HMS Iron Duke, and the Admiralty crowing about an additional five ships in production, bringing Britain's total to thirty-eight, fourteen more than the German fleet. King George's government seemed determined to win the race for domination of the seas by outbuilding his cousin, the German Kaiser.

She shook her head at the absurdity of spoiled royals unable to resist intrafamilial conflict, or maybe their advisors were to blame. What did anyone really know about the inner workings of governments and international intrigue? With that thought, the odious Bumpy's departing words at Christmas flashed through her mind. If war was on the horizon, it didn't bear thinking about. She needed all her energy to bring this baby into the world. The concerns of nations must wait. She threw the paper aside and turned her attention to the mundane.

She watched Althea through the open bedroom door going about her normal morning routine of making the bed, putting away the nightgown, setting the breakfast tray by the door for easy removal—all the little tasks India found daunting because they required bending and stooping. Althea was a treasure, and she loved her. Mama found this devotion to her maid disconcerting and beneath her standards, but India held firm.

Althea dropped the corner of the counterpane and rushed to the window. No doubt she had caught sight of Robbie James crossing through the garden. Nothing else would draw her from her duties with such alacrity. India smiled to herself. Robbie was sure to propose before the summer was out. India would bet her eyeteeth on it. The thought of helping to plan a wedding warmed her through and through. Althea deserved happiness and a family of her own. Best of all, in marrying Robbie, she would stay on the estate never more than a few yards from the castle. Charlie would have to find a house for them in the village, or maybe build one. That would be an excellent use of her fortune.

She slapped the arm of the settee. Enough of this idleness. She needed movement, and walking down to the garden was always a pleasant distraction. With the weather finally beginning to warm, spring was truly with them. The daffodils were fading, and the roses were setting their buds. May and June had become her favorite months in England. Back home in North Carolina, she had loved autumn best because of the glorious, vibrant foliage, but here, forests were not as prevalent. Yorkshire's meadows and dales in spring and summer, however, were glorious covered as they were in bluebells, marsh orchids, foxglove, yarrow, harebell, and more.

As she rose from the settee, something deep within her lower belly tugged, followed by the feeling a champagne bottle must experience when its cork pops. Clear fluid gushed from between her legs, ran down her thighs, and soaked into the carpet at her feet.

India froze where she stood. She wouldn't be going on any walks for the foreseeable future. After all the wishing this moment would come, she was suddenly unsure she was prepared. She knew very little of human childbirth. What little information she had came from Dr. Millhouse. He had done his best to explain and reassure her, but he was sixty and a man. What did he really know of the realities of giving birth? He had explained the physiological side of things, but had clammed up when she started asking about what she would feel. He patted her hand and said not to worry. Easy for him. He was not the one who would have to push a stranger the size of a great fat hen out from between his legs. She had seen enough of birthing foals and calves on the farm at The Falls to know there would be pain and blood.

Mama had been no help. The woman who never balked at speaking truth no matter how rude or painful had turned a rosy pink and said polite people did not speak of such things. Althea could only share what her own mother had told her, and that was precious little.

India shook her head and slumped back down on the settee. Ready or not, she was on the verge of getting her wish. She prayed her labor would be short.

***

Despite her water having broken, the contractions were too far apart. Already twelve hours had passed in which India went from drowsing to crying out in pain. She was exhausted, with nothing to show for her efforts.

Dr. Millhouse drew back from examining India and frowned. "I'm afraid this baby is taking its own sweet time. It seems your body is reluctant to give it up just yet."

Althea stood at the head of the bed, mopping India's face with a damp cloth. "My mother had eleven children. The last one didn't want to be born, just like Her Ladyship's baby. The midwife had Momma get up and walk."

The old man harrumphed and nodded. "Lady Kilnsey, if you are up to the task, I have seen pacing help."

India grimaced and struggled to the side of the bed. With her hand on the small of her back, she made circuits of the bedroom until she couldn't take another step. She stopped by a sideboard, leaned on it for support, and panted, trying to draw sufficient air into her lungs, crowded as they were by the baby. Every breath was an effort. It felt as though the child was tired of being balled in the fetal position and had stretched his arms over his head, pressing into her diaphragm while his feet stomped on her bladder.

A stiletto of terror pierced her heart. Dear Lord, please don't let this be a breech birth. Surely the doctor would have said something if the baby was in the wrong position. She glanced at Dr. Millhouse, who smiled and nodded. His display of confidence and encouragement did nothing to dispel her fears. Despite her exhaustion, or perhaps because of it, India's mind raced out of control with images of births gone terribly wrong. She slumped down onto the settee and buried her face in her hands. What should be the happiest time of her life was turning dark and frightening.

Unable to sit comfortably, she walked to the western windows, peering out into the night in search of what she could not say. Beams from a full moon danced over the boxwood hedges in the Chinese garden below and turned the stone terrace and pathways into rivers of silver. Beyond the garden, a light breeze rippled the moorland grasses, creating pockets of shadow and light where they danced to a tune only they could hear. Nothing sinister lay beyond her window and yet she felt as though she stood on a precipice looking into an impenetrable void that threatened to destroy her happiness and alter her life forever.

She leaned her forehead against the glass. These depressing thoughts must be quelled. They helped neither her nor the baby. The long hours of unproductive labor had played havoc with her emotions. Completely depleted, she trudged back to the bed and lay down. Through closed eyes, tears trickled onto her cheeks.

Dr. Millhouse patted her hand. "There now, Lady Kilnsey. No need for weeping. Let's check your progress." With the examination completed, he lowered her nightgown and smiled. "Good news. Things are progressing again. I think we should have a baby before dawn."

Whether it was the exercise or nature simply finally understanding the task, India's contractions began in earnest. Within the hour, the wail of a newborn filled the room. Althea swaddled the baby in a blanket and placed it in India's arms. All the fears of the previous hours melted as she gazed upon the face of her perfect child.

Dr. Millhouse nodded to Althea. "Tell the others they may come in now."

Charlie rushed to the bed and knelt beside her. Taking her free hand, he kissed it then brushed her temple with his lips. Peering at their child, he said, "In all the excitement, no one has said. Do we have a son?"

India glanced at the doctor, who busied himself with his instruments and medical bag. She then looked at Althea, who drew a long breath before saying, "The baby is perfect and healthy. That is what matters. She looks like Her Ladyship, so she will be a beauty."

India hugged the little bundle tighter to her breast. The expression on Charlie's face could only be described as dismay. It cut to the quick to think she had disappointed him.

He would love their daughter, of that she was sure, but he had counted on a son. Girls were useless to an entailed estate such as Kilnsey. Burying her face in the baby's blanket, she allowed the stress of the last hours to pour onto the cottony softness. Poor baby. Poor little girl, from birth a disappointment to everyone except her mother, whose love mere words were inadequate to express.

CHAPTER 9

India watched her mother-in-law's face as she learned the baby was a girl. God bless Mama. She did her best to hide her disappointment, but despite her superb skill at concealing her true thoughts and emotions, Mama missed the mark this time. India caught her in an unguarded moment when everyone else was focused on the baby. The expression in the older woman's eyes said it all. She looked tired and defeated. Like Charlie, Mama would love the baby, but it did not change the fact that both desperately wanted a son and heir. A wave of protectiveness swept through India.

She tore her eyes from Mama's face and smiled brightly at the doctor and Althea. Pulling the blanket back, India let her fingers drift over the downy dark blonde fluff on the baby's head. The little bundle's eyes flew open. Unusually, instead of the muddy nondescript color she had been told to expect, they were a deep, clear navy. She sighed with adoration and pride. "I think she's the perfect combination of our best features. Who do you think she looks most like?" The question was directed mostly to Charlie.

Leaning closer, Charlie knit his brow and stroked his chin like an Oxford don about to deliver himself of profound judgements. "Yes, I predict she will be a great beauty." Looking at Mama, he continued, "I think there is a likeness to Great-Great Grandmother Adeline's portrait, the one hanging in the gallery. What do you think?"

Mama adjusted her *pince-nez* and leaned forward. "I believe there is." She stepped around from the foot of the bed, coming to rest beside India. "Yes, she has Adeline's eyes. You know, Adeline was the greatest beauty of her generation. During her debut season, it is said that her attendance at a ball ensured all the eligible young men would attend. There were duchesses who purportedly invited her solely on that account despite her family's tenuous connections. The late earl once confided that Adeline's mother had to cobble together a somewhat suspect connection to a Scottish title. It was manufactured by bribes paid to the childless incumbent, if rumors are to be believed. At any rate, Adeline was invited to the best balls and caught the eye of the then Lord Kilnsey." She glanced at Charlie, maternal pride and affection slipping out from behind her normally controlled visage. "My son owes his good looks to Adeline."

India looked from her husband to the baby and back. Yes, even as a newborn, one could see the little girl looked like her papa. Perhaps her imagination and fears were heightened by the exhaustion of a long labor, but the realization of how much the baby looked like Charlie sent a wave of relief through her. Relatives tended to favor children who exhibited a strong family resemblance, which pretty much guaranteed Mama would adore the baby.

India blinked. The Baby. They couldn't keep calling her that. The sweet little mite needed a name. She and Charlie had discussed boys' names on end but had not even mentioned one for a girl. Adeline? Why not? It was a pretty name and was also a family one.

Cocking her head, she gazed down at the angelic face of her infant daughter. She was small for such a big name, but somehow it suited her. It was both strong and feminine, with a history dating back into the ages. Now for the middle name. Mama's given name was Maude. Yes, it fit nicely. Three syllables followed by a single. Mother would never survive having a granddaughter named for Charlie's mother and not her, so Petra Elisabeth was necessary. Lady Adeline Maude Petra Elisabeth. It was quite a mouthful, but the English nobility were accustomed to such.

***

Althea found Robbie in the estate office. Instead of entering immediately, she stood at the window and watched him, his head bent over the accounts with a shock of his lovely dark hair falling forward as it was wont to do. At age 45, he was a devastatingly handsome man. The weathered lines around his eyes and the touch of gray at his temples only added to his good looks. She still marveled that he had noticed her, a mere lady's maid. He must have felt her eyes on him, for he looked up and grinned. Laying his pen on the blotter, he beckoned her join him.

He rose as she entered the office. "I take it by your smile the baby has arrived, and all is well with mother and child. And do we have an heir?"

Althea's smile faded a little. "Unfortunately, no. It's a little girl, but she is beautiful and His Lordship seems to be in love with her despite her sex."

Robbie's face grew solemn. "They're young. I'm sure there will be more babies. One of them is bound to be a boy." He stretched his back and rolled his shoulders. "I'm in need of exercise. Walk with me?"

They left the courtyard by the postern gate and were soon ambling hand-in-hand toward the open moors. As they walked in comfortable silence, Althea considered India and Charlie's plight. While Althea prayed Robbie was right, a worm of anxiety inched its way into her heart. As her courtship with Robbie grew, Althea had come to understand just how desperately estates like Kilnsey needed a male heir. This business of entailment had been totally foreign to her when she first arrived in England. She had only a vague understanding and thought it was like the American tradition of passing farms down to sons instead of daughters. If there were only girls in the family, then the girls got the farm. What she had come to realize is that only first-born sons could inherit an entailed English estate. He got the title, the land, the houses, and the money. The rest of a nobleman's children were completely left out unless there was some other resource outside the entailment. If there was no first-born son, then the estate passed to the nearest male relative in the line of succession. It seemed so very unfair. Here, you had children raised in great luxury who were left to fend for themselves once they were adults. No wonder the debutante season was important for the girls.

As the path rose, Althea sensed a solemnness falling over Robbie. She cast a sideways glance and studied him from beneath her lashes. Yes, his usual jovial expression had been replaced by one more somber. The corners of his mouth had turned down slightly, and a crease had formed between his eyes. He appeared deep in thought. Whatever distracted him, it must not be pleasant for his expression deepened. His brow furrowed as though he pondered a most complex problem.

Althea stopped and placed her free hand on his arm. "What's troubling you? You've gone far away."

Robbie blinked a couple of times as though to remind himself where they were. Lifting her hand, he kissed her palm. "My apologies. I did not mean to appear to ignore you. Quite the opposite, in fact. You are much on my mind."

Althea cocked her head. "How so?"

Robbie chuckled, then his smile dissolved. He turned to her and with his fingers ever so lightly lifted her chin until his eyes gazed deeply into hers. The unspoken communication caused her heart to beat a little faster.

Robbie's expression softened with a small, self-deprecating smile. "I have been thinking about what I'm about to say for months. I've argued with myself that you deserve better, that the difference in our ages is too great, that you may feel only friendship, but in the end, I always come to the same conclusion—that I must ask the question regardless of the potential danger to my heart." His words tumbled to a halt, leaving Althea on the verge of bursting. He seemed to be casting about for encouragement.

She paused long enough to ensure a firm grasp on her emotions and tone. "Go on. Don't leave me hanging."

He looked at the toes of his boots for a few seconds, then met her gaze with one so fraught with emotion it stilled her breath. "You have owned my heart for some time now and will forever. Despite all arguments to the contrary and against better judgement, it is my dearest wish that you do me the honor of becoming my wife. I love you body and soul and cannot imagine life without you by my side."

When she did not answer immediately, he went on. "Of course, you may need time to consider. I will put no pressure on you, but I could go no longer without speaking to you."

Althea wiped away tears from her cheeks. When she saw his distressed expression, she blurted, "Of course I will marry you. I was beginning to think you would never ask. I'm just so overcome with happiness I could not find my blasted voice."

Robbie's hurrah bounced off the surrounding hillsides and rolled through the valleys. Then, he hugged her tightly. Remembering decorum, she pushed back from the embrace. With a small curtsy, she continued, “It would be my greatest pleasure to become Mrs. Robert James. I love you and the life we will have together.”

***

While splashing cold water on her face from the basin in the bathing room, India could have sworn she heard someone shouting. It sounded like joy rather than crisis. Curious all the same, she grabbed a towel and went to the window looking northward over the moors. Movement on the hill nearest the castle caught her eye, and she waited until the cause drew nearer. It was Althea and Robbie. Her heart swelled. By the expressions on their faces and the way Robbie stopped and lifted Althea’s hand to his lips then kissed her in earnest, it appeared he may have finally popped the question. Well, good for him. It was about time.

India hummed happily as she went back to the bedroom. Bending over the antique cradle with its Kilnsey crested canopy and frills, India kissed Adeline’s cheek. The baby stirred for a moment then drifted back into the dreamworld only infants inhabit. India hugged herself and spun in a circle then grabbed a bedpost to keep from falling. The dizziness lasted a second or two more before she felt steady enough to crawl back into bed. This was probably not the best time to be dancing around, but her energy and equilibrium would return all in good time. Shouting her joy would feel fantastic, but it would bring the household running. For now, she would rest and take care of her baby. Life was coming right for everyone she loved and she couldn’t be happier. The world lay open before them and everything in it looked perfect from her vantage point.

CHAPTER 10

India tiptoed into the nursery and peered down at her six-week-old daughter. Her heart swelled with pride. She was prejudiced, of course, but Adeline was surely the most beautiful, the smartest, most wonderful baby in all creation. Bending low, she cradled the infant in her arms and lifted her from the bassinet. Beyond them, a disgruntled harrumph sounded in the entry connecting the nursery to Nanny's sleeping alcove.

"Really, Milady. You'll spoil that child the way you fuss over her all the time. Coddled children are a trial to everyone. Now, just give her to me."

Mama had insisted on hiring Nanny Philby on the recommendation of a great friend whose daughter no longer needed the services of a children's nurse. Not for the first time, India suspected she would come to regret allowing her mother-in-law to influence her in this decision. Nanny Philby was proving to be quite domineering and bossy. India set her mouth in a thin smile and turned to greet her antagonist.

"Good morning, Nanny. Thank you for your concern, but I'm not sure one can spoil a little baby. Besides, I want His Lordship to see Lady Adeline before he heads out for the day. With the summer planting well under way, he will be out until dark. Please have her ready to be taken down. I shall return presently." India passed Adeline into Nanny's outstretched arms and turned on her heel without waiting for a reply.

Although it went against her nature, India had learned how to handle impertinent servants by observing her own mother, and after her marriage, Mama. One must not give in no matter how much one's knees knocked together during a confrontation. If she was honest, India had to admit Nanny Philby scared her. Being a first-time mother left one with a certain amount of insecurity, but she refused to be cowed. Adeline was her baby, and she would care for her in the way she thought best, even if it flew in the face of generations of tradition where leaving the care and rearing of one's children to others was the norm. India returned to the nursery after allowing enough time for Nanny to get the baby clean, dressed, and ready to greet her father.

Swishing into the dining room, India was pleased to see Charlie's plate still full of food. He would be at table longer than anticipated. India paused at the end of the table and frowned. Unusually, Charlie had not looked up when she entered. In fact, he seemed completely unaware of her presence. The morning edition of the York Herald lay folded on the table beside his plate. Robbie leaned over Charlie's shoulder. They both appeared glued to the front page. She slipped up behind Robbie and peered around him for a glimpse.

Archduke Franz Ferdinand, Heir to the Austrian Throne, and His Duchess Murdered screamed from gigantic letters beneath the newspaper's masthead. The subheading shouted *Will Europe Go to War?* At India's audible intake of air, both men glanced in her direction.

She gripped Charlie's shoulder. "Do you really think there will be a war? I had hoped Bumpy was just being his usual obnoxious self when he talked about it at Christmas. For heaven's sake! King George and the Kaiser are first cousins."

Charlie placed his hand over hers but did not look up. "Unfortunately, at present family connections count for little. Unless exceptional diplomacy occurs, I am very afraid this tragedy will result in armed conflict."

The feeling that the world had suddenly become a very uncertain place slithered around India's heart. She hugged Adeline closer and kissed the top of her head. The baby's eyes flew open, and she graced her mother with a gummy smile then cooed. It sounded so much like language India smiled despite the alarming headlines. At least some things would remain certain no matter what happened beyond the walls of their home and borders of the estate. The most certain of all was the unbounded love she felt for her child and husband.

Bending so Adeline was within her father's line of sight, India said, "Did you hear that? I swear she's trying to talk. I know it's much too early, but still, it sounded like she wanted to say something." When he did not respond, India tapped his shoulder. "Charlie, did you hear?"

Charlie glanced up. "What? Oh, yes. She is a darling baby." He leaned over and kissed Adeline, then returned his attention to the newspaper. Having reached the end of the article, he looked at Robbie. "We must make rounds of the farms. If war comes, the army is going to need all the food we can produce. Let's look at where we can grow more grains and how the breeding program can be improved. The Home Farm will certainly agree to increased production, but we need to ensure the tenants are on board as well. "

Robbie stroked his chin and cut his eyes at India before replying, "Yes, we do, but I don't anticipate any real resistance except perhaps from Holden." Robbie paused as though reluctant to continue. "I . . . I believe there may still be some awkwardness there."

At the name Holden, memories of their wedding and the week afterward came flooding back. For such a long time, Charlie had believed himself in love with Farmer Holden's daughter, Annie. Then, even after she and Charlie married, he still thought Annie's child was his. It took a very uncomfortable hour over tea in the Holden farmhouse inglenook to set Charlie straight. Thank goodness Annie turned out to be less than Charlie thought her to be. Her baby was the offspring of her husband, a cousin on her mother's side, to whom she was engaged while she was carrying on the dalliance with Charlie. When she realized she could not catch an earl after all, she fled to Ireland to marry her longtime fiancé. Farmer Holden apparently still held Charlie responsible for his daughter's sullied reputation.

With a distracted kiss from Charlie and a nod from Robbie, the two men marched from the dining room. India went to the window and watched as they strode across the courtyard and through the main gate. No doubt they were going to get saddle horses from the estate stable in the village. They would speak with the farmers and secure their cooperation. Of that, she was sure.

Not long after they married, India discovered something about her husband she had not previously realized. Charlie had shown himself to be a natural leader, and it was not simply because he was the lord of the manor. The men on the estate looked up to him, liked him, enjoyed his company. The fact that he worked alongside them in the fields must have contributed to their view, but there was something more. There existed within him an indefinable trait, a sort of charisma, that elicited other men's respect and desire to follow him.

Adeline stirred and whimpered. India shifted the precious bundle's weight and swayed slowly from side-to-side. The baby yawned and settled into a gentle sleep. Lucky baby. She could dream of whatever babies dreamed secure in her mother's arms, loved and protected, unlike her parents whose own sense of security had just been shattered by a newspaper headline. An uneasiness lodged itself in the pit of India's stomach. Their happy, safe world felt as if it might slip away at any moment and there was nothing either of them could do to prevent it.

CHAPTER 11

India looked around the third-floor tower room and gave herself a little hug. This was perfect for an art studio. The light beaming in from the corner windows was exactly right. With a good cleaning, cabinets put in place, and art supplies gathered, she could spend a few hours here each week in much-needed solitude. With nothing but talk of impending war on everyone's lips, stress had become her constant companion. A month had passed since that idiot murdered Archduke Ferdinand. All over the continent, sabers had gone from rattling to clanging. All anyone spoke of was how the boiling Balkan pot was going to drag all of Europe into conflict. Austria and Serbia were already at each other's throats. If she allowed it, despair could easily overtake her. She gave herself a mental shake. Dwelling on something over which she had no control was pointless.

She had found the room quite by accident while searching for unused furniture they might give to Althea and Robbie to furnish their soon-to-be home in the village. Charlie had suggested she set one of the footmen to the task, but India wanted to make the selections herself. It was a small gift to her dearest friend, and it gave her an excellent excuse to go exploring on her own. With the wedding set for early September, Charlie had seen to the renovation of a sweet cottage with roses framing the door. The contractor who did the stable-to-garage conversion was glad to stay on for the cottage redo. Charlie took his duties as best man seriously, as did she as matron of honor. Between wedding planning, caring for Adeline, and trying to keep everyone's spirits up, she was exhausted. If she didn't have something positive and creative in which to lose herself, she would surely go crazy.

Placing a hand on each hip, she surveyed the room again and envisioned herself slipping away in the afternoons while Mama napped and Charlie was out on the farms with Robbie. The room was right above their private parlor with easy access from their apartment. Yes, it would do splendidly. At least this one small thing would be right in a world seemingly on the verge of losing its collective mind.

Simply having decided upon a space of her own buoyed her spirits. Now, all that remained was a trip into York to purchase art supplies. While pregnant, she hadn't traveled farther than the village of Kilnsey. Charlie, Mama, and Dr. Millhouse had been adamant. It was time she resumed her normal activities.

Tomorrow was Tuesday, a good day for shopping. She and Althea could take the early train to York and make an overnight of it. They would visit the dressmaker to order Althea's wedding clothes and a matron-of-honor ensemble for India. On Wednesday afternoon, she would drop by the Women's Social and Political Union office before they took the late afternoon train home. It would make a lovely outing, the first she had had since the baby's birth.

She and Charlie had reached an uneasy truce on her involvement with the suffragists, operating on a "no news is good news" plan. As long as she kept her involvement confidential, she could assist the effort on a limited basis. It was not the complete independence she craved, but it was more than most of her contemporaries enjoyed. Charlie was far more progressive than most Englishmen, but in the end, he was still a man and a peer of the realm.

***

With breakfast completed, India skewered her hat in place with the lovely mother-of-pearl hat pin Mama had given her for Christmas, then admired her reflection in the bedroom's cheval mirror. She ran her hands over her waist and hips, turning this way and that, sighing with relief. The last of the baby weight had disappeared. She had her figure back, but with some subtle differences. Her bosom was fuller, her hips more rounded, and there was a little pooching at the belly where it had once been flat. Altogether, it was not bad for being two and one-half months postpartum. Just last night, Charlie had remarked approvingly. Exchanging her girl's figure for that of a mature woman was the price she would gladly pay a thousand times over for their beautiful Adeline. At the rate she and Charlie still lusted for one another, baby number two might come sooner rather than later.

With a final adjustment to her hat, she ventured downstairs headed for the auto where Barton and Althea were already ensconced. Today would be a good day, one she planned to enjoy to the fullest.

Mama awaited her at the foot of the grand staircase. "Are you sure this journey is wise, my dear?"

India's heart rate kicked up a notch at the note of warning in the old lady's voice. Keeping her nerves in check, India raised a brow in feigned surprise and innocence. "Why ever not? Surely there is no danger in an overnight stay at York's finest hotel. Just because Austria and Serbia are at war, it does not follow that terrorists now roam the English countryside."

Mama harrumphed and pursed her lips. "It is unseemly to make light of a war that may soon involve all of us. That being said, it is not foreign affairs which concern me. Do you plan to pursue your personal interests while in York?"

India glanced at the door and took a step toward it. She had neither the time nor the patience for an inquisition. "Of course. Althea really must order her gown now. The wedding is only five weeks away. Our appointment with the dressmaker is right after luncheon, so we must be off. We cannot miss the nine o'clock train."

India turned to leave, but Mama waylaid her with a hand on her arm. "Do not be disingenuous. You may have Charles fooled, but I suspect this little jaunt has a dual purpose. It does not take two days to have a dress fitting for a servant's gown. You are going to the suffragists' office, aren't you?"

India's eyes widened before she could stop them. Drat. It was as though the woman had read her mind.

Mama pursed her lips then continued, "Yes, I can see the truth in your face. Have a care, my dear. While I may be in some sympathy with their cause, pouring phosphorus down pillar boxes, as was done so recently, is beyond the pale. It is a miracle the postman opening the box wasn't killed in the ensuing explosion. We wish to see neither your face nor your name in the press nor should you be the subject on gossips' tongues."

Heat crawled up from India's throat until her cheeks burned. Was it embarrassment at being caught in a lie or anger at being ordered about that sent her emotions into such a spin? Mama could be an insufferable tyrant when she chose.

India crossed her arms under her bosom and met Mama's gaze with determination. She would not be treated like a wayward child. The vote was too important. "I will keep my part of the bargain, but I will not be dissuaded from supporting the cause where I am able. I will work for a few hours in the office and make another donation from my personal funds. It is what we agreed. Charlie has no objections."

A little jab of guilt pricked India's conscience. In truth, Charlie had no idea she planned to visit the W.S.P.U. office on this trip. He was so consumed with organizing the estate's farms for increased production she had not wanted to upset him with plans which might add to his worry.

***

On Wednesday afternoon, India left Althea at the dressmaker's for fittings and hailed a taxi. The driver frowned when she gave her destination, but he had the good sense to not comment upon it. The taxi pulled away from the curb and India settled back against the seat. This was usually her favorite drive—down Petergate past the Minster, then right onto cobbles that passed between Tudor blocks leaning out over the city's oldest streets. Today, she watched the passing scenery in increasing agitation. The morning's headlines had been alarming. While there was no immediate danger, future events might well shatter the hopes and dreams of every British family, whether high-born or low. As they rounded the last corner, India's mid-section churned at the sight of the W.S.P.U. sign hanging above the office door. These trips to York represented independence, her chance to be the woman she wanted to be.

It wasn't just for herself that these days meant so much. She loved Charlie deeply and wanted his happiness, but she loved Adeline just as much, actually more in one important way, with a mother's fierce desire to protect. Adeline's generation deserved better than their mothers' experience as second class, near non-citizens dependent on their fathers' and husbands' goodwill. She aided the movement for herself, her child, and all women. How much longer that might be possible was anyone's guess.

India paid the driver and stepped through the door of the W.S.P.U. into a whirlwind of activity and an atmosphere of anxiety. Typists pounded frantically. Telephones shrieked as soon as a call ended. Anyone wishing to be heard was forced to yell. Women ran to and fro, carrying boxes and piles of file folders.

In the back of the cavernous room, several women gestured in the most dramatic fashion around the group's president. Faces that were visible wore scowls, their mouths open in snarls. It did not take a sixth sense to discern what they argued about. It was surely the topic screaming from the headlines of every newspaper in the land—*Great Britain Declares War on Germany: Summary Rejection of British Ultimatum Regarding Invasion of Belgium.* At present, the snatches of discourse India heard indicated the immediate concern was the potential impact on the movement.

She hesitated in the reception area, straining to get a firm grip on her emotions before charging into the fray. Oddly, the tension accompanying the buildup to war had disappeared overnight, replaced by a strange sense of relief that the waiting was over but also dread of what war would mean for the family, for Charlie.

Instead of requesting an assignment, India moved toward the group. Their shouts grew ever more frantic the closer she got. The beleaguered president watched India's approach with something near elation. Or was it relief written across the woman's face? Probably some of both. India's position and title had been a welcome addition to the membership rolls since the day she communicated her interest in the cause. Being a countess gave her a definite cachet among the other ladies. Her opinions were given the utmost respect despite her being only twenty-two and an American. Perhaps she could help the poor woman out.

The president waved and shouted above the din, "Lady Kilnsey. How delighted we are to see you. Please join us."

India hid a smile as the ladies stepped aside to make room for her. The Red Sea parting at Moses's command could not have moved faster. India nodded to the group, which fell silent. "Thank you, Mrs. Goodman. By the amount of activity today, I fear I may have come at a bad time?"

The president shook her head vehemently. "Oh, no. Never. In fact, you are just in time to assist us in making a most difficult decision. Perhaps you might share your thoughts."

"And what decision would that be?"

Mrs. Goodman's hands fluttered. "Oh, dear me. Please forgive my thoughtlessness. Of course, you have no idea what we discuss."

India smiled and nodded. The poor woman was already upset enough without being corrected. "Please, go on."

"Yes, the subject at hand is what to do now the nation is at war. Do we continue the fight or do we abandon it in deference to the war effort? How do we balance patriotic duty with the justness of our cause?" Mrs. Goodman's speech ended with the whine of pleading.

India blinked. Yes, those were definitely the right questions, but now that they had been voiced, the answers weren't as clear as one might have hoped.

CHAPTER 12

India drew a long breath and exhaled slowly. All eyes were trained on her, awaiting answers to questions she felt ill-equipped to address. Remembered newspaper photographs of women being imprisoned and force-fed for demanding their rights flashed through her mind followed by battlefield pictures of previous wars presented in history books from her school days. Both patriotism and suffrage were critical issues, but which took precedence now? As she pondered the question, an image of a far more personal nature pushed aside those memories. Charlie, dressed in military khaki, stood before her as though she could reach out and touch him. It was not a memory but a foreshadowing of her greatest fear. Her pulse raced as Charlie fell to the ground wounded and bleeding.

She blinked and tilted her head back for a moment then let her gaze sweep the group, pausing just long enough to meet the eyes of each lady before speaking in a voice hoarse with unshed tears. "I truly believe our husbands, fathers, brothers, and sons will soon be in uniform. The call for volunteers may come at any moment. Our men are patriots and will answer the call to duty. How can we women do any less? I propose we table our quest for the vote until peace has been declared, however long that may take."

Some ladies appeared taken aback and angry, their eyes narrowed and lips pursed. Others seemed awestruck by realities they had not yet considered. They looked to one another for solace, nodding and clasping one another's hands.

A well-dressed lady beside Mrs. Goodman scowled. "Don't be absurd. This will all be over by Christmas. My husband has friends at the War Office, so he should know. We should continue as we are."

A low roar ensued until an older woman dressed in the sensible garb of genteel poverty held up a hand, demanding silence. "All of us are old enough to remember the Boer Wars and the tactics used by both sides. Those conflicts were on and off for years. We have no real assurance of how long this present war will last. It may indeed be over quickly or it may not. I suggest we adopt a wait and see attitude. Madame President, I believe it is much too soon to make any decisions regarding our cause." The speaker fixed Mrs. Goodman with a firm expression.

"Perhaps you are correct. Let us wait and pray it is a brief conflict." Turning to India, the president continued, "Thank you, Lady Kilnsey. You have certainly given us something to think about."

India forced a smile, nodded, and turned away. The leadership of York W.S.P.U. might be unsure how to proceed, but she certainly knew where she stood. It was firmly by Charlie's side no matter what the future held. She left the offices without offering either her time or her money.

India instructed the taxi driver to drop her at the Minster. She wanted some exercise before meeting Althea in a little tea shop nearby. A leisurely stroll would calm her nerves and help her decide how much of what had just transpired she would relate. Althea, who usually followed India into all adventures, drew the line at getting involved with the suffragists. She valued her position and refused to endanger it. It rankled, but all staff were Charlie's employees, people he could dismiss without reference if he became angry enough. The thought of Althea being forced to leave Kilnsey Castle was not to be borne. Perhaps Althea needed to hear the whole story to protect her from unintended blunders if questioned about their time in York.

***

At the tinkle of the shop bell, Althea looked up from a magazine spread open before her on the table. She placed her teacup on its saucer and eyed India as she approached. "Well, that didn't take long. I was all ready for a nice read." She studied India for a moment. "You look like you could use a cup of tea." She signaled to a waitress while India took the seat opposite. "And have a scone for energy. They're delicious. The owner said the cream and strawberries came in from a local farm just this morning."

As Althea listened to India's description of events at the suffragists' office, her mind turned to Robbie and their wedding just over a month off. Robbie felt the difference in their ages was a negative, but it was really a godsend. He was surely too old to enlist. The army would never accept a man in his mid-forties. Of course they wouldn't. While Charlie was of prime military age, she need not worry where Robbie was concerned. Even if His Lordship chose to fight for his country, Robbie would remain on the estate. He would manage the tenants and Home Farm as he always had. Together, they would stand by India in Charlie's absence.

They left the shop with only enough time to rush for the only remaining first class compartment. Breathing heavily, Althea shoved their packages onto the overhead rack and plopped down on the seat opposite India.

Flapping a handkerchief near her face, she said, "As soon as the train moves out of the station, I will lower the windows. It's stifling in here." India looked at her as though she had heard the words but did not comprehend them. After an uncomfortable pause, she nodded, a blank expression in her eyes.

The train trip home was a silent affair, with Althea casting intermittent glances at India, who seemed lost in worry. A crease drew her brows together and her mouth turned down at the corners. As they pulled into Grassington Depot, India did not stir. In fact, when their carriage lurched to a stop, she sat as though she had no idea where they were or what they should do next.

Althea laid a hand over India's bunched fists and squeezed. "We need to gather our things. Barton is headed this way." When India did not move or respond, Althea rose. Bending slightly, she grasped India's shoulder and gave it a shake. "It's time to get off the train."

India blinked twice and seemed to finally surface from whatever dark hole her mind had lodged itself. "Oh, yes. Of course. Please open the door and let him know where to find us."

Once ensconced in the Rolls, India fell silent again. Althea glanced at her mistress and prayed this did not portend what the future held. If so, Robbie would have an even greater burden in keeping the estate running. If India slipped into melancholia, she would be of little use to anyone, not even the baby.

They arrived in the castle courtyard to find His Lordship racing from the castle and coming to rest in front of the Rolls. Barton had to slam on the brakes to avoid a collision.

Charlie strode to the passenger door and flung it wide. "Mama tells me you decided to pay a visit to the suffragette office while you were in York." He turned his glare upon

Althea. "Please take Her Ladyship to our apartment. I will meet her there presently." Having given what could only be described as an order, he turned and marched away toward the estate office without a backward glance. The office door opened and slammed shut before she dared look at India.

Althea glanced across the footwell to where her mistress sat on the opposite seat. Never had she heard His Lordship speak that way to his wife. He appeared truly angry. India's lips were set in a thin line, and she scowled at nothing in particular.

Althea started to speak, but India waylaid her with a fist striking her palm. "If he thinks he is going to order me about like some chambermaid, he has another think coming. I'll make my own way to our apartment, thank you very much. I do not need a keeper. When he deigns to join me, he will get the fight he obviously wants."

Althea glanced at Barton, who stood at attention awaiting India's hand to assist her in descending from the auto. He refused to meet her gaze. Ignoring his proffered hand, India jumped from the vehicle and steamed toward the castle's entry, leaving Althea to place her hand in the chauffeur's.

As she stepped down, Barton whispered, "His Lordship has rowed with the Dowager Countess. He defended Her Ladyship when his mother criticized the York trip. Just thought Her Ladyship should know."

Althea removed her hand from the chauffeur's grasp and smiled. "Thank you, Barton. I appreciate the information." She turned and started toward the castle entrance.

Barton cleared his throat loudly. Althea stopped and looked back at him. "Is there something else?"

"Begging pardon for the cheek, but I think Her Ladyship should know that we, that is the other members of staff and me, we all think she is a grand lady. She has our loyalty because she is kind and generous." He stammered to a halt, his cheeks turning the color of her favorite deep pink roses in the cutting garden. "Just thought she should know."

"Of course, and I'll tell her. Thank you." She resumed her journey to the castle, but the estate office door flew open and Charlie rushed out, no doubt headed for India. Unsure whether to speak or follow, Althea stood motionless as her master marched past.

Charlie frowned and called over his shoulder, "Go to the office. Robbie wants a word."

So, she was not to be privy to what India and Charlie had to say to one another. Just as well. She wanted to tell Robbie about the perfect wedding gown she had ordered. It was simple and elegant, just right for a country wedding in a village church. India and Charlie's generosity with them made Althea's heart glow with happiness, but with a goodly amount of humility, as well. Growing up on a mountain farm in an unpainted dogtrot cabin, she never envisioned the life she was about to embark upon. There may be a war on, but she and Robbie would be safely tucked away together on this lovely Yorkshire estate.

She dashed through the office door, all bubbly excitement, until she saw Robbie's face. He looked like a man who was about to be executed. The desolation darkening his eyes sent a jolt of terror through her.

"What is it? Has something terrible happened? Surely the Germans have not invaded already. That seems impossible."

Robbie got up, walked around his desk, and took her hands, kissing each in turn. He drew his lower lip between his teeth and sighed. "My darling, I believe we should rethink marrying."

Althea gasped and took a step back. "Why? What on earth has made you change your mind? Have you decided you don't love me after all?"

He shook his head slowly, gazing at her with such longing that she wanted to cry out. "Far from it. I love you with all my heart, but I feel I would do you a complete disservice by marrying you now. No one can predict what this war may do to the nation or our people. It would not be fair to tie you down under such circumstances."

Althea's hand flew to her mouth to stifle a scream. Robbie's integrity was one of the many things she loved about him, but this was taking it too far—way too far by any measure. Her heart and head thumped in time together. What could she say to rid him of this ridiculous notion? She swallowed hard and fought back the anguish his words had brought. When she had a better grip, she stepped close and laid the back of her hand against his cheek. She looked into his eyes, hoping he could see the depth of her love and the truth of what she wanted to say.

"While I appreciate your sentiments, I reject them completely. I want to be tied to you forever no matter what comes. I will simply not accept what you say. You may think it gallant, but it breaks my heart. I will not bear life without you. That is the sum of it. You are stuck with me. Period. End of discussion."

His desperation and icy determination of just moments ago melted away. Looking at her askance, he studied her with such longing that she started to speak again, but he put a finger to her lips and continued to stare into her eyes.

Finally, he nodded. "I can see you are in earnest. I do not have the will to resist you. Against my better judgement, we will proceed with the wedding plans. I am a selfish cad for allowing this, but I love you too much to do the right thing."

Exasperation flooded Althea. She put a hand on his chest and gave a little push. “You men can be so infuriating. Marrying the person you love is the right thing to do, the only right thing.”

He swept her into a deep, passionate kiss that took her breath away. It was only after he broke the embrace that it occurred to her to wonder why he thought giving her up was the right thing to do.

CHAPTER 13

India heard Charlie's boots thudding on the hall runner. She dropped the magazine through which she was absentmindedly flipping, stiffened her spine, and turned toward the door. The tramping stopped, and he banged into their private parlor with all the grace and charm of an enraged bull. Setting his sights on her, he charged with eyes blared. "We are at war. What ·were you thinking going to that office? Those women may well now be viewed as aiding the enemy with their demonstrations and anti-government claptrap."

India's eyes narrowed. She stood with fists balled at her sides. "In no way are they aiding the enemy. If anyone is acting the traitor, it is Parliament that refuses to grant to us what is ours by right. By denying women the vote, Parliament is denying our humanity, making us less than the bootboy who shines your shoes."

They stood leaning toward one another with flushed faces, anger radiating from their bodies, neither willing to give way.

Charlie was the first to bend. "Look, I understand your desire. I really do, but there are greater things at stake now that Britain's declared war. Please tell me you realize this."

India gave herself a little shake and flexed her fingers. "Of course I do. And for your information, just today I suggested to the W.S.P.U. that we suspend activities until hostilities cease. Whether they will take my advice is anyone's guess, but I will stand by our country and its fighting men."

Charlie visibly relaxed. "I should have known better than to believe less of you." He wrapped her in an embrace, which she at first resisted, then eased into until her cheek rested on his chest. Kissing the top of her head, he continued, "I pray the braggarts in London are correct and this will be over by Christmas, but I fear it somehow may last far longer and change all our lives for the worse. In all likelihood, there will be a call for volunteers. When it comes, I will do my bit." The last sentence came in a near whisper, his voice catching on the last word.

India stuffed a knuckle into her mouth and bore down. She had known he would feel that way, but hearing the actual words seared her mind, heart, and soul.

***

The days of August crawled by with a succession of reports on how the British Expeditionary Force, made up of 120,000 professional soldiers, was faring in France and which nation was the most recent to declare war on a neighbor. Before the month ended, conflict engulfed nearly the whole of Europe. German troops were crashing through Belgium on their way to take Paris, and just as Charlie had predicted, Lord Kitchener was calling for volunteers to grow the British ranks. As much as she supported Britain in the fight, India dreaded the start of each day and the casualty reports it brought.

Charlie looked up from his newspaper as India took her seat at the breakfast table. His face was grim.

“Is there bad news?” She didn’t really want the answer, but better to have done with than allow it to hang in the air like the odor emanating from a cesspool.

He nodded and breathed heavily. “A good friend from my school days is listed among the casualties. He was killed at Mons. After our time together, he entered Sandhurst and became an officer.” His gaze drifted to the dining room windows overlooking the Chinese boxwood garden. It was as though he could not meet her eyes.

India watched him for a moment, her heart beating faster with each breath she took. “Tell me what is on your mind. I can’t bear the suspense a second longer.”

He replied in a smile tinged with sadness and conviction. “You know me too well. I had hoped to delay telling you about a decision I’ve made, but I see trying to save you from the truth for a few days longer is futile.” Infuriatingly, he stopped speaking and took a sip of coffee.

India’s fist hit the table, setting the china rattling. “Don’t stop there. By God, go ahead and tell me. You are volunteering, aren’t you?”

He finally met her eyes. “Yes. As Lord Kitchener has asked, I am forming a Pals unit made up of men from the county, including Cragfast Mastiles and Kilnsey villages. We will train together and be sent abroad as a unit.”

“And you will be their captain?”

“As it stands now, I will. If a more capable officer emerges during training, I’ll be happy to step aside and follow rather than lead.”

India’s stomach roiled. The food on the sideboard no longer held any appeal. “How much longer will you have at home?”

“Not much, I’m afraid. The quota for the company is almost complete. When I’ve secured the final few recruits, we leave for Breary Banks Camp at Colsterdale. We’ll join the

15th Battalion, West Yorkshire Regiment with some lads from Leeds."

"And just when were you planning on breaking this news? It seems you've been recruiting for quite some time now. Did you think I would be uninterested? You've gone behind my back and made plans that have a tremendous impact on my life and that of everyone on the estate without so much as a by your leave."

"I didn't mean for it to be this way. I thought it would take much longer to recruit the number of men needed. I thought there would be time for you to get accustomed to the idea, but as it is, things are simply moving much faster than I anticipated."

One corner of India's mouth lifted in irony. "It seems Yorkshiremen are a patriotic lot. Will you be taking any of the household staff?"

"Several of the footmen and Barton have signed on as has Yarboro. He will serve as my batman. For him, at least, nothing much will change. A batman's duties are almost identical to a valet's."

India blinked in surprise. In no way could one equate serving in a manor house with being on a battlefield. It was unthinkable, but she was grateful to the valet. She softened her tone. "I'm glad Yarboro will be with you. He is reliable and has a lot of common sense." What she did not add was unlike Charlie, who had been known to let his emotions govern his head on more than one occasion.

How could he be so loving a husband and father and yet such a thoughtless ass about his leaving to go to war? He actually believed he would spare her by keeping this a secret for as long as possible. Unbelievable. If she stayed another moment, she would start shrieking at the stupidity and senselessness of it all. But as angry as she was, sobbing and shouting at Charlie would do neither of them any good. She rose and shoved her chair back.

Charlie looked at her in surprise. "Are you not eating?"

She managed to choke out a "no" before she fled the room. Despite her emotions running at full flood, he must not see how truly devastated she was by his thoughtlessness. He was going to war with every possibility of never returning. It would only make his burden greater if he saw her wailing and screaming like a banshee. As terribly difficult as it would be, she must buck up and face head-on what was coming. She must have courage and show everyone she, too, could bear hardship with a stiff upper lip. It would be expected and would be what was needed. The needs of others became a great weight threatening to crush her, but she would bear it.

Charlie needed her. Adeline and Mama needed her. The whole damned estate would soon need her. Thank God Robbie was too old to enlist.

***

Althea gazed at her image in the cheval mirror in India's bedroom, feeling out-of-place and exhilarated at the same time. The young woman who looked back was almost unrecognizable. She was dressed in a wedding gown of ivory cotton lawn, the same India had worn for her wedding. With His Lordship scheduled to leave for training shortly, she and Robbie decided to move the ceremony forward so the best man could be present. In the end, she canceled her order for a wedding gown. The dressmaker said she could not possibly finish the chosen design in time with the date changed. It was probably for the best. She really had no need for a dress that she would only wear one time.

Althea turned this way and that, gauging where India's gown might need alteration. Surprisingly, it was a pretty good fit as was. Just let out the waist and hem a little and it would be perfect. The matching veil complimented her better than she had dreamed. Thinking about India's and His Lordship's generosity swelled Althea's heart. No newlyweds could want for more. Now her mistress was acting as lady's maid, fluffing the veil and straightening the train.

India poked her head around from behind. "You look beautiful, so why do I see tears in your eyes?"

Althea swiped a finger under each eye. "I guess I'm feeling a little overwhelmed. Robbie and I have been engaged for such a short time. The world is falling apart, but we're so happy. You've been kind and generous. Somehow it feels thoughtless and unfair, especially to you and His Lordship." Her eyes locked with India's reflected gaze. "I feel like such an imposition with the troubles you're facing. Maybe we should wait."

India stepped from behind, coming to rest between Althea and the mirror. "Do you love him?"

"What?"

"I said, do you love Robbie?"

"Of course, more than I ever dreamed it is possible to love someone."

"And he feels the same about you. I ask you, which is better? Being happy or not getting married because it feels like an inconvenience for others?"

Althea noticed that India's eyes were brighter than usual. "Here I am going on about petty stuff when you're so worried about His Lordship. I don't know what has gotten into me."

"Wedding jitters. Every bride has them. Put the silliness out of your mind. I'm having fun in my role as matron of honor." A crease formed between India's brows. "I need something to focus on besides my own troubles. Charlie is so distracted these days, it's hard to talk to him about anything."

***

India stood at the altar with the Reverend Howard, Robbie, and Charlie, all eyes trained on the church door. In a moment, the strains of the bride's processional would begin and Althea would be escorted down the aisle by Ainsworth, substituting for a father who had neither the money nor the inclination "to haul hisself halfway 'rount the world jist to see his daughter marry a jumped up, confounded furriner."

When Althea had read aloud her father's response to the wedding invitation, she mimicked his pronunciation perfectly, sending India into fits of laughter. The next line, however, brought tears and anger. "Any man who don't own the land he works ain't worth a plug nickel. You and your young'uns ain't gonna amount to nothing if you hitch yorself to such. Since you got your mind set, good riddance. Daughters ain't nothing but trouble, no how." At that point, Althea had dropped the letter into the fireplace and set a match to it. The ash was removed quickly and the topic not discussed again. India prayed Althea had put the whole sorry episode away without giving it another thought.

Fortunately, the sister to whom Althea was closest had written on behalf of all the sisters a wonderfully supportive letter expressing their best wishes and congratulations on making a miraculous escape from marrying a man like Daddy. That second letter had brightened Althea's spirits immensely. India made a note to offer the girl passage and a position in the castle if the need ever arose for her to make a similar escape.

The organist sounded the trumpet voluntary, and the bride began her journey to the altar. India smiled and winked at Althea then glanced at the groom. If ever a man loved a woman to the point of worship, it was Robbie James. His eyes saw only his bride, and they were filled to the brim with love, joy, and pride. Althea gazed at her groom with a demurer expression, but one just as joyful and loving.

Feeling someone watching her, India looked to where Charlie stood slightly behind the groom. His eyes were brighter than normal. They, too, communicated a love that cherished the beheld, but instead of joy, shadows of longing and disquiet darkened them. He was so distracted these last weeks it felt as if a chasm yawned between them. He had ignored their child to the point she feared he might not really love Adeline because of her sex. India's heart had become Janus, the Roman god of transitions and duality. It swelled with joy for Althea and Robbie, but ached for what lay ahead for Charlie and herself.

Althea reached the altar and Ainsworth placed her hand in Robbie's. To India's great relief, the wedding party could finally turn to face the vicar. No one in the congregation would see the tears threatening to spill down her cheeks. She sniffed and forced herself to concentrate on Reverend Howard as he droned the opening words of the service.

"Dearly Beloved, we are gathered here in the sight of God, and in the face of this Congregation..."

CHAPTER 14

One week to the day after the wedding, while Althea and Robbie were still on their honeymoon in a Scottish Highland cottage by the sea, India stood on the platform at Grassington Depot with her hand clinging to Charlie's arm as though he might disappear in a puff of smoke. Her heart ached knowing he would soon do exactly that. Along with the fifty local men he had promised Kitchener's recruiting officer, he would board a train carrying him away in a cloud of coal smoke belching from the engine's stack.

He wore the rank of captain. As an earl, it was assumed and then confirmed that he would lead the men he recruited. The bespoke uniform fit him beautifully. It was amazing what a good tailor could do with thick wool twill fabric. The puttees wrapped his ankles and calves looked odd to her eye but were apparently an important safety measure. The polished brass insignia badge on his cap flashed in the sun. He looked every inch the gallant soldier and leader of men. It seemed impossible he was even more handsome in drab khaki than in his gray and black morning suit.

It took all her strength not to scream and cry, begging him not to leave her alone to shoulder the responsibility of the estate. Although she had been around crops and livestock all her life, she had been an observer, never a farmer. Robbie would manage the day-to-day operations, but any major decision would fall to her as Countess of Kilnsey. Her knees buckled, and she gripped Charlie's arm even harder.

He looked at her with concern. "Are you all right, my dear? The day is uncomfortably warm. Perhaps you should sit in the depot."

Heat spread across her cheeks. "I'm fine. I just stumbled on the pebbles. They rolled when I shifted my weight. They really should do something about this gravel. Why they haven't paved the platform is a mystery." Babbling. Again. Whenever she became flustered. Would she never rid herself of the habit?

He raised a brow, studied her for a moment, then nodded, satisfied what she said was true. "If you are sure you aren't becoming ill, I must confirm that all the men have arrived and are ready to board. It won't take long. I'll be back in a few minutes to board myself. Will you be all right waiting here?"

Unable to speak without betraying her true feelings, she simply nodded. She refused to add to his worries with a display of emotion or by becoming hysterical. He shot her a grateful smile and left her standing by the door to his first-class compartment.

Pride mixed with terror flooded India as she watched Charlie marshal his men, starting with those of their household. He stopped briefly with Barton, their chauffeur, Yarboro, his valet, and the footmen who stood in a small group smoking and chatting, then moved on to the farmers, shopkeepers, and their lads. Charlie stood out not only for being the only man in uniform, but in the way he moved among the men and how many of them tugged their forelocks at his approach. He presented every inch a respected and trusted leader.

Charlie stopped beside a man smaller than the others. He lifted the man's chin with a finger, then shook his head. After they exchanged a few words, Charlie patted the man's cheek and pulled a cap off his head. The "man" was only a boy of probably fifteen. Charlie took him by the shoulders, turned him toward the road, and gave him a gentle push.

The boy trudged away with hunched shoulders, throwing disgruntled looks over his shoulder every few steps. The other volunteers chuckled, but they did not laugh outright. The boy had offered himself in service of his country, which they clearly respected, though one did call out, "Come back in three years, sonny, if we ain't already whipped them Germans by then." As the boy passed India, he surreptitiously swiped at tears. With a maternal sigh, she turned away. Maybe he would eventually realize how lucky he was to be too young to go to war.

When his men were aboard, Charlie returned to India's side. Taking her in his arms, he kissed her with a passion that spoke of longing, desperation, and finally resignation. He held her so closely the breath whooshed from her lungs, making her dizzy. She squirmed against his chest until he broke the embrace and met her eyes.

"I'm sorry, my darling. I'm afraid the tensions of the moment carried me away. I'll miss you terribly. This will be our last kiss for some time. I wanted, nay needed, it to convey all that my British upbringing causes me difficulty in expressing." He lifted her hand to his lips. "Please say you understand."

"Of course I do, but it would be nice to hear you try to put your feelings into words. I'll help you by speaking first. I love you with all my heart and soul. Being without you will be torture, but I know it's necessary. I will write to you every day so you will know what is happening on the estate. I will show Adeline your picture, so she will not forget her papa." When her voice betrayed her by shaking, she stopped speaking and swallowed hard. Through tears, she continued, "We will all be waiting for you and loving you and praying for your safe return. You are the love of my life. I cannot imagine one without you. You better take care of yourself." A sound somewhere between a laugh and a sob colored her final words.

He was silent for several seconds, then lifted her face, kissing each cheek and her forehead. "Oh, my dearest love. Mere words are inadequate to express my feelings. My love for you and our child is beyond any emotion I ever expected to experience. It is simple and enormous all at once. You are my love and my life." He smiled wistfully and traced her jaw with his fingertips. "How was that? Not too bad, I hope, for a stiff British officer."

He was ever one to resort to wry humor when life was at its most serious, but he could not hide the very real tears shimmering in his eyes. India's heart split open. She buried her face in his uniform tunic to hide her own tears. He kissed the top of her head, released her, climbed into the carriage, and was gone. India stood among the other wives and sweethearts waving until the last carriage disappeared in the distance.

India returned to the Rolls, where Ainsworth stood at attention. Charlie had learned quite by accident that the butler knew how to drive an automobile and had pressed him into service for this trip and for the day Robbie and Althea would return from their honeymoon. Ainsworth adopted an expression of one being greatly put upon, bowed slightly, and stated he would be only too happy to oblige. His facial expression belied his words with every hair of his raised eyebrows. He wore the same aggrieved expression now. The memory of the previous encounter brought an involuntary chuckle that became a sort of sobbing laugh. Her body heaved to the point of stress-driven hysterics. She shook so hard she could not step up onto the running board. Ainsworth harrumphed and gripped her elbow.

"My Lady, I believe you are overwrought. It would not do for the public to see you thus. Please allow me to assist you." His tone was that of a schoolmaster correcting a wayward pupil. India glanced at him and sniggered. He frowned and gave her elbow a little upward push. She collapsed onto the seat and buried her face in her hands. The engine's roar concealed the wail of her sobs.

***

India stepped down onto the castle's cobblestoned courtyard and breathed in heavily. Crushed by the emptiness only his absence brought, how could she stand being here without him? Fear of shouldering all the responsibly of the estate without him filled her with dread. A tremor trailed from her shoulders to her hands, which she clasped and held firm. She must not have a fit of nerves when she saw Mama. The old lady was stoic enough, but beneath the veneer of calm, India sensed turmoil. Mama was Charlie's mother, after all, and no matter how much she might try to hide her emotions, she had to be as distraught at his leaving as India.

Ainsworth cleared his throat. "Would Her Ladyship approve the storage of the vehicle in the garage?"

India smiled imploringly. "Could you, please?"

If ever a man's body communicated the same sentiment as the rolling of one's eyes, Ainsworth moved in just such a manner. India sniggered softly as she watched him steer the auto toward the converted stable. Better to laugh at his expense than shake the castle walls with anguished screams.

She was halfway to the front entrance when the parlor maid came running from the door. "Milady, the tenants are all in the Great Hall wanting a meeting with you. I tried to tell them you wouldn't want to talk to them today, but they wouldn't listen."

"Did they say what they want?"

"No, Milady, but that Mr. Holden seems like the leader."

Annie's father. Wonderful. That was all she needed right now. He had no doubt waited for Charlie to leave before stirring up his neighbors. Farmer Holden had never forgiven Charlie for his affair with Annie. India sighed. Her trial by fire had begun. She wiped at her cheeks, squared her shoulders, and marched toward the castle.

CHAPTER 15

India strolled into the Great Hall and eyed the gathering of estate tenants with what she hoped was a relaxed attitude. It would not do for them to think her nervous in their presence. Most of the farmers wore expressions of discomfort and embarrassment. Holden, on the other hand, stood stiff-backed with fists balled at his side. He stepped forward with hard eyes and a grim, down-turned mouth.

"Lady Kilnsey, we want to know how we are to get the harvest in now that His Lordship has taken all the lads to war. We want to know what you plan to do."

India's pulse kicked up a notch. She inhaled slowly and concentrated on removing her gloves. The ordinary task gave her time to get a grip. Meeting his aggression in kind would benefit no one. "Good morning, gentlemen." She fixed each man with a friendly, but intentionally superior smile while she tucked the gloves into her suit jacket pocket. Interlacing her fingers, she held her hands at her waist. These men must not see her shaking. "To your question, Mr. Holden, why did you not discuss this with His Lordship prior to today? Surely, you realized the harvest would become an issue when we declared war. What provision have *you* made?"

Holden looked slightly stunned as he took a step back. He opened his mouth, shut it, and opened it again. "We expected Lord Kilnsey to take charge as he's the landlord."

"And when he didn't, you failed to mention this to Mr. James? You must surely have realized His Lordship had a great deal on his mind while recruiting men to serve their country. He is doing his patriotic duty. What have you done in aid of the war effort? I know my husband and Mr. James discussed plans for increasing the acres under production with each of you early in the summer. Wouldn't that have been the appropriate time to discuss labor issues?" Again, she cast a steely gaze upon each man. Most of them had the good grace to drop their eyes.

"Maybe, but we didn't think he'd be taking all the lads with him." Holden attempted an aggrieved tone.

The front door opened and clicked shut, followed by the tread of Ainsworth's shoes on the stone floor. Thank goodness she no longer faced these men on her own. "I see. When there has been a shortage of help in previous years, how has the issue been addressed?" She knew the answer, but she was damned if she would make this easy for Holden. He was trying to bully her since Charlie and Robbie weren't around. Fine. She would see who had the last word, and by God, it wouldn't be him.

"We ain't never had this problem before."

The man had the effrontery to lie to her face. "Really? I believe you are mistaken. Think again."

Holden's face turned the color of a ripe fall apple. "I don't take orders from no woman an-"

India interrupted him with a raised hand. "But you wish for a woman to solve your problem? What an interesting outlook you have. As it happens, I know exactly how such labor shortages were solved and I am surprised you have apparently forgotten." She looked at the younger men. "Will you give permission for your older children to help with the harvest as they have in the past?" There were several affirmative murmurs and nods. "Excellent. I will speak with the schoolmaster about allowing the older children to take time away from school until the harvest is completed. I will arrange a similar school break when planting time arrives. Will this be satisfactory?"

All the men responded favorably, but Holden was not finished. He fired one more volley. "It's just like the gentry to want us working folks' children to go without a proper education, so they can be kept down."

India's jaw grew rigid. "Apparently, you have also forgotten summer terms. The schoolmaster has always conducted one for those students in need of it. He certainly will not object to the extra income. I will speak to Mr. James about a summer stipend from the estate accounts." India gave each man a curt smile and adopted an attitude of dismissal. "With your problem solved, I now must see to the Dowager Countess. She has just sent her only son to war and needs the comfort and support of those who care for her."

Sensing the butler hovering behind her, she continued, "Mr. Ainsworth will see you out."

Most of the men tugged their forelocks and murmured their thanks, but not Holden. He glared a couple of times over his shoulder as he stomped from the hall. She had won this battle, but it was apparent there would be more to come. Robbie and Althea would be home soon. He could deal with the troublesome Holden from now on.

One of the younger farmers lingered, shooting India imploring looks while the others trooped past. The third time he looked her way, India nodded slightly and signaled to Ainsworth. He waylaid the young man with an excuse that the housekeeper wished to send a message to the farmer's wife, who occasionally helped with the castle's laundry.

This was the first India had heard of extra help being needed with the laundry, but she was grateful to the butler for his quick thinking.

When the door closed on the main group, India turned to the young man. "It's Billy Grant, I believe?"

"Yes, Milady."

"You wish a private word?"

"If you be forgiving the liberty, I can't let you go on believing all of us think like Holden."

"And how does your thinking differ from his?"

Billy looked at Ainsworth. The butler nodded encouragement. "You may speak with confidence. Her Ladyship will thank you for your honesty."

Billy looked at the floor and shuffled a foot like it would help him form the words. Apparently finding what he needed, he looked again at India. "I don't think any of us should be trusting him. He wants everybody to think he's looking out for us by trying to make you and His Lordship look bad." He stopped speaking but clearly was not ready to depart.

India's senses sharpened. "Go on."

"He's saying with His Lordship away, the estate will go to rack and ruin and that we shouldn't pay the rents unless you do what he says."

"And exactly what is it he wants?"

"He's after Mr. James's job, Milady. Begging your pardon for saying this, but he thinks everything would be different if His Lordship had married Annie. He would have moved from the farm to the estate office or even the castle itself."

"And what do the other tenants say?"

"They don't like him or the way he talks, but we're all afraid of him, so we try to stay on his good side. I'm ashamed to say it, but there it is. There's talk he's got connections with a bad sort who don't mind burning folks out when they cross him."

India blinked in shock. "What you describe is a crime. Why has he never been arrested?"

"Cause it can't be proved. Maybe he just says stuff to scare people, but a few years back, there was a man over to Kilnsey Village who got in an argument with him in the pub. Made Holden real mad, it did. Said the man would be sorry. Not long after, the man's barn burned down with his prize bull inside."

"I see. Thank you for this information."

"I was raised to know right from wrong. You and His Lordship been good to us tenants. Holden ain't grateful to His Lordship, working like he done in the fields alongside us all them years. He don't see what you done to improve the school and making sure the cottages got they roofs fixed. He's always studying on what he ain't got and complaining about the least little thing that don't go his way."

"I truly appreciate your loyalty. I will not tolerate criminal behavior or bullying. If ever you or your family are in need, please come to me."

"Thank you, Milady. He's a bad sort. You be careful, now." Billy tugged his forelock, nodded, and hurried from the castle to catch up with his fellows.

When the door closed on Billy, India wilted. All the tension drained away, leaving her limp and shaken. She turned to Ainsworth. "Thank you for being perceptive and alert just now."

"It is my job to protect the family I serve, My Lady."

India gave him a grateful smile. "It is and you do so with subtlety and skill. This interview would have been much more difficult without your support. You came to the castle at the same time I did, but it feels like you have been with the family for generations. You've proven yourself a treasure many times. Today is certainly no exception." India paused to gauge the effect her words were having. The butler, never effusive, allowed a gentle smile to light his eyes. India continued, "Servants always know more than anyone what is happening on an estate. You will keep me informed?"

"Of course, My Lady. With your permission, I will also enlist Mrs. Wilson's assistance. She is more likely to overhear anything the maids say. They are generally good girls, but they do love to gossip. Anything worthy of your notice will be brought to you immediately."

"That would be most helpful. Thank you." India nodded her dismissal.

Now to deal with Mama. Sometimes Mama's stoicism led her to behave in a manner that could only be described as cold and unyielding. Early in India's marriage, that attitude had felt like a personal affront until she realized that under the hard exterior beat the heart of a woman who had survived much adversity and had prevailed because she had no choice. To have done otherwise would have meant failing her children, something Maude Clarence Browning Westmoreland, the Dowager Countess Kilnsey, was not prepared to do. By Mama's lights, to give in was tantamount to treason to the family.

India moved from the Great Hall, strode through the dining room, and entered the drawing room where she found her mother-in-law ensconced on a sofa beside the fireplace. Her arrival did not seem to register, which gave India a moment to observe. It could have been the direct light pouring through the high windows, but it seemed Mama had aged overnight. There were dark smudges under her eyes that had not been there only a week or two before and her cheeks appeared sunken with new creases in the formerly unlined porcelain surface of her skin.

Mama's attention finally focused on India. She patted the cushion beside her. "Come sit here and tell me how it was."

For the next few minutes, India tried to put the best face possible on Charlie's leaving, ending with the young boy who had tried to enlist and how sweet Charlie had been.

Mama nodded. "That sounds just like my son. He has always been kind where it counted. As a little boy, he was forever bringing injured wildlife into the castle and hiding them in the scullery much to the distress of Cook and the maids." A wistful expression played across her face. "I pray his soft heart will not be a hindrance in battle."

India could stand it no more. Tears broke and streamed down her cheeks. To her surprise, Mama did not criticize. Instead, she wrapped India in a maternal embrace and patted her back. "That's right. Let go now while there are just the two of us. No one understands more than I the depth of your feelings. Together, we will face what is to come. I saw the estate through bad times in the past. You will have my full support for this one, as well."

When the storm passed, India pulled back. "Thank you, Mama. Your words give me courage. I admire your strength and will try my best to emulate it. I must if we are to deal effectively with the Holdens of the world."

Mama raised a quizzical brow. "What has the old blighter been up to now?"

India swallowed her surprise at the language Mama used and related her recent encounter.

Mama harrumphed. "He thinks he should have Robbie James's job, does he? As if such as he would ever have been allowed to occupy the estate agent's office, much less the castle. The man clearly does not know his place. We will remind him of it when the time is right."

"But Charlie says he is the best farmer of all the tenants. I don't want trouble with him."

"That may be the case, but what Charlie apparently did not tell you is that Holden and his wife are rabid republicans. She's Irish, you know. The pub incident Billy Grant mentioned was the subject of much speculation at the time. Even I heard of it. Holden beat his opponent senseless with a cane because the man denounced the Irish quest for home rule." Mama pursed her lips and breathed deeply. "If the Holdens in any way prove disloyal to us or the crown, they must be turned out. We cannot have traitors in our midst."

India stiffened at the word traitor. She had no idea the potential trouble with Holden ran so deep. For the millionth time, she said a prayer of gratitude that Robbie would remain on the estate with them.

CHAPTER 16

Althea watched the rock and gorse covered hills of the Highlands sweep past her compartment window with more than a little wistfulness. It had been a lovely three weeks in the cottage overlooking Dornoch Firth, but now they were returning to the reality of wartime Britain and the uncertainty of a world that felt on the verge of disintegrating. As the train rounded a bend, a burst of coal smoke partially obscured the view, leaving her unsettled as though this was an omen of things to come. She dropped her head against the seat back, determined to push away such fanciful thoughts. Nothing must be allowed to mar the memories of their honeymoon. Feeling Robbie's eyes on her, she gazed up at him.

He raised her hand to his lips. "Happy, my darling?"

Althea nestled her head against his shoulder. "Exquisitely. If I had known how much pleasure was to be had, I might have married earlier."

Robbie placed his hand against his chest in mock alarm. "But then you would have married someone else."

"True and certainly a man who could not match your charm and prowess."

He slipped his arm about her shoulders, pulling her close so that his lips brushed her ear. "It is you who inspire me to heights I never imagined possible."

“I know I started it, but I think we better stop.” Althea giggled as heat rose in her cheeks. “I would be mortified if anyone overheard us. We sound like a couple of randy adolescents.”

Robbie glanced at the compartment door leading to the corridor. “Between a closed door and the train’s noise, I doubt anyone passing could hear. Furthermore, you make me feel like an adolescent.” He paused and kissed her temple. “Will India expect you to resume your duties as soon as we return?”

“I suppose she might be willing to wait. What do you have in mind?”

“I want you to be settled in our cottage before you return to the castle. It is the first time you’ve had a home of your own, and I want you to enjoy it for a little while.”

“Will you be returning to your duties immediately?”

“Of course. I can hardly leave the burden of running the estate solely to India longer than necessary. I haven’t shown her anything.”

“Then you will understand my desire to return to the castle immediately, as well. India is going to need all the support we can give her.”

***

India sat on the drawing room sofa absentmindedly flipping through the latest Tatler. Its contents held little interest for her, but she needed distraction while she awaited Althea and Robbie’s return. The fate of the estate could not rest in her inadequate hands any longer. Anxiety had become her constant companion since Charlie’s departure for military training two weeks past. The encounter with the tenants had brought home to her just how dependent on their friendship and cooperation the estate was and how little she really knew of its business. She had plowed her way through the interview with them on sheer willpower and bravado.

She threw the magazine on the floor and drummed her fingers on the occasional table at her side. Their train was meant to arrive over an hour ago. Ainsworth had not been pressed into further service as chauffeur after all. India simply did not have the heart to ask, and he did not offer. The hired pony cart and driver should have had them home by now. She rose from the sofa and strode to the windows overlooking the courtyard. Nothing stirred except the swallows and martins flying to and fro among the castle's crenellations. Marching back to the sofa, she plopped down, slumped into the cushions, and crossed her arms over her bosom. If Mama came into the room and saw her less than proper posture, too bad. She was in no mood for criticism.

The slap of a cart's wheels on the courtyard's cobblestones drifted through the panes. Thank goodness. Now she could at least hand the day-to-day management to Robbie.

***

It had been a restless night. India tossed and turned, unable to sleep for more than what felt like minutes at a time. As happy as she was to have Althea and Robbie home, their return was one more confirmation that Charlie was gone from home for God only knew how long.

She sat alone at the breakfast table missing him more than ever. Even her earlier visit to the nursery and Adeline's delight at seeing her had not raised her spirits for long. As she forced a forkful of egg between her lips, the door opened and Robbie strode in with a cheery good morning. He poured coffee for himself and joined her at the table.

Clearing his throat, he said, "I thought we might go over the rents book today. Charlie and I always set aside the last Monday of the month for the task." While his tone implied a relaxed attitude, it missed the mark. She could hear a touch of anxiety beneath his outward calm.

Frowning, she said, "Why ever would you need me for that? I thought you would handle the day-to-day running of the estate."

Robbie scooped two sugar lumps into his coffee, paying undue attention to the whirlpool his spoon created. "With Charlie away, it's important a member of the family stay informed."

India dabbed her lips with her napkin and returned it to her lap. "Did you discuss this before he left? He certainly said nothing to me about it."

"We did. At length." Robbie refocused his attention on India. "He was adamant, and I agreed wholeheartedly."

India's mouth formed a thin line. Charlie had been so distant before he left. It was infuriating he did not just talk to her. "Then why did he leave it to you to give me the news?"

Robbie didn't answer. He added cream to the now cooling beverage and observed the spoon's circuit once more. Drawing a fortifying breath, he said, "I was unaware you had not been brought into the picture. I apologize for springing this on you. I do know he wanted your final days together to be unmarred and as happy as possible."

Her shoulders stiffened, and she stared him down with narrowed eyes. "I see. He didn't trust me to not have hysterics, or was it that he couldn't bear talking to me about it?"

Robbie had the good grace to appear embarrassed. "I'm sure I can't say, but we both know he had much on his mind before he left. Perhaps he simply forgot you were unaware of the plan."

A sliver of guilt slid through India. “Yes, he was terribly distracted. I’ve never faced anything like going to war.” She shot him a watery smile. “Perhaps I expect too much.”

“No, he should have told you, but I’m sure his failure was unintentional. He always spoke as though you knew. As it is, you know now, so we should begin your introduction to estate affairs today if you feel up to it.”

“Affairs?” India’s hand flew to her mouth. “As in how the entire estate is run?”

“Why, of course.” Robbie blinked several times. It was a moment before understanding dawned. “Oh, I see I’ve been unclear. Charlie wants you fully apprised of every aspect of estate business down to the smallest detail. He believes having only one person holding such knowledge unwise and I agree. We are at war. As much as we may not want to think it, the future is uncertain. We must prepare for all eventualities. I’m sure you can see the wisdom.”

Of course, she could see the wisdom, but just because she knew something in her mind did not mean her heart was ready to accept the reality.

CHAPTER 17

India placed her elbows on the desk and rested her head between her fists. The pile of assigned readings Robbie had given her grew daily. It was as though the paper and ink conspired to produce as many offspring as possible. The mere sight of it made her head spin. Robbie and Charlie might find seed, weed, feed, and breed articles fascinating, but she found them deadly dull.

Until now, she had not fully understood how closely involved Charlie was in the day-to-day running of the estate. With their marriage and the injection of cash that came with it, she thought he had evolved to the style of management cherished by his peers—making the important decisions and overseeing the general direction of things but leaving the mundane details to their estate agents. Obviously, that was not at all the case.

The estate office door opened and a smiling Robbie strode through it. "How is the reading going?" He stopped when he saw her face. "I hope I'm not overwhelming you. That is not my intention."

India pushed her paper antagonist away and shot Robbie a disgruntled look. "I'm doing my best, but there's just so much about farming I don't know. Who knew there were so many diseases sheep can contract? Is it really necessary for me to know about cheesy glands or how to prevent tetanus during shearing? Don't the farmers keep abreast of best husbandry practices? Surely not all the veterinarians in the country have volunteered for active duty."

"No, not all, but our vet left for France last week. That leaves old Dr. Sims the only vet in the county. He may be retired, but he is being called out to farms, nonetheless. He is beyond doing the more intense manual labor, like dislodging a calf stuck in the birth canal, but he can still do palpations and treat diseases."

India's heart sank. "Good Lord. Please tell me you don't expect me to stick my arm up a cow's posterior."

Robbie chuckled. "Of course not, but it will be well for you to know what is involved. There may come a time when Dr. Sims will call on you to make a decision. You need to have accurate information to make the best choice."

"Robbie, I appreciate you want to educate me in animal husbandry and crop cultivation, but I don't think I need to learn all of it, especially not in one sitting. After all, you know what needs to be done in those areas. Can't I just stick with the financial side of estate management? Balance sheets are much easier to comprehend."

Robbie laughed aloud. "Charlie is right. You inherited your Grandfather Ledbetter's business sense. I first saw it when you questioned Charlie about dipping into your fortune's principal for improvements to the castle. He wanted to do them all at once, but you were alarmed at the outflow of capital. You were angry, and rightly so, I might add." Robbie picked up the farming journal open before India and closed it. "Perhaps you've done enough reading for today. Let's get Althea and go for a drive. Fresh air will do us all good. While we are at it, we can begin your driving lessons."

"Driving lessons?" India's voice bounced off the walls.

"Oh, didn't I mention? Charlie wants you and Althea to learn how to drive. We'll start with his Vauxhall."

"Whatever for?"

"Because the solicitors have been unable to find a replacement for Barton. We thought you would be more comfortable learning in the smaller auto instead of the Rolls."

"Will they stop looking for a replacement if I agree to this?"

"No. I will instruct your solicitors to keep at it, but with every able-bodied man needed for military service, the pickings are virtually nonexistent. And by the way, they suggest you come up to town at your earliest convenience."

"Why?"

"Charlie instructed them to acquaint you with the terms of the entail and his will. He wants you fully prepared should the worst happen."

India went numb. There was so much Charlie had not told her before he left. So very much. And then there was the four-word phrase that drove a stake through her heart—should the worst happen. This was not what she had signed on for—no wife or mother had—and yet here they were discussing the unimaginable as though it was last week's market report. The world really had gone completely insane.

She looked at Robbie through a mist. "I know Bumpy is his heir until we have a son of our own." Her voice cracked on the word son. "What else is there?"

"I believe it has to do with the terms of maintenance for you and Adeline. Your lawyer in New York insisted on certain accommodations when your marriage contracts were drawn up."

India nodded. "I see." At the mention of her New York lawyer, memories of the weeks before she left America for the last time tumbled through her mind. She and Mother had been estranged at the time, but David Havemeyer, her mother's first love and now husband, seemed to have looked out for India's welfare, nonetheless. Mother's marital bliss improved her nature, leading to an easing of the estrangement. Travel to meet her first grandchild was planned, but then the war came. She didn't want to leave neutral America where everyone was safe. The war was happening to other nations and other people. Heaviness settled around India's heart. How long might it be before grandmother and granddaughter finally met was anyone's guess.

India blinked several times. "Forgive me. I'm afraid I was lost in memories for a moment. Now, where were we? Oh, yes. Mr. Havemeyer. I knew he had seen to certain conditions, but I must admit I did not pay as much attention to the specifics as I should have. My mind was on other things at the time. "

"Of course it was. Your father had passed away unexpectedly and then you were planning a wedding an ocean away in a place you had never visited. It was a lot to deal with." Robbie pointed to a pad of paper and a pencil. "Perhaps you should send a telegram to London requesting an appointment. Write it out and we can send it from Grassington Depot whilst we are out."

"Yes, I suppose I must see them. I'll see what can be arranged for next week or the following. I would like for Althea to go with me. Might you accompany us?"

"I don't think both of us should be away at once, but have Althea with you by all means."

"I will feel better knowing I won't face the solicitors alone. I always feel at a disadvantage. They are so stern and humorless."

"That may be, but I would venture to say you are a match for any dreary old lawyer. Shall I send for Althea and bring out the Vauxhall?"

Fifteen minutes later, Robbie stood bent toward the auto's radiator with his hand on the crank handle putting it to the task. Three rotations of the device and the engine sparked to life. Turning first to India, then to Althea, he said, "You see, it's really quite simple once you get the hang of the thing. Now, which of you will be first to give it a go?"

India and Althea looked at one another and rolled their eyes.

"Well, who will it be?" When they still did not answer, he said to India, "It's your auto. You go first."

Her mouth formed a disgruntled pout. "If I must."

"You must." He stepped aside and gestured toward the handle. "Go on now. Give it a turn."

She bent down, grabbed the thing, and gave it a push. It refused to budge more than a fraction of an inch.

Robbie put his hand over hers. "Here. Put your whole upper body into it. You can do it."

She pushed. She shoved. She yanked. She pulled. Finally, she swore a very unladylike oath and gave it every ounce of strength she had. The handle made an entire circuit. She gave it one more turn, and miraculously, the obstinate beast roared to life.

She stepped back, massaging her arm. "I think I may have pulled my shoulder out of joint and I'm quite sure I've torn a ligament. If this is what it takes to get the blasted auto going, I doubt we will take many trips with me as the driver."

Robbie was undeterred. "You did quite well. It will become easier the more you practice. I promise." He disengaged the engine by removing the ignition key. He reinserted it, turned it, and looked at Althea. "Now, your turn, my love."

***

Althea finished buttoning India's blouse and helped her into her suit jacket. She ran the clothes brush over the dark blue gabardine ensemble and admired her work. When she had a baby, she hoped her figure would return with the same speed as India's. It continued to surprise that she now found herself interested in babies and all things domestic. She had worked hard to get away from the life her mother knew. It was a little scary. The same things Momma always focused on now dominated her waking moments. Feeling eyes on her, she met India's gaze in the cheval mirror.

India secured her hat with a pin, then frowned. "Is everything okay? You seem far away."

"Everything is actually quite wonderful." Althea grinned and waggled her eyebrows. "I finished the curtains for our kitchen and they look great, if I do say so myself. The cabinetmaker over in Kilnsey sent word that our kitchen fittings will be ready this week. Life is good."

India grabbed her handbag and adjusted her hat. "I guess I'm ready. Have our cases been taken to the auto?"

"Yes, Ainsworth attended to it with his usual efficiency. I suspect he is feeling pretty put upon having to do the footmen's jobs, as well as his own, but he didn't complain."

India's lip curled. "We have all had to adjust, so he can just deal with it. Ready?"

Althea put on her hat. "As ready as ever will be. Our chariot awaits."

Robbie stood in the courtyard beside the auto. He saluted as India and Althea passed through the front door, but made no move to open the Vauxhall's passenger door for them. "India, I believe it's your turn to drive today." When she made a face like a foul odor had just descended, he continued, "You are really doing quite well. Althea can take over at the halfway point if it will make you feel better." When neither girl moved, he said, "Oh, all right. I'll crank the handle. India, just get behind the wheel. Grassington isn't far, you know."

Althea watched India from the corner of her eye. She could always tell when India was nervous. Anxiety hung around her today like an expensive cashmere shawl, necessary in winter, but itchy and unbearable in summer's heat. It had been abnormally warm all week. The climate today was definitely uncomfortable in more ways than just the temperature.

India fidgeted with the ignition key, missing the hole several times, until she finally jammed it in with a whispered curse. She swiped at a bead of moisture on her upper lip.

A trickle of sisterly concern ran through Althea. This trip to the solicitors was wearing terribly on India. It could only be due to the nature of the discussion. The chief topic would be Charlie's will. Such things brought home just how precarious a soldier's life was.

Althea made a decision. "Now that y'all have done the hard work of getting the engine cranked, I think I'd like to do the driving. What do you say?"

India shot her a grateful look. "If you really want to..."

Althea nodded. "I really want to. I think I'm getting the hang of it and I want to cement my skills. Let's exchange seats."

The trip to the depot and the train ride to London passed uneventfully, unless India's quiet withdrawal and her lack of attention to her surroundings were considered an event. The train pulled into the terminus just before teatime.

***

A hand on her arm jerked India back to the present. She had been in a sort of waking dream where she and Charlie were on the train to Ripon and The Old Orchard Inn where they spent their three-day honeymoon. It was such a beautiful memory. She didn't want to give it up simply because they had arrived at Kings Cross.

Althea tapped her arm. "It's time to get off the train. Ainsworth called Kilnsey House from the village post office and informed them we would arrive in time for tea, so we've got to hurry."

"I wish he hadn't bothered the London staff. We will be here for so short a time. We could have stayed at a hotel."

While Althea gathered their cases from the overhead rack, she said, "He thought the hotels might be full with all the coming and going through London these days. In fact, Robbins said as much during their conversation, if it can be called that." Althea giggled. "I can just imagine the stately Robbins speaking into a telephone. Ainsworth said he barely delivered his message before Robbins rang off. I think Ainsworth rather enjoyed telling the tale."

India grinned. "We must remember Robbins started in service around the time the Yankees finally left the South with the end of Reconstruction. We must make allowances."

Althea chuckled and opened the carriage door. "Anyway, the London staff needs something to do. You and Charlie haven't been to town since before Christmas. Now with the war and all, they may be feeling a little anxious about their employment. At least that's what Ainsworth seems to think."

"Robbins has been the butler and Mrs. Thorne the housekeeper at Kilnsey House since before Charlie and Clarissa were born. They should know they will always have jobs as long as Charlie has anything to say about it." India's hand flew to her mouth. She had inadvertently given voice to her darkest fear. The humor of moments ago died, destroyed by the waking nightmare of what the future might hold. She gave herself a mental shake. It was this damned need to see the solicitors that had her in such a state.

Althea smiled gently. "Yes, you are fortunate in your staffs in the Grosvenor Street house and the castle, as well. It's too bad Clarissa and Jonathan canceled their visit over the summer. I don't blame them, what with the war and all, but America is neutral. Seems like they could have come anyway."

India stood and grabbed her handbag from the seat. Tucking a stray strand of hair back under her hat, she replied, "Jonathan was the one who put a stop to the trip. Charlie's brother-in-law is the most practical of men. Clarissa has her practical side, too, but she really wanted to come. She's afraid it will be a long time before she can come home again. She wants to spend time with Mama, who, as Clarissa pointed out, is of an age where nothing is guaranteed. Jonathan was afraid they would get here and not be able to get back to New York. I guess I can see his point, but I can't bear to think it could be years before we see them again." India shuddered. During the months leading up to her marriage, Clarissa had become as much an older sister to her as she was to Charlie.

Althea put an arm around India's shoulders. "Come on. Let's go find the hired chauffeur. It's been a long day. We'll both feel better with some food and a bath."

India gave Althea a watery grin. "Yes, we really must hurry. You know how Cook gets when she thinks her food is unappreciated. If we don't do justice by her tea, we may pay for it at dinner."

They found their driver and left the station in a hired auto. Even Charlie realized it was a colossal waste having a full-time chauffeur cooling his heels in London with no one to drive around most of the year. Since the train was much faster, they never asked Barton to drive them to London.

The now familiar trip from Kings Cross to their London townhouse at Number 34 Grosvenor Street, Mayfair passed the usual points of interest. Nothing about London had changed since the declaration of war unless one counted men in uniform on every sidewalk and military lorries trundling along with the taxis on Euston Road. They edged Regents Park and took a left on Park Street and then another onto Grosvenor where they stopped at the door of the loveliest townhouse on the block. Its three stories rose nearly as high as the four-story structure abutting it. Its rooms were spacious and inviting.

India had been upset with Charlie for spending a small fortune to buy back Kilnsey House while they were only engaged, but on days like this, she was glad the family owned the house once more. It had gone out of the family for a few years after Charlie's wastrel father, the fourteenth earl, had sold it to pay for his women and gambling debts. It now felt just as much like home as the castle, in some ways more so.

Being several centuries younger than Kilnsey Castle, Kilnsey House had the design and appearance of an actual residence. The rooms were where they were supposed to be instead of carved from the layout of a stone fortress. Every detail from the cantilevered stone staircase in the entry hall to the beautifully carved plaster cornices of acanthus leaf scrolls and rosettes, to the rich oak paneling and wainscoting spoke of a home built with attention to detail. It was most fortuitous that Charlie's five times great-grandfather had been a member of the same club as the Grosvenor who first leased land for residential development back in the early eighteenth century. Kilnsey House was one of the earliest and best. India loved it nearly as much as she loved her childhood home, The Falls, in Pisgah, North Carolina.

As they alighted, India glanced at her brooch watch and said, "Ah, good. Just in time for tea. We are saved from Cook's wrath. First, something scrumptious, then a long soak in my lovely tub. I think dinner should be something light and simple. Will you tell Cook?" When Althea nodded, India continued, "You know, I'm glad we're staying here. I feel the stress melting away just knowing I will sleep in my own bed. We will beard the lions tomorrow after a good night's sleep."

CHAPTER 18

India and Althea arrived at the offices of Smythe, Britton, Savage, and Gray twenty minutes early. India's hands clasped and released until her gloves were a twisted mess. She would explode if she remained seated much longer. Smiling at the reception clerk, she casually rose from her chair and went to the windows overlooking Berkeley Square. The desire to flee to the leafy expanse with its lovely benches, sculptural fountain, and statues was almost overwhelming. A voice calling her name saved her from the spectacle of pacing the room.

They were ushered into a large office lined with bookcases and anchored in the center by an enormous desk behind which sat an elf of a man, his balding head bent over a thick file. He stood at their approach. The edge of his desk hit him at stomach rather than hip level. Gesturing toward the chairs opposite his own, he said, "Please be seated, Lady Kilnsey. I have your documents here. Were you offered tea?"

He looked at Althea with interest while India introduced her "friend" Mrs. James. When no further explanation of Althea's presence was given, he bent toward the file lying open on his desk, giving a full view of his shiny pate.

India glanced at Althea, who refused to meet her gaze. Mr. Savage's bushy eyebrows and fringe of white hair completed the image of a well-dressed gnome. A fit of giggles bubbled, but India managed to tamp them down. Rudeness would in no way help matters.

Smiling more broadly than the situation required, she responded, "Thank you. We were offered refreshment, but we have only just come from breakfast."

"Very well. Shall we begin?"

For the next half hour, the lawyer went over the terms of the entail, all of which India already knew. Mr. Savage was so earnest in his desire for her to understand she did not have the heart to interrupt. Basically, she and Adeline got nothing from the estate. All would pass to the odious Bumpy, His Grace, the Fifth Duke of Hawik and Charlie's distant cousin, unless she produced a male heir. Any desire to laugh fled as India thought about how the likelihood of a son diminished daily as war spread throughout the continent.

Setting aside the entail documents, he shuffled through the file and retrieved a single page. "Ah yes, here it is. Did His Lordship happen to mention that your solicitor in York and I have been in recent communication?"

"I'm afraid not."

"I see. Then I will give you the background of this document before its particulars. Before your American attorney . . ." He paused, seeking the name. ". . . Mr. Havemeyer would approve the marriage contracts, he ensured there would be provision for Your Ladyship should His Lordship predecease you. He was most adamant on that point, as I recall, in view of your fortune being designated a dowry and thus becoming part of the entail. The document I am holding fulfills the requirement." He stopped apparently to gauge India's comprehension.

She nodded. "I see. Please go on."

"I will summarize for you rather than read all the legal language. Saves time, you know." Tapping the document, he continued, "This is His Lordship's last will and testament. He directed his York solicitor, Mr. Mitchell, to draw it up, whereupon His Lordship signed it. The document was then transferred to our offices here in London, as we are the principal firm for the estate and the family." Again, he paused to judge India's understanding.

"Mr. Savage, please do not keep me in suspense. I know what a will is." A twinge of shame at her imperious tone pinged India, but her patience with Savage's plodding was nearing an end.

A pink glow suffused the lawyer's face. "As you wish, My Lady." He cleared his throat and adjusted his pince-nez. "The main and most important point contained herein . . . " He tapped the will again. "Should His Lordship predecease you, Kilnsey House here in London will pass to you completely without impediment."

India blinked several times. "How can that be?"

Mr. Savage graced her with a somewhat superior smile. He was clearly enjoying having caught her off-guard. "The situation is thus. When the fourteenth earl found it necessary to sell Kilnsey House, it passed out of the entail. When the present earl purchased it, the house became solely His Lordship's property, with no attachment to the entailed estate whatsoever. His Lordship made the purchase before your fortune officially passed into the estate and has since paid the mortgage with a small inheritance from his maternal grandmother, hence ensuring there will be no confusion regarding the house vis-à-vis the entail. Part of your marriage contract provided that His Lordship must secure for you and any offspring of the marriage, other than a direct male heir of course, a permanent home of suitable quality and size. Kilnsey House became available and it will become yours should . . . ” He stopped speaking as the pink glow returned.

India picked up his theme with a sinking heart. “His Lordship predecease me.”

“Exactly.” His voice was quieter and less authoritative. “Now, as to income and maintenance, a portion of your fortune, again courtesy of Mr. Havemeyer, has been set aside and invested for your future use. It should prove adequate for your maintenance and the upkeep of the house. This is in addition to whatever may come to you upon your mother’s passing. I understand that you also continue to receive a modest allowance from your grandfather’s estate that was explicitly excluded from the moneys that came to His Lordship upon your marriage.” He stopped again to scan the will. Apparently satisfied, he said, “I believe that correctly summarizes your expectations. Have you any questions?”

India shifted and leaned forward. “So, let me get this straight. I will have a house and enough money to live here in London, if I wish?”

The lawyer began gathering the papers and shuffling them into a neat stack. “Precisely.”

“And there’s no way Lord Hawik can touch any of this?”

“Correct again.” He gave her what could only be described as a conspiratorial smile. “I doubt His Grace has been apprised of these terms. Perhaps you wish me to convey the information?”

India was silent for several seconds, then returned his smile. “Thank you, but no. That will not be necessary. I believe we should wait until such time as we must. I see no need at present to disturb His Grace’s peace-of-mind.”

Mr. Savage chuckled, then swallowed hard. “As you wish, My Lady. Is there any other way I may be of service?”

The gentleman clearly wished to draw the interview to a close. India replied in the negative, thanked him, then led

Althea out of the building. She waited until they were seated on a bench in Berkeley Square before bending double with laughter.

Althea became caught up in India's mood. Together, their peals of laughter had passersby staring and whispering.

Wiping her eyes, India gasped a couple of times before saying, "Isn't the idea of keeping a secret from Bumpy Carlisle delicious?"

Althea nodded. "When are you planning on breaking the happy news?"

"Try never. Should Charlie be killed, it may provide me with the only happy moment in an otherwise horrendous time." She laughed until her tears were driven by sobs. Althea put her arms around India and patted her back. India's storm eventually passed.

She retrieved a handkerchief from her handbag, dabbed at her cheeks, and blew her nose. "All this time, I thought Charlie bought the house for purely selfish reasons. I was even angry when he did it without discussing it with me first. I wonder why he never told me about his will and how the house will be mine?"

Althea looked thoughtful for a moment. "Maybe because he has only recently had his will made? That's how Mr. Savage made it sound."

"Perhaps, but surely he knew about the provision in the marriage contract." India placed her elbow on the bench back and rested her cheek against her fist. "Why didn't he tell me he had a reason for wanting the house back besides returning it to the family's possession?"

Althea shrugged. "Men are funny creatures. Their pride is as fragile as the finest crystal. After you got so mad, maybe His Lordship was too proud to tell you."

"That doesn't make much sense, does it?"

"No, not really. I guess you will simply have to ask him if he gets to come home before his unit ships out to France."

***

Althea pulled her shawl close around her throat as she picked her way across the courtyard's icy cobblestones. Robbie and India were late again for luncheon and the Dowager was none too pleased. She smiled at the little vignette playing out in the estate office window. The heads of the two people she loved most in the world were bent together in concentration over some book or farming journal. Robbie said that India had learned a lot in the past three months. He said she was smart, quick, and a hard worker, qualities that at first surprised him. He now praised India so often Althea had to remind herself not to be jealous, that she had nothing to fear where either Robbie or her mistress were concerned, for they loved her with the same devotion she gave them.

With Christmas Day hard upon them, everyone was feeling happier than they had in months. A huge fir tree stood decorated in a corner near the Great Hall's enormous stone fireplace and garlands were strung among the rafters. Yew, holly, and juniper sprays added a seasonal touch to mantels in the castle's public rooms. The place was alive with the fragrance of fresh evergreens, all in anticipation of holiday festivities.

She stopped just short of the door to watch the pair in their earnest pursuit of learning. India frowned while Robbie tapped the pages before them, turning them back and forth apparently by way of comparison regarding some topic they were discussing.

She could read his lips. "See, there is nothing contradictory..."

She waited to enter the sanctum sanctorum as she thought of Robbie's office. It held many activities in which she did not take part, but she accepted this as his job, a job he loved and a duty he took seriously. Robbie must have felt her eyes on him, for he suddenly looked toward the window and rewarded her with a broad smile.

Althea opened the door and stepped into the warmth of the small space heated by a coal stove. "Mrs. Bertrand has luncheon on the sideboard. The Dowager wants you in the dining room right now. Her exact words were, 'They must arrive post haste. I will not countenance Cook's food being ruined by their tardiness.' Y'all better come on."

India looked at Robbie. "I don't think I can bear coming back to this mess today. My head is spinning."

Robbie nodded. "I've pushed you and you've done very well. Before long, you'll be nearly as good a farmer as Charlie."

India rolled her eyes and sneered. "If my brain doesn't explode first. You're a hard taskmaster."

"I say, that's a tad unfair. It's your estate, yours and Charlie's." Robbie's chuckle belied his words. He patted the journal open on the desk. "As a reward for your hard work, let's take time off from farming until after Christmas. What do you say?"

"Fabulous," Althea and India said at the same time. "Jinx," they cried in unison and erupted in giggles.

Robbie must have thought Althea's attention was solely on India because in an unguarded moment, grimness darkened his handsome face. There seemed to be some secret he held from them. All the humor of the moment melted, replaced by an unnameable fear. Althea glanced at India to see if she noticed his mood shift. Thank goodness India seemed oblivious. The girl did not need more stress than she was already handling.

CHAPTER 19

Christmas Day turned out to be a quiet affair with just India, Mama, Robbie, and Althea gathered in the drawing room watching Adeline crawl among the wrapping paper, ribbons, and boxes. Everyone laughed at her seven-month-old antics. She was far more interested in scrunching the colorful paper and banging small boxes together than she was in the dresses and toys that were her actual presents.

India observed her little family with gratitude and a peaceful heart. All talk of Mama moving to the Dower House had ceased when Charlie left for war. Mama acquiesced without argument when told India's peace-of-mind was at stake.

As lovely as it was to have Mama within the household, she held tight to her opinions. That would never change. She had been appalled when India wanted her maid at Christmas luncheon. She only relented when India insisted Althea was no longer a lady's maid but rather her lady's companion who just happened to help her dress on occasion. India explained further that as the estate agent's wife, Althea's position was even more elevated. Robbie had always been invited to Christmas luncheon and other celebratory meals. Her final point revealed how deeply Mama cared for her. India tearfully asserted that Althea was now the closest connection she had to her American family and home. Having Althea treated as part of her English family would bring India some joy in the bleakness of Charlie's absence.

After dinner on Twelfth Night, the adults gathered around the dying embers of the Yule log, a tradition long ago moved from the cavernous Great Hall to the drawing room. While the timber used was now smaller than the entire tree trunk of olden times, having a large log ablaze for several days made for a lovely tradition which India had grown to cherish.

Robbie rose from the sofa where he had been sitting beside Althea. "It's gone ten. I think we should start back to the village before our route becomes any icier." Looking at the Dowager, he asked, "May I add attend to the fire before we go?"

She replied with "yes" and "thank," but the "you" became lost in the swoosh of the drawing room door and the figure who strode through it. Seeing Mama's expression, India jerked around, then raced to Charlie, who lifted her off the floor in an embrace that left her gasping for air.

When he put her down, she studied him, letting her fingers glide along his jaw. "You're so thin. Are they not feeding you in that wretched camp?"

Charlie kissed her and replied, "We get plenty to eat, but the hard physical training burns it all away. I think this is the most fit I've ever been."

He grabbed India's hand and pulled her to the room's focal point where his mother sat posture-perfect beside the fire. He bent and planted a kiss on her cheek. "Mama, you look regal, as always." If he noticed his mother's failure to answer, he did not show it. He turned and grasped Robbie's hand with both of his.

Robbie placed his other hand on Charlie's shoulder. "By God, it's good to have you home. How long is your leave?"

Charlie's smile faltered. "Only three days, I'm afraid. My unit will be at the front by mid-month. After a week in Southampton, it's off to France."

India watched her mother-in-law carefully. The color had ebbed from Mama's cheeks, and her eyes were brighter than normal. Mama always had a firm grip on her emotions, but tonight even she seemed close to losing control. India bit down on her inner cheek. Tears must not mar Charlie's homecoming and the little time he had with them. For the next three days, everyone must put aside their fears and make this the happiest time possible.

A cloud passed over Robbie's features, which he quickly tried to hide before clearing his throat. "I see. So short a time. Well, we must make the best of it. To that end, we have excellent news. You are going to be very proud of India. She's becoming quite the farmer and land manager. You will have no worries on that account."

India's eyes narrowed. Charlie would have no worries about the estate, whether she was knowledgeable or not. Robbie was the consummate manager. This was not making sense. The men seemed to be colluding. Whatever it was, she would not ask. Charlie did not need to deal with an emotional, demanding wife as he prepared to march off to war. She would broach the subject of Kilnsey House gently when the time was right, but would go no further into areas of discussion that might cause stress. Tonight, all he needed was to be held in her arms and loved until they both fell into an exhausted sleep.

***

India awoke at dawn. Despite the exertions of the previous night, her dreams had played havoc with her rest. Images of men shooting one another, cannons firing, and bodies flying haunted her dreams. She had been only a child during the Spanish-American War, but she remembered the newspaper front page reports. The lurid pictures created by editorial artists and reports coming out of Cuba and the Philippines had left an impression on her seven-year-old mind.

Charlie looked very peaceful. She did not want to wake him with her fidgeting. Fighting the temptation to run her hands over his beautiful body, she tiptoed to the bathroom, turned the sink's tap to a light flow, and splashed water on her face. She grasped the edges of the sink and leaned toward the mirror above. Sallow. That was the only word for her complexion. Or maybe haggard better described the woman who looked back. This would not do. She pinched her cheeks until they glowed as pink as the dawn kissing the snow-covered hilltops outside her window. After running her lips between her teeth several times to bring back color and twisting her hair into a loose bun, she tilted her head and evaluated her efforts. Not too bad, if she did say so herself.

She went to the wardrobe and removed her best day dress. Althea would arrive with Robbie before breakfast, but that was at least an hour distant. Since Althea and Robbie's move to the cottage in the village, India had adopted a habit of dressing herself in the morning. Her costumes for a day of Robbie's lessons in the estate office required little effort, so completing the small task came easily. She finished buttoning up the simple shirtwaist and stepped to the cheval mirror. Although her hips were more rounded after Adeline's birth, her waist had returned to its pre-pregnancy contours. If anything, she looked better now than before the baby. Her figure had filled out nicely. Gone was the lanky girl's body, replaced by that of a fully developed young matron. She ran her hand over a wrinkle in the skirt and nodded. This was better. She wanted the three days with

Charlie to be as perfect as she could make them, and that meant doing her best with her appearance. He should leave home with visions of beauty and tranquility for his dreams at the front.

She opened the bedroom door and closed it as gently as possible, but its click echoed across the room all the same. Charlie rolled over and rubbed his eyes. His mouth lifted in a crooked grin. "Stop where you are and let me look at you." She did as bid and returned his smile. He propped himself up on an elbow. "Now give us a spin 'round." When she had complied, he patted the side of the bed. "You're even more beautiful than the day we married. I am one lucky sod. Come over here and give me a proper good morning."

India's brows rose at the word sod. She sat beside him, kissed him, then wagged a finger. "You seem to have picked up some new expressions."

He laughed and slipped his free arm around her waist. "I've always known them. Between the older lads at school and working with farmhands for years, one could not help but pick up some of their language. It comes in handy with the enlisted men. Makes me seem more like an ordinary bloke."

She ran her fingers through the mop of hair that had fallen over his eyes and pushed it back in place. "You must be a wonderful officer and I'm sure your men love you, but you will never be an ordinary bloke. You are my beloved husband and Adeline's papa. That makes you very special." She stopped speaking and kissed his forehead. Maybe this was the right time to discuss Kilnsey House and have her question answered. "You thought of us first, even when you had so much on your mind. I love you for it."

He sat up and stretched. Locking his fingers behind his head, he leaned back against the headboard. "I take it you have seen the London solicitors. Good. I wanted you to be aware of the terms of my will before I leave for France."

“Yes. Mr. Savage insisted. Althea went with me.” She regaled Charlie with the details of the interview, making him laugh at her descriptions of the lawyer. “Mr. Savage seems to hold the odious Bumpy in the same esteem as you and I.” She paused and drew her lower lip between her teeth. It might as well be now. There might not be another opportunity as good as this one. She placed her head against his shoulder and traced the hollow of his throat with her finger. “If I ask you a question, will you promise not to take it the wrong way?”

“Depends on what you ask.” He wrapped both arms around her and nuzzled her ear. “What are you offering in exchange for my cooperation?”

She sat up and pushed his arms away. Looking into his eyes, she said, “I’m serious. I need to ask a question, but I don’t want you to think there is an implied criticism in it.”

He frowned. “That sounds ominous. Out with it, but I warn you. I will allow nothing to ruin our time together. You may ask, but I may choose not to answer.”

She nodded. “Fair enough.” She drew a deep breath and let it out slowly. “You know I love Kilnsey House. It’s beautiful and feels like home. I’m glad it is in the family again. I’m just wondering why you didn’t tell me it is not part of the entail.”

All humor faded from his eyes while he studied her. After several seconds, he took both of her hands in his. “I could be very noble and say I didn’t want to resurrect a sore subject. I might say I bought the house knowing it would fulfill the obligation of the marriage contract, but that would be dishonest. You were pretty angry when you learned of the purchase. The dangers of spending principal and the fact that we were not yet married were your main points, as I recall.”

He fell silent again while his gaze drifted to the windows. He appeared in a quandary. Finally, he looked at her and said, “In truth, I bought Kilnsey House because I wanted it.

Plain and simple. I committed a large sum based on the expectation of gaining your fortune. You were right to be angry and suspicious. I should have been honest. I was a thoughtless cad for not discussing it with you, but losing the house for a second time was beyond endurance. It was only when war was declared that I thought about what might happen to you and Adeline if I do not return. Had I used money from the estate to repay the mortgage, the house would have returned to the entail. As it is, it may become yours free and clear. If you like, I can have Savage draw up the legal documents and sign it over to you now. Would it make amends for my earlier deception?"

His final words engendered a wave of guilt. He looked earnest and wistful, as though he believed she thought less of him for his admission.

She shook her head. "Please don't think like that. I don't need the house in my name, nor do you need to make amends. Kilnsey House belongs to the Earl of Kilnsey, as it should. That's all that matters." She lay her head on his chest so he would not see her tears. "I love you terribly. I'm sorry I asked, but thank you for answering honestly. I don't want secrets between us. Promise me there will never be any, no matter the circumstances."

He kissed the top of her head. "Never again. You have my word."

Despite her regret, a small part of her was glad to know the truth, glad he loved and respected her enough to be honest. There would be no secrets between them from now on. They would truly be one, as the marriage vows said.

CHAPTER 20

The days with Charlie slipped by in a blur. Charlie ate like he wouldn't see food again for a long time, sending his compliments to the kitchen after every meal. They made love like honeymooners, the first two days leaving their apartment only to take meals with Mama and spend time in the nursery playing with Adeline. If Charlie's mother resented their shunning the company of others, she gave no sign. India suspected the Dowager understood their desire for seclusion. More than once in the past, she had told India how grateful she was to see her son happy in his marriage. It touched India deeply to hear her mother-in-law's praise, especially knowing how unhappy Mama must have been with Charlie's reprobate father. The third day, they emerged from their cocoon at Robbie's insistence to discuss any potential decisions Charlie wished to make regarding the estate before he deployed. The men heaped praise on India's grasp of management, which she appreciated, but it seemed overmuch. Something unspoken lurked beneath their banter, leaving her uneasy.

The fourth day, the sound of an army lorry trundling into the courtyard awakened them. After dressing hurriedly, Charlie grabbed a couple of pieces of toast from the dining room sideboard, shoved half into his mouth, and headed for the front door. India followed, with Adeline in her arms and Mama at her heels.

As India passed through the door, a strange sensation settled over her. Her sense of place grew so keen each movement felt disjointed, isolated, as though everyone was caught in a series of photographic stills. The salute Charlie exchanged with the lorry driver and his handshake with Robbie might have been the jerky actions of automatons. Not until Charlie wrapped his arms around her did time snap back into place. Then, it raced at lightning speed.

He must have sensed her confusion, for he pulled back and held her at arm's length. "Please don't worry. The lads and I have had good training. We know how to take care of ourselves and one another. I will be fine, and I promise to write as often as I can."

India's voice caught on a sob. She swallowed hard. "I can't help but worry. Don't expect me not to. That would be impossible."

His expression brought her up short. He did not need her negative emotions, not now when he was headed to the Western Front. She had to put a brave face on his leaving and on her dread of overseeing the estate. She absolutely must. His life might depend on his believing all was well at home.

She mustered the best smile she was able. "I expect at least a letter every few days, and I promise the same. I want to know what you are up to." She gave him a crooked smile that belied unshed tears. "And stay away from those French girls. They can keep hands off. Got it, buster?"

He looked surprised, then laughed. "No danger there, my darling. You are the only girl for me. You are my beautiful, most beloved wife." Cupping a hand around Adeline's soft baby fuzz, he continued, "Look at the beautiful child you've given me."

With a final embrace, he kissed her and the baby, then swung up into the passenger seat. The engine roared, and they were gone. India followed the lorry to the main gate, coming to rest under the portcullis.

Swaying from side-to-side in the unconscious motion of all mothers holding babies, she stared at the road until not a wisp of the lorry's exhaust floated on the calm, frigid air. Nothing of Charlie remained in view. His time with them felt like a dream—unreal, ephemeral. Her motion stopped. She was numb. She had become ice without the ability to move mind or body.

She might have stood there forever had Robbie not placed a hand on her shoulder and given it a gentle squeeze. "Best come inside. We can't have you or the baby becoming ill."

***

With the hours of work involved in running the estate and carving out a few minutes each day for her child, time had a way of passing so rapidly she hardly noticed. Rapidly, yes, and yet agonizingly slowly. With Charlie in her thoughts continually, the hours dragged into days, the days into weeks, and weeks into months—forever.

True to his word, Charlie wrote often. India cherished his letters despite the alarming details in some of them. For her part, she wrote every day. Some communications were only quick postcards, others were longer missives detailing the progress in her relationships with the tenants or Adeline's adorable accomplishments. She told him only the positive. Adeline's first steps and her infant babbling that everyone said sounded like words featured large in her letters.

There were things she did not write, things over which he had no control but would worry about, nonetheless. She did not tell Charlie that Mama had suffered a severe cold which the doctor feared would turn to pneumonia or about the concern over where Farmer Holden's allegiance lay. Rumors of traitors and spies were rife in the county. She did not complain about the difficulties of running the farms with nothing but old men and schoolchildren to tend the fields and livestock. The shortages and privations she kept to herself.

On a blustery April afternoon, Althea burst through the estate office door waving a stack of envelopes. "Here's today's post and there is a nice fat one with a military return address."

India whooped and jumped up from behind the desk. Rifling through the stack, she called out, "Bill, bill, bill . . . Charlie!"

She plopped down in her chair and tore the envelope open. The fact that Robbie and Althea moved toward the door did not register until it clicked shut. A soft sigh escaped. She was alone with the man she loved even if it was only words scribbled on cheap paper.

My Dearest Darling,

The wonderful food package you sent has finally arrived. I cannot say the small cakes and biscuits were completely intact, but their taste was in no way affected by the jolting they received on their journey. Please thank Mrs. Bertrand and tell her my men and I enjoyed every morsel. The delicious food was an outstanding change from our daily rations. I suspect she used the last of her pre-war sugar supply, for which I am humbly and deeply grateful. It lifted the men's morale immensely, as anything from home does.

Your descriptions of our darling Adeline delight me no end and lift my spirits. I carry the photograph of you two in the pocket nearest my heart. Please write more of you both and your activities.

While I cannot reveal our actual location, the chap with whom I share censorship duties approved what I am writing. One of our duties is to read the letters written by the men in our units and censor anything that might be of use to the enemy if the letters fell into the wrong hands. It is a chore neither of us relishes, but it is part of being an officer in charge of a unit. We exchange censorship duties for each other's mail.

Our unit is dug in, safe down in the six-foot-deep valleys that are our trenches. Two aprons of barbed wire protect us from any advancing Germans who are equally dug in, so one might say things are fairly quiet here. The drainage system is holding any runoff from rain at bay for the time being and the duckboards make travel along the line bearable. The officers' dugout is somewhat snug, if one can say that about an underground dwelling. The Kilnsey men are hale and hearty. We are doing well. Please share this with the families of the men who are illiterate. Those of us with educations do what we can to dash off notes for the men who cannot write, but time for such is limited.

I must leave off here. Please kiss Adeline and Mama for me. I have enclosed a note for Mama, which I know you will not mind passing on to her.

With all my love,
Charlie

***

Althea turned at the castle door and observed India through the office window. She might be a wife, mother, and landlord responsible for the running of a large estate, but she was still a girl in some ways. Every letter from Charlie brought out girlish shouts of hope and delight. The thought of what lay ahead darkened any pleasure Althea had in the vision of India's joy over Charlie's letter.

When they stepped into the vestibule, she waylaid Robbie with a hand on his arm. "When are you going to tell her? It can't wait much longer."

The knowledge Althea carried pierced her heart and soul. It affected her most, but it also would have a mighty impact on India. Althea hated keeping it secret, but Charlie had insisted, so she acquiesced.

CHAPTER 21

Ainsworth hovered at India's elbow. "The morning post and London Times, My Lady."

India placed her teacup on its saucer and took the letters without even glancing at the newspaper. Shuffling through the mail, she found one she would read immediately, but not the one she most hoped for. She could not expect Charlie to write daily, but she always searched for his formal script on the exterior of every envelope. Letters from the front arrived in an unpredictable pattern, sometimes several all at once and then nothing for weeks.

Laying the bills and business correspondence aside, she tore open the envelope with a New York City return address. Mother's missive began with its usual greeting, as if India might have forgotten her position in their relationship. India scanned the letter before reading it in full. Her stepfather, David Havemeyer, was mentioned several times. This did not bode well as he was also her American lawyer.

Dear Daughter,

I hope you and Baby Adeline are well. The news we receive from London is most alarming. David and I have concluded it is best that you bring the baby to New York and remain here for the duration. You have an agent to run the estate, so there is really no reason to put yourself in harm's way.

Your sister-in-law, of course, disagrees. Lady Clarissa does not want her mother left alone in the castle. I suggested the Dowager come also and live with her and Mr. Rivers. Neither of them seemed very pleased at the prospect. I believe the topic has become a source of tension between them.

You and Adeline may have the Washington Square house. It will be most convenient. With my dear mother's passing, David sees no reason to keep it, but Number 5 has been in my family since it was built. I rue the day he persuaded me to purchase the Fifth Avenue townhouse. Of course, he refused to live with Grandmama. I suppose you may understand, though I never will. 5th Avenue is a more modern establishment, but I simply cannot bear to part with Washington Square. Your living there would preclude any notions of putting it up for sale.

Let me know your travel arrangements and David will have our chauffeur meet you at the dock. He will bring you to us first, then you can settle into Number 5 at your leisure. You will need to hire servants as we let the ones you knew go when Grandmama died. I look forward to your reply.

With affection,
Mother

India shook her head. How like Mother. She never changed. Her interests lay behind any and all gestures toward others. Her plans too often turned to demands on those around her. It was foolish to think India and the baby must rush to America to avoid the effects of war. Kilnsey was far removed from any danger save for a full-fledged German invasion, which was most unlikely. India folded the letter and shoved it back in its envelope. She had no choice but to reply. That task, however, could wait until later in the day.

Unusually, the butler still hovered.

"Ainsworth, is there something you wish to discuss?"

"No, My Lady, but I thought it best I stayed until you have read the morning headlines. I fear there has been a tragedy, and I did not like to leave you alone with such dreadful news."

India sagged in her chair. What on earth could stir the stoic Ainsworth so? India dropped the envelopes and grabbed the Times. The headline covered a full quarter of the front page. *German U-boat Sinks R.M.S. Lusitania.* Of the nearly 2000 passengers and crew, only 761 survived. Among the lost were 123 Americans. India dashed through the pages to reach the casualty lists. It took only moments to discover the name of someone she knew. She blinked and read it again. William Connor, Esq. of Boston and New York.

A need to be alone came over her. "Thank you, Ainsworth. Is the staff aware of the sinking?"

"I have awaited your approval before sharing the information. May I inform them?"

"Of course." India closed and folded the paper. "Is there danger any of the staff had family or friends on board?"

Ainsworth hesitated before replying, "One of the maids has family in America. Her brother may have been on the ship, coming home to do his patriotic duty."

"Please take the Times to the servants' hall. This news should not be kept from anyone who has suffered a loss." India paused before releasing the paper. "And if the worst has happened, tell the maid she will have as much time with her family as needed."

The butler tucked the paper under his arm. "Thank you, My Lady. I believe there is only an aged mother remaining in England. If arrangements are to be made, I fear they will fall upon the girl."

"Very well. Let's hope for the best, but if it is bad news, please keep me informed."

After inclining his head, Ainsworth left her alone with her thoughts.

My goodness. Billy Connor was among the lost. Since coming to England, she had given him no thought whatsoever, and yet . . . He was her first real experience of romantic attraction. She had thought he was the one. He had led her to believe his courtship was genuine. He had showered her with attention and feigned affection all the while having been engaged for two years and on the verge of marrying. She had been naive and silly. His reluctance to call for her at the door should have raised suspicion. It should have warned of an unflattering duplicity in his nature, but she was unwilling to see it at the time. He used the excuse that her family would not approve of his Catholic faith to entice her to secret meetings in Washington Square Park. She had been such a stupid girl. While he behaved respectfully in other ways, he was nonetheless a self-acknowledged cad, a bounder, and thank God, a mere shadow in the past. Hopefully, he left his wife and any children well provided for.

India eyed the eggs and bacon congealing on her plate. Scooping up a mouthful, she chewed and swallowed despite their unappetizing consistency. Even the wealthy could no longer afford to waste food. War touched almost all aspects of their lives now.

The dining room door opened, pulling her back to the present. Robbie went to the sideboard, poured coffee for himself, and took a seat without his usual cheerful greeting. How odd. He was always the most affable of men.

India studied the slump of his shoulders for a moment. "Is everything all right? You seem troubled."

He did not answer immediately. Instead, he considered the addition of cream and sugar to his coffee far longer than the task required.

When he finally spoke, self-deprecating humor colored his voice. “Please forgive my rudeness. Althea has just given me a rather severe dressing down, which I deserved. Her words are still ringing.”

India’s lips twitched in a rueful smile. “I doubt you could ever do anything to deserve such. Tell me. What has her so upset?”

He resumed stirring his coffee until it slopped over the rim. Discomfort radiated from every pore. “There’s something I feel you should have known long ago, but which Charlie did not want discussed. I think he couldn’t bear having a moment of your time together marred. You have my sincerest apologies. Althea is right. I should have stood up to him on this point.”

“I think you had better tell me right now.” India’s forehead furrowed. “The effect of bad news is rarely eased by delay.”

He moistened his lips, dragging out the seconds before replying, “I know everyone thought my age would excuse me from active duty. It’s true as far as going to the front is concerned, but there are other areas where I may serve. I cannot sit here safe when our friends and neighbors are in such danger. I must do my bit. I’ve volunteered and been accepted to a clerk’s position in the War Office in London. An old school chum has risen in the ranks and he pulled some strings to have me attached to his command. Please forgive our deception.”

His revelation pushed all thoughts of Billy Connor and the *Lusitania* from her mind. Stunned hardly described how she felt. Everything now made sense. All the hours spent studying crop best practices, treatments for animal diseases, learning to drive, all of it had been in service of the moment she would truly be left to run the estate on her own. Through a falsely calm smile she asked, "How long has Althea known?"

"Not terribly." Robbie broke eye contact, shifting his gaze to the nearest window. The pastoral scene beyond did not appear to ease his discomfort. "Althea is not happy about this, but she understands my desire to make a difference."

"And when did you and Charlie cook up this little scheme?"

"Right before he left for training. I showed him a letter from my friend in the War Office asking if I could see my way to join him there. Charlie agreed that all of us must go where we're needed. Life at the front is difficult for our men. I believe I can make a difference in my small way. I will be processing supply requests from the various commanders in the field and coordinating deliveries to the front."

"And when do you desert us?"

His face flushed when he met her gaze. "I'm to report in two weeks. Again, you have my deepest apologies for the deception. It was ungentlemanly and unkind. However, I can assure you neither Charlie nor I have any fears about the estate. You have all the skill and knowledge you need." He pushed his chair back. "If you will excuse me, I should go to Althea. I left her in tears."

India gave him a curt nod, for she was beyond speech. Betrayed, stunned, and enraged best described the impact of his revelations. She stared at the departing Robbie as she boiled within, but he was not the sole target of her anger.

In times of emotional turmoil, Charlie tended to retreat into himself. Too often, he became uncommunicative, even brusque and rude when called upon to face unwelcome situations. His behavior when they spotted Annie and her baby on the train platform at the end of their honeymoon attested to his self-absorption. He had dashed away to confront Annie about the baby's parentage without so much as a by your leave. In fact, he had refused to speak to India until she confronted him in the Holdens' parlor. His behavior had nearly ended their three-day marriage.

She now found herself in an impossible position. It was not that he and Robbie expected her to do her part and hold things together here at home. No, it was the skullduggery and subterfuge that set her temper ablaze. What does one write to a husband with whom one is furious, but who is also in mortal danger? Charlie's life and those of his men depended on his full attention to the war and her assurance all was well on the home front.

The urge to smash things became overwhelming. She picked up her coffee cup and hurled it against the marble fireplace surround. An explosion of china shards littered the hearth.

If she had needed an excuse to refuse Mother's demand, she now had it, but at what cost?

CHAPTER 22

Althea wiped her cheeks and blew her nose into a linen handkerchief. She traced its silk embroidered pattern with her thumb—roses for June, her favorite flower and her birth month. When she opened India's Christmas gift, she found twelve pieces of fine linen, each embroidered with a different flower, one for each month. June and its lovely roses now lay in Althea's lap, a crumpled, soggy mess.

Robbie had no right to ask her to keep important information from India. The situation had caught her between the two people she loved most in the world. Her relationship with India was more like that of sisters than employer and employee. Robbie was all she had dreamed of in a husband, something she doubted she would ever have until he miraculously entered her life. She could never love another man the way she loved Robbie, and he loved her just as deeply in return. How could he do this to her?

His footstep sounded in the passageway leading to the servants hall. He asked her to await him there until he had informed India of his imminent departure. He came through the doorway, nodded, and held out his hand. Althea studied him as he approached. Distress darkened his handsome face. Well, too bad. He and Charlie had both acted badly.

She took his arm, allowing him to lead her toward the back entrance and the courtyard beyond. As they entered his office, he murmured, "You have been crying again. I'm so sorry." He assisted her with a chair, then kissed her cheek.

She stiffened and asked, "How did India take it?"

"About as well as you would expect. She tried to hide it, but I could tell she is angry."

"Do you blame her?" Althea heard the anger in her own voice, but at the moment, she did not care. These men had deceived them, shamefully so.

"No, of course I don't blame her or you either for that matter." He picked up her hand, turned it palm up, and brushed it with his lips. "How are you doing, my darling?"

His solicitude and sad eyes elicited more tears. In a shaky voice, she said, "About as well as can be expected." Sarcasm might be mean-spirited, but she could not stop it from coloring her reply.

He brushed a stray lock of hair from her cheek and tucked it behind her ear. Kissing her throat, he murmured, "Hurting you is my biggest regret. Please forgive me, but I beg you to understand that every able-bodied man must do his patriotic duty. Who would I be if I failed my king and my country?"

She sniffed and wiped her eyes. "You would be here with me in our sweet cottage helping India run this estate. Are you sure she can handle it?"

He moistened his lips and swallowed. "She's learned everything she needs to make a go of it. The biggest problem will be a labor force. That wouldn't change even if I stayed. The Home Office is rumored to be formulating a plan to give farmers assistance with the planting and harvest. I will, of course, alert India immediately if this proves accurate."

"With all the men going to the front, who are they planning to recruit? Invalids and the elderly?"

Robbie chuckled. "Not exactly, but if what I hear is true, our tenants may have to adjust their views."

"In what way?"

"I would rather not say in case it's all just fanciful nonsense dreamed up by over-eager bureaucrats. I promise India will be the first to know if it becomes a reality."

"You are certainly being mysterious." She poked his chest. "It better be something good or you will be in big trouble."

"And if it's only make-believe?"

"Then you have nothing to worry about, do you? I will never know what we might have received."

***

Two weeks later, Althea stood on the Grassington Depot platform, waving until the last wisp of engine smoke disappeared. Only then did she burst into tears. Robbie was truly gone. The war had swept him away on a tide of patriotic duty. It was hard, very hard not to be bitter. He did not really have to volunteer. It had been his choice to leave her alone in a place that felt much less like home without him.

Dabbing her eyes, she turned to India. "I feel such a fool blubbering like this. None of the other women are making a scene. You must be embarrassed to be seen with me."

India slipped her arm around Althea's shoulders. "Don't be ridiculous. I can assure you no one understands better than the women of this county how you're feeling right now. Come on. Let's head home."

As they approached the auto, Althea felt India's eyes on her. "I'm okay. I promise not to make another scene."

India smirked and cocked her head. "Oh, I had no worries about a scene. I'm just wondering which one of us worthy motorists will crank and who will drive. Shall we flip a coin? Heads will drive. Tails must crank."

Althea shot India a watery grin in reply. "I don't have a coin. Do you?"

India reached in her handbag and shook her coin purse. "Not even a half penny."

Althea scrunched her shoulders and raised her hands palms up. "Well then, I guess we just sit it out until Ainsworth arrives in the pony cart to see why we didn't get home. Even though he thinks driving the auto is beneath him, he can do it. Dibs on the passenger seat. You can drive the cart."

India laughed and slung an arm around Althea's waist. "Tell you what. If we can persuade the stationmaster to crank, I'll drive. In your current state, you might run us off the road."

Althea rolled her eyes. "You can use me as an excuse if you like, but I am not in a state." She held out a hand. "See? Steady and calm as the windless sea."

"Uh huh. Very poetic. You go ask him then. He likes you better than me."

"Ah, but you are the lady of the manor. He can hardly say no to you."

India huffed in mock irritation. "Oh all right, if I must."

Althea pointed toward dark clouds gathering in the west. "You must. Looks like it's going to rain."

As Althea settled into the passenger seat, waves of sadness and dread washed over her. Robbie and Charlie were both gone now, and in all probability would not be back until this bloody war was over. Who knew how long that would be or what they would all have to go without for the duration?

CHAPTER 23

India placed her teacup on its saucer and selected a cucumber sandwich. The china rattled a little due to the uneven ground upon which the table and chairs sat. Her gaze lingered on the moorland where the slanting sun had painted the waving grasses with a deep rose-gold brush. These warm, languid afternoons of taking tea alfresco would soon come to an end.

This summer of 1915 had passed pleasantly, for the most part. The weather came in the right mix of sun and rain. The farmers were predicting the best harvest in years. Lambs and calves were born in prodigious numbers, from birth frolicking in the fields on strong, well-shaped legs. The moors, pastures, and verges of the lanes donned their colorful patchwork of native flowers, which danced in mild breezes.

Given such glorious weather, she, Mama, and Althea often took tea here on the lawns beyond the formal gardens under the shade of a single giant oak standing guard at the entrance to the wild, untended moors. With sunset coming after nine p.m., the Chinese garden provided a pleasant place to enjoy pre-dinner drinks. They made it a habit to gather about seven and enjoy a sherry or cocktail before going to the dining room around eight for a simple, summer meal. When winter descended, she would miss these lovely days and evenings.

Some in the household raised a brow at Milady's companion being included in every meal, but India could not have cared less. She wanted Althea with her and so she was treated like family. It eased the loneliness of Charlie's and Robbie's absence for both of them. If it had not been for the war and the growing shortages in even the simplest supplies, the summer of 1915 would have been a perfect season.

To everyone's delight, Baby Adeline achieved her infant milestones with a precocious ease that kept everyone on their toes. She walked at ten months and ran at twelve, causing her nanny to give chase, huffing and puffing with every stride. More than once, Althea reported catching Nanny Philby scolding the child for acting like the toddler she was. While the words Nanny used did not amount to abuse, India was left feeling let down and suspicious. If Nanny acted thus when others were within earshot, what was she doing when no one could see or hear her? Despite Mama's continued claims that Philby was the best possible choice, India watched her nursery nemesis with care.

India sat at the office desk going over cultivation and harvest figures when a feeling of unease descended without warning. One minute the numbers marched down the ledger page written in a neat, orderly hand. The next, they disappeared, replaced by a nameless, shadowy dread. Something was wrong with the baby. She felt it as clearly as the pen her fingers grasped. She dropped the pen and dashed to through the castle's front entrance.

India's old nursemaid back in North Carolina had claimed to have second sight due to her Scots-Irish heritage. As India ran up the flights of stairs toward the nursery, she wondered if she had caught a touch of the "fey" from the woman she credited with raising her. After all, India was descended from Scots Highlanders on her father's side. Adeline should have been napping peacefully, but instead, infant screams rolled down the hall as India reached the nursery floor.

She lightened her step upon the hall runner and crept to the open door. What she saw made her heart stop and then race. Adeline's head snapped back and forth while Philby's hands encased her little ribcage. The baby's face turned from fiery red to a purplish hue. She gasped for air.

Fighting a desire to throttle the monster, India bellowed, "Put my baby down and pack your bags. Be gone within the hour or I will have you arrested."

A look of alarm spread over Nanny Philby's face as she dropped Adeline into her crib. "Milady, I was just trying to get the little lamb to stop crying. She has been a trial this afternoon."

"You believe shaking a child until she can't breathe is the way to stop crying? I am not sure why my mother-in-law insisted on having you, but it ends this minute. Get out of my sight."

A more confident gleam settled in the nanny's eyes. She straightened and drew herself up to her full height. Stepping toward India, she leaned in. "We'll see what Her Ladyship has to say about this. The Dowager is who I listen to." She raised her index finger and shook it in India's face. "Why, you. You're just an upstart, lowbred American pretending to be a countess."

A loud bang sounded just beyond the nursery door. India and the nanny jerked toward the noise. Mama stood in the entry, a scowl hardening her eyes and mouth. She must have been drawn to the nursery by India's shouting, and she had clearly heard the most important parts of the confrontation.

Laying a hand against the doorjamb, she raised her walking cane and pointed. "Philby, you heard Her Ladyship. You will be gone before the hour is out or face the Kilnsey constabulary. Furthermore, you will leave without a reference." Looking at India, she continued, "Take the baby downstairs. Send Ainsworth and Mrs. James to see that our orders are followed forthwith. I will join you in the drawing room presently."

Leaving Mama alone with Philby did not feel right, but seeing the set of the old lady's jaw and receiving a decisive nod, India picked up Adeline and headed for the stairs. Mama was a force when she set her mind to something. Letting her handle the situation for which she bore considerable responsibility might go some way toward assuaging the sense of guilt she must surely feel. If Mama's guilt came even close to her own, it would be a burden she would bear for a long time.

Having dispatched Ainsworth and Althea to the nursery, India settled into the sofa by the fireplace to await Mama. Adeline gave her a toothy grin and climbed onto India's lap for a game of peek-a-boo. The baby giggled and tried to imitate India's silly faces. She really was a sweet child. It took a hard heart to fail to see Adeline for the adorable little girl she was. Philby was definitely blind to her baby's charms. In fact, there probably wasn't a child on earth who would be calm and quiet enough for the old bat.

Adeline tugged on India's arms. "R-pwane, Mummy. R-pwane."

India stood up and lifted the baby into airplane position. Flying her around, India chanted, "We're glad she's gone away. We're better off this day. We'll be happier from now on, for the bad old crow is gone." India laughed at the silly rhyme that had popped into her head, but she would not repeat it. Adeline picked up language quickly these days. It would not do for the baby to call every older woman she saw an old crow. Arms aching, she lowered the baby to her hip. Her heart held a lightness she had not felt in months. Today, right had been done for her precious child and they were better for it.

But then reality reared its unsettling head. Their found solution had simply created another problem. She slumped onto the floor, placing Adeline on the carpet beside her.

Being estate agent and owner combined took massive amounts of her time. Who would care for the baby now? She could not do both. Having the baby in the office would prevent any real work being done, and Mama was physically beyond caring for an active toddler. She had replaced one problem with another.

The minutes dragged, marked by the mantel clock's chiming of the quarter hours, without an answer presenting itself. At long last, a muffled commotion drifted to the drawing room from the service area of the castle. India rose and went to the windows overlooking the courtyard. Nanny Philby, back stiff and face rigid, climbed into the pony cart. With one scathing glance at the window where India stood, the old biddy nodded to the village boy holding the reins, and she was gone from their lives, never to hurt Adeline again. But what now?

A gentle hand on her shoulder broke India's reverie. Althea waited until the pony cart passed under the portcullis, then said, "Glad to see the back of her. I'm just sorry she didn't show her true colors sooner."

The baby tugged on India's skirts. She bent and gathered Adeline up, kissing her dark golden head. "Me, too. If Adeline has any lasting harm, I will never forgive myself. I should have stood up to Mama and chosen someone I liked." She looked away from the window. "Where is Mama?"

"She is taking a rest in her room. I suspect the confrontation took more out of her than she wants to admit."

"You're right. When Mama lifted her cane, there was a tremor which she managed to control, but it took a lot of strength." India led the way to the sofas. When they were seated, she waggled her brows and grinned. "I wish you could have seen Philby's face. I doubt anyone has ever threatened her with a cane. She went white. I thought she might faint."

Althea placed a hand on her chest in feigned shock. "Faint? That old battle-ax? Never." She pursed her lips, crossed her eyes, and sniggered.

India giggled, then launched into uncontrolled laughter. Wiping her eyes, she gasped, "I must have been more upset than I thought. I think I was on the verge of hysterics." She giggled again, huffed, and hiccupped. In the next moment, the humor died away. She swallowed hard. "As glad as I am that Philby's gone, I have no idea what I'm going to do about the baby. I can't care for her and run the estate. Neither one would get the attention they deserve. Oh, what am I going to do?"

Neither of them heard the light tapping of a cane on the carpet. "That is an excellent question." Mama apparently was not in need of rest after all. She moved toward the fireplace, looking at India in apparent contrition. "Would you be interested in an old woman's ideas after having received such poor advice from her in the past?"

It would have felt good to agree with Mama's self-ascribed criticism, but rubbing it in would serve no good purpose. India patted the seat beside her. "Of course. We hired Nanny Philby based on the excellent reference of your close friend. You could not have known what she was like."

Mama gave India a grateful smile. “Your generosity does you credit, my dear, and I assure you the mistake will not be repeated.”

“You have an idea that might solve our problem?”

“Indeed. I believe we should look closer to home for a nurse. Perhaps a woman with a small child of her own who would welcome the income. I doubt we could persuade her to live in, but it would solve your daytime problem, and I know the girl to be an excellent mother and possessed of a kind and generous nature.”

“Please, tell me. Who is this paragon and when can she start?”

“You will need to discuss this with her husband, but I believe Billy Grant might be willing for his wife to come here during the days. They have a little girl only a month or two older than Adeline. Unlike so many of my peers, I have always believed a child of privilege benefits from associating with those less fortunate.”

This was the first India had heard her mother-in-law express such egalitarian views, but the plan seemed a godsend with only one drawback. “What will we do at night?”

Mama fixed Althea with an appraising look. “You must surely be lonely in the cottage with your husband away in London. It would be a kindness if you would return to the castle on a permanent basis. I know India would not object. She really cannot be expected to care for the estate all day and then care for her child all night. Your daytime duties cannot be very taxing since we do not entertain or go about as we did before the war. If Mr. and Mrs. Grant agree to the arrangement, surely it is best for everyone.”

India looked at Mama from beneath lowered lashes. This was most uncharacteristic. While she loved and respected Charlie’s mother, she also knew Mama could be somewhat devious when she wished. “I must say I’m delighted with the idea of having Althea living in the house again, but I am surprised you're not anxious for us to seek a nurse through one of the reliable London agencies. Why do I suspect you of harboring ulterior motives?"

Mama's cheeks flushed. "If you must know, I believe we should have greater access to the feelings of our tenants regarding the war effort. The Grant girl can provide a conduit to her husband, and thus the community, without raising suspicion."

India blinked as her head snapped back. "What on earth has brought this on?"

"Cousin Archibald called on me a few days ago. He enjoys a good gossip, which is usually off-putting in a vicar, but he has his finger on the pulse of the community. He is well-liked by his parishioners. They feel they can trust him with their concerns. He imparted some rather disturbing information regarding our tenant, Holden. I have been considering our best course since his visit. Philby's departure presents a solution. Billy Grant showed his loyalty when he warned you about Holden's motives for stirring up the tenants. I believe Billy will welcome the extra income and be a willing participant in our covert interests."

India tried to keep her irritation from finding an outlet in her voice. "I see. Is there a good reason you kept this to yourself? Exactly what did Cousin Archibald say?"

Mama shifted on the sofa so that her gaze met India's. Placing a hand over India's, she replied, "You carry the load of the entire estate and its future on your shoulders, my dear. I did not want to add to your burden until there was need."

"That still does not explain what has alarmed you."

Mama arched a brow. "Archibald has heard rumors. He frequents the pub in Kilnsey. Normally, I do not approve, but in this case it has proven beneficial. Joseph Bennett, the farmer whose land abuts Holden's and with whom he shares the lane to and from the village, has observed odd movements around Holden's farm, always after dark. When returning home from the pub, Bennett has seen figures creeping to and from the cottage on several nights when the moon was especially bright. Given Holden's propensity for violence, Bennett has not approached the men, nor has he mentioned the sightings to anyone other than Archibald. Whatever Holden is doing, it cannot be above board. Otherwise, why the need for the cover of darkness?"

India drew a deep breath and exhaled slowly. "Holden is not someone with whom to trifle." She mulled what Mama had told them for a moment. "I believe we must be on our guard. Your plan to bring Mrs. Grant into the house is excellent. Pray she and her husband agree to it." She placed a hand on Althea's arm while she searched for the right words. "This will not work without your help. Can you bear leaving your dear cottage? It's a lot to ask, I know."

Althea placed her free hand over India's and smiled. "The cottage feels rather empty since Robbie left. It would be my pleasure to return to the castle and help with Adeline."

A lightness in heart and mind settled in India, a feeling she had not experienced in a long time. "I must be honest. Having you in the house with us will be wonderful. We'll share the night duties. I promise." Kissing the baby's head, she continued, "My sweet girl sleeps through the night and hardly ever wakes before seven. I really think this will work. Now, when and how do we approach the Grants?"

CHAPTER 24

India lifted Adeline from her hip and placed her on the rug beside little Ruth Grant. The babies giggled and hugged like they had not seen one other for a very long time. In reality, they had been separated for about thirteen hours. Mary Grant and her baby left the castle each day at six and arrived for duty each morning at seven. As predicted, Billy Grant had been very happy for his wife and child to become part of the Kilnsey nursery. He welcomed the steady income it brought and was relieved at the prospect of getting information to India without drawing attention to himself. The arrangement benefitted all. Thus far, all had been quiet in the moorland community as the farmers prepared for the harvest.

Harvest. The word brought both gratitude and anxiety. They were on the verge of the largest bounty in recent memory, but who would do the actual work of scything and gathering on the Home Farm? India had assigned all the workers available to the tenants. As that particular labor force was made up of the tenants' older children, she could hardly syphon them off for her own use. Mr. Smith, Home Farm manager, was beside himself with worry. With those thoughts humming in her mind, she kissed the babies and headed for the estate office.

As she crossed the courtyard, her spirit sank at the sight of who was coming up the castle drive from Mastiles Lane. Manager Smith's pony cart rumbled under the portcullis and drew up beside the office door. He tugged the brim of his peaked cap while she lifted a hand in half-hearted greeting. Without opening his mouth, she knew what he would ask and she thus far had not found a solution. It would be the same question he asked every time they met. She increased her pace. Might as well get the interview over with. The faster she sent him on his way, the quicker she could finish the accounts reconciliation she had begun yesterday.

Smith removed his cap and nodded. "Good morning, Milady. I was hoping for a word."

"Of course. Please come into the office." After they entered, India took her seat behind the desk, pretended to adjust papers on the desk, then fixed him with as kind a smile as she could muster. As if she did not know what he was about to say, she asked, "How may I help you?"

Smith shuffled his feet, stared at the floor, and met her gaze. "It's the harvest, Milady. I simply cannot get it in by myself. We got to find some lads somewhere."

Keeping a firm grip on her temper, India replied, "We have covered this territory several times already. I have placed advertisements as far away as York, Leeds, and Carlisle. I have made inquiries in every town, village, and community far and wide. If men are not at the front, they are all employed. The other tenants have offered you their children's services as soon as they complete their own harvest. Exactly what more do you expect me to do?"

"Begging your pardon, Milady, but using the local children will be too late. We've got to get the harvest in now or lose it." He was clearly trying as hard as she to control his anger, but he lost the battle. "If His Lordship was here, he would know what to do."

India stood and glared. If it was a shouting match he wanted, by God he would get one. All the stress and frustration that had built since Charlie and Robbie volunteered exploded. Hitting the desk with her fists, she shouted, "But His Lordship isn't here, so you are stuck with me. Are you asking me to work alongside you in the fields the way my husband did before we married? Are you?"

The man looked thunderstruck. When he was able to reply, his words stumbled and tumbled over one another. "I . . . I never . . . That is to say . . . I never meant such. That wouldn't be proper. Not in the least."

They stood on opposite sides of the desk, their eyes locked until Smith dropped his gaze. "I should not have come to complain. I'll just do the best I can."

India's anger faded as quickly as it had risen. "This detestable war is not your fault, nor mine. I'll try again to find laborers, but don't get your hopes up. It is all I can do."

Smith nodded. "Try is all any of us can do. Thank you, Milady. I am sorry to have added to your troubles. I will take my leave." He trudged to the door and turned. With a final nod, he headed to his cart with hunched shoulders and a downcast gaze.

As she watched him climb into the cart, her spirits sank to their lowest point of the day. Who knew what new hardships and complaints would present themselves tomorrow? She slumped down into her chair and put her elbows on the desk. They must not lose the harvest. The nation needed everyone at home to do their bit. Their soldiers' very lives depended on it. Placing her chin on her balled fists, she stared off toward the castle's parlor windows in the hope an answer might flash in the glass. None appeared. Foolish to have thought such. In her plight, she was becoming fanciful. That would not do. Problem-solving required clear thinking.

A brisk walk usually helped her mood. She grabbed Charlie's old field coat from the hat stand by the door and headed for the postern gate. Perhaps she could slip out to the moors with no one the wiser. Solitude without explanation to others was in order.

As she neared the top of the first moorland rise, she heard laughter coming from the other side of the hill. Clearly, girls were enjoying something, perhaps a joke or maybe just being young and alive. India was only twenty-four, but the load she now carried made her feel at least twenty years older. Oh, to feel young again. She smiled and pushed on to the top.

Beyond the rise, she came upon girls sitting on a blanket enjoying a picnic. India glanced around her. She had not realized it was such a glorious day. Why not have a picnic if one had nothing better to do, no obligations calling upon one's time, no one demanding labor where there was none to be found? India shook her head. That was unfair. It wasn't the girls' fault they had free time to lounge in the mild fall sunshine. She must not let bitterness overcome her.

She pursed her lips and continued to observe the girls. Their backs were toward her, so they were unaware of her presence. They were three of several unmarried girls who lived with their parents in Kilnsey and Cragfast Mastiles villages. They had finished all their schooling and spent their time helping their mothers at home. When the housework was finished, some of them did a little work for charity, but they mainly were free to spend time as they wished. With all the boys their age in the army, they really had nothing better to do. *Nothing better to do.* The words first whispered to her, then sprang to life and shouted. Yes, that just might be the answer to her prayers. If things worked out as she hoped, Mr. Smith was going to have to make some adjustments in his thinking.

CHAPTER 25

India approached the girls and cleared her throat loudly, hoping not to startle them. "Hello, ladies. It is a glorious day to be out-of-doors, is it not? However do you find the time?"

The girls jumped to their feet and looked afraid they had been caught doing something they shouldn't.

The oldest one took the lead. "Indeed, it is, Milady. A glorious day, I mean. We've finished our work for our mums. They gave us permission to have a picnic. If we're trespassing, we're sorry. We didn't mean any harm."

"And you have done none. These wild acres may belong to the Kilnsey estate, but they are to be enjoyed by everyone. Do you often finish your work this early?"

"Yes, Milady. We're fast workers."

"And do you ever do chores that are not in the house?"

The youngest sniggered. "Cor! I do the milking and work in the garden. My mum says my back is a lot younger than hers. We even help in the fields when our daddies need us." The other two nodded in agreement.

"Have you ever thought about getting jobs?"

The eldest replied, "There aren't any jobs for girls like us."

India ran her gaze over each girl. They appeared healthy and strong. "If I could find good, honest work for you, would you be willing to take it no matter what it was?"

The eldest replied, "Yes Milady, as long as our parents don't mind."

India smiled as she drew her ever-ready little notebook and pencil from a pocket. "I've made a note of your names. Tell your fathers I will call upon them presently with a proposition of national importance. You girls are patriotic, aren't you?"

The third girl nodded fiercely. "Oh yes. We all got brothers away fighting the Hun. If we can help king and country, we're willing."

"But you don't know what I wish to propose."

The eldest stepped forward. "It doesn't matter. I'd rather be doing something that will help my William than just sit around waiting. I'll do anything if it will keep him safe and get him home faster."

"I take it William is a beau, not a brother?"

The youngest giggled. "That's right. They've been sweet on each other nearly all their lives. He's asked her to marry him."

"I see." India nodded wistfully. "I know something of missing loved ones and fearing for their safety. William is a lucky man to have you waiting for him." The moment of shared emotions passed. India smiled and continued, "Well then, it's settled. I am very glad you are such fine patriots."

***

Late afternoon sunlight streamed through the cottage window as India shook hands with the last of the girls' fathers. It had not taken too much persuasion to secure the girls' labor for the duration of the harvest. After all, the farmers had sons and other loved ones at the front.

India bid the family farewell and strode to the paddock where she had left Zara. The little mare whinnied and tossed her head as though to ask what had taken so long? India climbed into the saddle and tapped the Arabian's sides with her heels. They moved out into the lane and soon were moving along at a fair trot. India gave Zara her head and urged her into a canter in the hope exercise and fresh air might banish the dark cloud hanging over her. The next step would be telling Mr. Smith the happy news that the harvest was saved. She could just imagine his response when he learned the source of his salvation.

Presently, the single track to the Home Farm came into view. India squared her shoulders as she pulled Zara back to a quick walk and turned onto the lane. No matter Smith's reaction, she would stand firm. It would not be an offer. It would be a directive. She was the estate manager, whether he liked it or not. He would have no choice but to accept the only labor available to him, by golly. She hit the saddle's pommel with her fist, making Zara skitter sideways. India leaned forward and patted the mare's neck. The action calmed one of them, but India's heart still thumped in anticipation of the confrontation about to ensue. In the end, Smith would just have to accept change and there was no time like the present to ensure that he did.

India slowed Zara at the Home Farm cottage's garden gate. She looped the reins through the ring of a stone hitching post and marched toward the cottage door. It was teatime. Mr. and Mrs. Smith should be sitting down at this moment. She rapped upon the door and waited. No movement sounded within the domicile. Buzzing with impatience, she knocked again with more force. The sound of shoes scurrying across a stone floor came from the other side of the door. The latch clicked and the door flew back, revealing the farmer's wife breathing hard and frowning.

Mrs. Smith's expression dissolved quickly from irritation to one of anxiety. "Milady. We wasn't expecting company. We just sat down to tea. Please come in."

India tried to control her breathing and smiled in as reassuring a manner as she could muster. She had caused undue alarm in a woman she liked to think of as something more than a tenant. They could never be social friends, but they shared mutual goals and concerns.

India followed Mrs. Smith into the house. "Please forgive my intrusion. It is an awkward time to call, but I have excellent news for Mr. Smith. Perhaps he might come into the parlor?"

Mrs. Smith nodded. "I'll send him in." She pointed to chairs beside the parlor fireplace. "Please make yourself comfortable. Would you like tea?"

"Thank you. That would be lovely if it's not too much trouble."

"No trouble. It's already steeped in the pot." Mrs. Smith left for the back of the house.

India settled herself in a worn, but comfortable, chintz-covered armchair angled by the inglenook to allow for both warmth and conversation. Her fingers tapped a nervous tattoo on the arm's lovely blue, pink, and green flower pattern. She eyed the mantel clock as she shifted and recrossed her ankles. Mr. Smith was taking his sweet time in appearing.

She distracted herself by surveying the room. The curtains over the front window were snowy and freshly starched. The rug on the stone floor, while frayed on one edge, was free of litter and dust. Mrs. Smith obviously took pride in her housekeeping. The house was welcoming and cozy in the way of the best English cottages. Not exactly chocolate-box perfect, but clearly a well-loved home. Charlie valued Mr. Smith as a farm manager and good tenant. Pray he would see fit to accept her plan without too great a quarrel. The sound of a male throat clearing sounded in the hall. Ah, here came the man himself.

Mr. Smith trudged into the parlor wearing a perplexed expression. "Milady, my good lady wife says you need to speak to me?"

India summoned her warmest smile. "Indeed. I have wonderful news. I have secured laborers for the harvest."

Mr. Smith returned her smile with a broad one of his own. "Oh, that is good news. When can the lads start?"

India shifted again, edging forward in her seat. "Won't you please sit?"

"Thank you. Mrs. Smith will be in with the tea directly." He took the chair opposite. "However did you find them? Can the lads start tomorrow?"

"Yes, they will arrive bright and early tomorrow."

"Thank you, Milady. You have pulled off a miracle. Who are these lads?"

"Well, you must see . . . that is to say . . . they are not young men."

"Age makes no difference as long as they can do the work. Lots of older fellers judged beyond their prime can still swing a scythe or drive a wagon."

India swallowed hard. "Mr. Smith, you must prepare yourself. The next part of my news is not what you expect."

His eyes widened. "Please go on."

"The workers are not young or old men. They are girls from the community who are not otherwise employed."

He looked like someone had slapped him across the face. "Girls? Girls? You cannot mean girls." His voice rose with each pronouncement. "By Jove, this is not right. You can't expect me to take on a bunch of girls. They'll interfere with what work I can do by myself. They will be our ruination." His shouts were surely heard in the kitchen and beyond the cottage walls.

India moistened her lips and breathed slowly. Patience and persuasion were needed here, not rejoinder in kind.

"First, it is not a bunch. There are only three of them. Second, they will not need training, as such. The girls help with their family's harvests when needed, just like the schoolchildren are helping their fathers now. All you need to do is direct them to the fields and explain what you want done."

Mr. Smith's eyes sort of glazed over. He failed to reply or give any indication he comprehended her explanation. He appeared incapable of speech. Perhaps her news had brought on some kind of fit or apoplexy. She leaned farther forward. "You do understand me, do you not?" She tapped his arm. "Mr. Smith?"

He shook his head and met her gaze. "Forgive me. It is the shock, I guess, after so much hoping and worrying. If these girls are all we have, then they'll have to do." The fight whooshed out of him, leaving him looking like a punctured balloon. He shook his head again. "I'll do the best I can. Three will not be enough, but that's better than none, I suppose."

"How many more do you need?"

"At least two. Five good workers and myself could do the harvesting in good time."

India's eyes narrowed. He only needed two more workers. She slapped the chair's arms and said, "Very well, I believe I can get you two more. Be prepared to start the harvest tomorrow. Your workers will arrive at first light."

India rose and shook hands with Mr. Smith. She chuckled as the front door closed behind her. The promised tea had never materialized. The shock of hearing her husband raise his voice to their landlord must have been forestalled Mrs. Smith—a wise woman who knew when a situation called for discretion.

CHAPTER 26

Althea eyed India in dismay. "You cannot be serious. Your mother-in-law will be furious. I have no problem with it, but oh my goodness. Please do not ask me to be in the room when you tell her."

India put a fist on her hip and pursed her lips. "Coward."

"Yep. Absolutely. You forget. No matter how much you treat me like family, I am still an employee."

India's eyes widened as she waggled her head. "If you must look at it that way, yes, I am your employer, but I need your support when I reveal my plan."

"Now who's the coward?"

India smirked. "Both of us." She jerked her head toward the master suite door. "Come on. Let's get it over with."

Althea followed India to the hall. That girl was going to get both of them a tongue-lashing, if they were lucky. A list of the Dowager's likely reactions included, but were not limited to, yelling, storming from the room, becoming dangerously quiet, writing a letter to her son brimming with vitriol, heart failure . . . .

As they trooped toward the drawing room where the Dowager Lady Kilnsey awaited them for pre-dinner drinks, Althea steeled herself for the interview. She would offer support with her physical presence, but under no circumstances would she become embroiled in the confrontation to come. India had cooked up this little scheme and she could darned well make her case without Althea's help. In truth, the Dowager had no real choice in the matter, but she certainly knew how to make life miserable for those who displeased her.

India pushed the drawing room door open, and they swished into the room. Althea kept two paces behind. India's back was stiff with determination. Althea glanced at Lady Kilnsey ensconced on a sofa, sherry in hand. The old lady looked like she suspected something untoward. Her mouth was set in a firm line, her brow was raised, and her nostrils flared as though she had just encountered an unpleasant odor. It was like she could smell disappointment or trouble drifting in the air. Maybe she had a touch of the second sight.

The Dowager's mouth turned slightly upward in a tight smile. "Sit here beside me, Daughter-in-law. You look as though you have something on your mind."

India glanced over her shoulder and rolled her eyes. It was never a good sign when the Dowager called someone by their position in the household. Althea hid her smile by making a study of an imagined spot on her sleeve. Displaying amusement would not help the situation.

India took her time crossing to the fireside sofa. Althea went to the drinks cart. Without being asked, she gave two sherry snifters generous pours. A glass in each hand, she made her way to India, handed her one, and then chose a chair facing the fireplace. Being able to meet India's gaze directly was not a good idea. She had no desire to be drawn into the scene about to play out.

From the corner of her eye, Althea watched India's chest rise and fall a couple of times. Deep breathing when gathering courage was one of India's telltale signs. Althea inched back into her chair until her face was partially concealed by its high, winged sides. If she tried to make herself invisible, maybe the old lady would forget her presence.

India rolled her glass between her hands. "This is excellent sherry, is it not?"

"Yes. I fear there mayn't be sufficient bottles to see us through. It may be some time before we are able to purchase more. Perhaps you should ask Ainsworth to hold several bottles of the good claret and one or two of the sherry in reserve for when Charles comes home on leave."

"Yes, that is an excellent idea. He has not mentioned leave in his letters, but surely he will get a few days at some point."

Both India and the Dowager fell silent, and the atmosphere in the room became strained. India's eyes darted about the room as though she searched for the right words and timing to share her news.

From the depths of her chair, Althea shot India a meaningful look. The girl was stalling. It would not be long before the old lady caught on. She was a sly old fox when she wanted to be.

Receiving Althea's silent message, India gave her mother-in-law a small smile. Actually, it looked more like a grimace, but it was probably the best she could muster. She took a rather large swig of sherry and placed the glass on the occasional table beside the sofa.

"Mama, I have excellent news. I have secured workers for the fields and alleviated Mr. Smith's distress. We begin the harvest at first light tomorrow."

Old Lady Kilnsey inclined her head. "This is good news indeed. Wherever did you find laborers on such short notice?"

"They are locals who are not otherwise employed."

The Dowager cast a look over India that bore the first signs of suspicion. "If they are not away fighting and not already employed, they must be feeble, or the dregs of the community. Are you sure they can be trusted to do the work?"

"Oh, yes. They are young and strong and eager to help the war effort."

The Dowager's eyes narrowed. "And who are these paragons?"

"Well, actually, they are five local girls."

"I see. And who are their families?"

India named the three community girls before adding in a small voice, "And Althea and myself."

The old lady looked like she might jump from her seat. "Did I hear you correctly? You and your companion intend to work in the fields like common laborers?"

A fire lit India's eyes. "We do. There is no one else. If we do not help, a portion of the harvest will be lost. Both of us grew up on farms and helped with work as kids. Charlie and Robbie left it to me to see that things do not fall apart in their absence. This is my decision, and I will not be dissuaded. If it causes ill talk, I suggest those doing the gossiping have too much time on their hands. They should get those hands dirty with good, honest labor. Our farmers need all the help they can get, and I will not be badgered or bullied." Her last words were delivered with a glare and at considerable volume.

A knowing smile crept across the old lady's face. She searched India for a moment, then grasped her hand. "Well, good for you. You are proving yourself worthy of the trust placed in you. I cannot say I approve of your laboring in the fields, but I am old and set in my ways. The world has changed and the estate must change with it. Will you tell Charlie what you are up to?"

India squared her shoulders. "Of course. We keep no secrets. I am confident he will understand, given his history of working the farms."

Althea observed India carefully. If she had to guess, she would say India was not as confident as she pretended. Charlie, on the other hand, was many miles away across the Channel. There was little he could do to stop his wife.

***

India rubbed her aching arms. Hauling on the reins of the horse-drawn reaper-binder had proven almost as arduous as helping to gather the sheaves. The last step of lifting the sheaves into the threshing machine had left her muscles shaking and exhausted at the end of each day, but the harvest was in and the grains were shipped out to feed the troops. Robbie, as a supplies coordinator in the War Office, had arranged for all the Home Farm's grain to be bought by the army.

India leaned back in the office desk chair and rolled her head from side-to-side while stretching her shoulders. Hard labor had felt good and had taken her mind off the letter she received from Charlie a few days ago. He meant well. She knew he did, but his request was nonetheless painful. She picked it up and read it for the umpteenth time. The message had not altered.

My Dearest Darling,

I am, as always, in awe of your courage, skill, intelligence, and persistence. I wish I could have been there to watch you and Althea working alongside the stalwart Smith. I am glad he did not refuse your offer of help. You two and the three girls made all the difference between failure and success.

I received a letter from Robbie expressing his gratitude and saying how impressed his commander at the War Office is with the size and quality of the Home Farm's harvest. You and Althea have made us proud. I hope Mama did not give you too hard a time about your enterprise. If she did, you have my most heartfelt apology. Please let me know if a letter of rebuke to her is in order.

If you are able to take Adeline to York for a new photograph, I would be most grateful. I feel like I am missing so many important milestones in her life. I am sure she looks more like a little girl every day than the baby I left. One of my great fears is that she will not know me when I come home and that I might not recognize her either. I have enclosed a recent photograph taken by a friend when we were in a village near our location. We look very gay, I admit, for a couple of men fresh from the trenches. We find respite when and where we are able. Please show our sweet girl her papa's picture so she won't forget me.

On a less cheerful note, I have come to the sad conclusion that there is more we can do for the war effort. Moving motorized vehicles over the muddy tracks and battlefields is ridiculously difficult. The horses the army bought are being worked beyond their endurance. I have seen several simply collapse in their traces, never to rise again. It breaks my heart, but I ask that you sell to the army all our horses not used for farming. This will include my hunters, the cart ponies, and carriage horses. Will you consider selling your Zara, as well? I am sorry to ask for your little mare, my darling, but we need every animal we can get. Please forgive me.

A Sergeant McFee will arrive within the month to collect the animals. I love you and miss you more than words are adequate to express.

With all my love,

Your devoted Charlie

Damn him. It was unfair. Why must he ask this? He arranged to have Zara brought from North Carolina as a wedding gift. Riding her has been the only escape from the responsibilities he left to me. Riding out on the moors, I can forget the war and the estate's problems for a few minutes. If I sell Zara, it will break my heart. If I do not sell, I will forever feel I have let my beloved down in his hour of greatest need.

India crossed her arms on the desk, buried her face in them, and sobbed.

CHAPTER 27

The sound of a lorry trundling into the courtyard drew India's attention away from the latest edition of the *Journal of the Royal Agricultural Society.* So much for the newest process in deworming sheep. She shoved the magazine away, rose from her office chair, and went to the window. A horse van squatted in the center of the courtyard. A mustachioed gentleman in army drab with the insignia of a calvary sergeant stepped down from the vehicle, a clipboard in hand which he placed on the lorry's running board. Her heart sank. Sgt. McFee had arrived. She watched as he clasped his hands behind his back and rocked on his heels. He made no move to approach the front door. Instead, he stood beside the van and surveyed the castle. He seemed to be enjoying the view, damn him.

She rubbed her eyes and rolled her shoulders, trying to clean away the cobwebs of a night spent tossing and turning. Sleep had proven elusive, stolen by worry and dread. How could Charlie even suggest she could part with Zara? The very thought was beyond endurance. She squared her shoulders and prepared to meet the enemy.

It came to her in a flash, staying her hand on the door's knob. One minute she was on the verge of tears, the next, a calm fury settled over her. It was as though another personality had entered her body and taken control. Charlie told her to sell his horses and she would, but she'd be damned if Zara would go with them. One little mare could not possibly make much difference to the war effort. Zara was only fourteen hands and light-boned, even for an Arabian. She would be dead within a month given the conditions Charlie described in his letters.

India marched from the office, a slam of the door announcing her presence in the courtyard. Sgt. McFee startled, but quickly regained his composure. He adopted correct military posture and gave her a crisp nod.

As she approached, he said, "Lady Kilnsey?"

India halted a few feet from him and planted her feet firmly, ready for a fight. "I am, and you must be Sgt. McFee."

The sergeant looked taken aback by her vehement tone. "Yes… indeed. I have come about the horses."

"I know why you're here. I'm prepared to sell my husband's hunters, as he requested."

The sergeant retrieved his clipboard and inspected a list. He cast a wary look India's way. "I see we are to purchase four thoroughbreds, three geldings and a stallion, some ponies, and an Arabian mare. Does that seem in order?"

India's pulse pounded. "No, it does not. My husband can sell his hunters and the carriage horses if he wishes, but you will not have my mare." India balled her fists and stepped closer. The man loomed over her by a good foot. She glared up at him and shouted, "She's mine. I will not sell her. Furthermore, the ponies will stay exactly where they are—pulling my staff and me about the estate in carts. I will take it to the highest court, if I must, but you *shall not* have them." She stamped her foot and shook a fist. "You shan't, I tell you." Her words bounced off the castle walls and echoed over the roof's slates.

Sgt. McFee took a step back. "Lady Kilnsey, I assure you this is not a forced sale. If you do not wish to sell the mare, I have no authorization to take her. Indeed, I would not in the face of such sentiment. Please calm yourself."

The fire elicited by McFee's opening comments died, snuffed out by the man's expression. Something akin to fear flickered in his eyes. He must think her demented. Maybe she was because a fit of giggles took hold. The more she tried to stop them, the harder they came, until tears streamed. The harder she laughed, the more alarmed the sergeant looked.

"My dear lady, may I call someone? It was never my intention to cause such . . . such . . . " His words faded away. He apparently felt it improper to accuse a countess of having hysterics.

India wiped her cheeks, placed her hand over her mouth, and hiccupped like a drunkard on Saturday night. Demented was perhaps the right word for the state in which she found herself. Finally catching her breath, she said, "Please accept my apologies. I fear the strain of His Lordship's absence momentarily overwhelmed me."

McFee cleared his throat while casting a suspicious glance in her direction, no doubt fearful of another outburst. He drew a cautious breath. "Indeed. No need for apologies. Understandable, of course." An uncomfortable silence descended. The sergeant shifted from foot-to-foot while he looked at everything in the courtyard except India. A pained expression flickered in his eyes as he settled his attention back on her. "Might we discuss the horses further?" His tone was hesitant, his inflection small and tight.

India gave him a crooked smile. "We must walk down to the village where the castle stables are located. Please wait while I let someone know where I'm going."

India turned toward the castle entry but did not need to go further. Ainsworth hovered in one of the vestibule's windows. Nothing escaped his notice. He raised a brow in inquiry. India nodded. It was all the communication required.

An elderly groom, grandfather to the boy who had left their employ to fight for king and country, met India and the sergeant at the stables. He brought out the horses in turn while McFee cast an evaluative eye over each.

"These are fine animals, Milady. Fine animals, indeed. Lord Kilnsey is a true patriot." What the sergeant did not say was that the horses probably would not come home. Charlie's letters had made it clear animals did not last long under the conditions at the front.

Zara stuck her head over her stall door and nickered, probably wondering why India was failing to give her the attention she was due. India laid her cheek against the mare's blaze and scratched her throat and chin. At least the little Arabian would be spared.

In the end, McFee said he would have rejected Zara and the cart ponies for service because they were simply too small. His words echoed her own fears, saying they would not have survived at the front long enough to have done any good. She watched the van and its burden pull out of the courtyard with a sinking heart. She was not the only one in the family who adored horses. Charlie cared deeply for his animals. In all likelihood, he would never see his beloved hunters again.

***

Autumn evolved into a quiet Christmas with little to celebrate other than the fact that they were all in good health, including Charlie. At nineteen months, Adeline had not noticed that her pile of presents was diminished over previous celebrations. She was delighted with her single toy and played happily among the discarded ribbons and wrappings. India had given the servants an extra day off and a little cash to help them enjoy it as best they could. While everyone feigned joy, the strain of shortages and absent loved ones had begun to wear. A war-weary sobriety had settled over everyone in the community. The New Year turned and the winter of 1916 settled in wet and cold. A heavy snow mixed with sleet in March left everyone in eager anticipation of warmer weather. Easter was late, not until April 23. The day gave Yorkshire its first taste of spring. The following week squashed any joy the milder weather might have brought.

India scanned the headlines of May 3rd's *Times* and shook her head. Final count: 485 killed, another 2600 wounded, and 3500 arrested. British forces had done their job and quelled the enemy, but what a cost. Such a waste. None of the deaths, however, occurred at the front in France. On Easter Monday, Irish republicans had risen in an armed attempt to drive the British from their soil while the empire's attention was focused on the war in Europe. The rebellion failed. Having been born an American, it was easy to sympathize with the desire for self-rule, but India would not express those views aloud. Mama, Charlie, the servants, and the neighbors would never understand or forgive. They were English to the core.

India dropped her napkin beside her breakfast plate, preparing to leave for the estate office, when Ainsworth appeared at her elbow brandishing an envelope. "This has just arrived by special post, My Lady." Instead of disappearing as was his norm, the butler stepped only as far away as the sideboard where chafing dishes still steamed.

India glanced at the return address, and her heart dropped. The War Office's standard and address were emblazoned in the upper left corner.

Dear God, please. It can't be. Please do not let it be Charlie. Her head swam. China and flatware rattled as she grabbed the edge of the table.

CHAPTER 28

India's attempt at opening the envelope failed. Ainsworth stepped forward and silently offered the small knife he used for slitting the foil on bottles of wine. She reached for it, but her grasp faltered and the knife bounced upon the carpet beneath the dining table.

He scooped it up and asked, "May I?"

"Yes. Please."

He slit the envelope open and handed its contents to India. She flipped open the folds and wilted.

War Office

Whitehall, London

Lady Kilnsey,

It is with sincere apologies for the inconvenience this will cause that I write to inform you the British Army requires the use of Kilnsey Castle as a hospital for officers suffering the mental strain of war. Kilnsey's pastoral setting and isolation will provide the appropriate environment and confidentiality their condition requires.

Major John Fraser, Royal Army Medical Corps, will arrive on or about May 24, 1916 to ascertain arrangements needed to accommodate the convalescents. Thanking you in advance for your complete cooperation in the performance of your patriotic duty.

Sincerely,
Herbert, Lord Kitchener
Secretary of State for War

India read the letter a second time. The trembling in her hands subsided. Thank God. It had nothing to do with Charlie. If she were alone, she would scream and cry with relief. It was most unkind to give her such a fright.

After scanning it once more, she frowned and passed the letter to Ainsworth. "It seems we are to have uninvited guests. Apparently, we have no choice in the matter. I would not have refused, but I do resent Lord Kitchener's tone."

"Indeed, My Lady." Ainsworth cleared his throat. "Might I venture a question?" India nodded and he continued, "Does it seem unusual a letter should come directly from Lord Kitchener?"

India thought for a moment. "Yes, it does. I ran into Lady Milford when I was in York before Christmas. The Grange is being used as a hospital for wounded officers. If she had received a letter from a cabinet minister, believe me, she would have let it be known. I wonder why we've been singled out for such honor."

India's eyes narrowed as she tapped the envelope cast aside near her plate. "Lady Milford boasted about how the request for the use of their house had been made voluntary. She complained vociferously of the inconveniences they were suffering, but under the surface, I could tell she was quite proud. Made a point of what a sacrifice it is having strange men in one's home, but one must do one's patriotic duty, don't you know." India waggled her eyebrows while Ainsworth's lips twitched with a conspiratorial smile. Her imitation of the haughty Countess Milford was spot on, if she did say so herself. "Well, I guess we will know more after this Major . . . ," She paused and scanned the letter, " . . . Fraser arrives. He will probably need to stay the night. Let's put him in the room closest to the Grand Staircase. I don't relish a stranger roaming around lost blundering into family rooms. And I suppose we will need to fetch him from the station, assuming the War Office deigns to give us his travel arrangements."

On May 24, India stood at the Grassington Depot, staring into the distance. Despite the moderate temperature, the lace on the collar of her spring frock chafed. She ran her fingers under it as her foot tapped a tattoo. It was just like the blasted train from York to be late. Nothing ran on time these days. Here she was cooling her heels awaiting the arrival of an unwanted guest as though she had nothing better to do than wait upon the convenience of the War Office. She kicked at the little mound of gravel her boot toe had stirred up. This Major Fraser best be on good behavior. She was in no mood to deal with the hubris and superiority that too often accompanied officers.

Ainsworth had offered to engage the elderly stable groom in driving the cart, but India decided she would take the measure of Fraser on her own. The drive from the station to the castle would provide an excellent opportunity to assess what they were going to be dealing with.

A train whistled and coal smoke drifted above the bend in the tracks. The locomotive's nose appeared, and the train chuffed into view. Finally.

Its wheels ground to a stop amid the squealing of brakes and clanking of couplings. Only one carriage door swung open. A passenger in military uniform alighted and scanned his surroundings. He carried a Gladstone bag and a valise that bulged at the sides. Wonderful. He must be planning an extended stay.

India watched him for a few seconds before walking to him and extending her hand. "Major Fraser? I am Lady Kilnsey. Welcome to Yorkshire."

The major looked both amused and perplexed as he shook her hand. "Thank you for meeting my train." His voice identified him as a son of the Highlands.

"You are welcome. We all do as we must. Do you have any other baggage?"

"No, our crates will arrive once I have the lay of the land."

"I see. I will arrange for a larger transport when the time comes. Today, I'm afraid you will have to endure a long ride in the trap." She gestured toward the pony waiting hipshot beneath an oak at the corner of the depot. "Shall we?"

Major Fraser smiled and gave a small bow. "After you, My Lady."

He followed her to the trap and hoisted his cases into it then jumped up and sat opposite India. She clicked to the pony and tapped the reins against its rear. The mare glared around at India, tossed her head, and snorted.

The major chuckled. "Looks like she resents her job."

If the man thought he was being funny, he was mistaken. India pursed her lips and gave the pony more forceful encouragement with the whip. The animal and trap leapt forward in a jerky dance that nearly upended them. India hauled on the reins and the vehicle righted itself.

Damn and blast the beast. Of all days to decide to be contrary. She gave a crisp shout. "Aila. Walk on."

An amused look played in Major Fraser's eyes. "Appropriate name for your little pony."

"How so?"

"In Scottish Gaelic, Aila means from a strong place or stubborn. I can confirm the meaning is accurate."

"Really?"

"Yes. Aila was my grandmother's name. She was a force to be reckoned with when she got her back up. I'm told I take after her."

India kept her voice flat and dry. "How interesting."

Major Fraser must have gotten the message, for he glanced at India and fell silent. Thank goodness.

When she was certain his attention was focused on the beauty of the countryside, India glanced at the major from beneath her lashes. His uniform fit his tall frame well, accenting the breadth of his shoulders and narrowness of his waist and hips. He wore a thin mustache over his Cupid's bow lips. His hair was black, but his eyes were vivid blue in the way those with Celtic heritage sometimes possessed. He was a good-looking sod, for sure. No doubt he left a string of broken hearts wherever he went. One more reason to resent his being thrust upon them. All she needed was the housemaids swooning and neglecting their work.

After several miles of silence, the major drew an audible breath. "The War Office is most grateful. Your willing sacrifice speaks of your patriotism. Castle Kilnsey is a perfect location to meet the needs of our convalescing officers."

India shot him a look she hoped communicated incredulity. "We are happy to be of service to our ailing servicemen, though I'm not aware the use of my home is voluntary." She should feel some shame about her tone, but she did not. Major Fraser either had not been put in the picture where the demand for Kilnsey was concerned or he was being disingenuous. She did not have patience for either.

He chuckled nervously. "I must apologize. I know you didn't have a choice. I hope you will not hold that against me or my men."

India shot him a grumpy look. "I'm not in the habit of persecuting people whose misfortunes are beyond their control. We will make your patients as welcome and comfortable as rationing permits."

He looked surprised. "Then you have not been told."

India raised a brow. "Apparently not." One would have thought it obvious she knew next to nothing about what to expect from the coming invasion.

"Perhaps this is good news, then. You will not need to feed us from your own provisions. The army will supply our needs, and I am authorized to share with you and your household, as well. My men will also be ordered to stay away from the family's quarters. I hope this meets with your approval?"

"Indeed. I look forward to seeing what the army will provide." They fell back into an uncomfortable silence.

As they drove on, India mulled over their conversation. Something felt off. Maybe it was the way he referred to his patients. He had twice called them his men and had made no reference to their conditions. Perhaps it was his way of maintaining confidentiality and showing respect. Still, it seemed odd.

India pulled back on the reins, slowing the pony to a crawl as they crossed the narrow bridge connecting the banks of the River Wharfe. She hunched her shoulders and rested her elbows on her knees. Not very ladylike, but her back hurt. Oh, what joy. Only another five miles to go.

***

Althea heard the postman before she saw him. His cart's wheels crunched upon the courtyard's gravel, drawing her to the nursery window. She swayed from side-to-side to comfort a fussy Adeline. Mrs. Grant had not come to work for a couple of days because her baby had a fever and she did not want to spread whatever her child had. The postal lad marched to the front door and pulled the bell. A distant tinkling sounded in the castle's bowels. Presently, the door opened and Ainsworth relieved the messenger of his burden. The lad hopped back in his cart, slapped the pony's rump, and they were off on their rounds again. So much for the day's excitement.

Althea placed a mollified Adeline on the carpet and sat beside her to play building blocks. She loved India's baby, she really did, but the babysitting got old in a hurry. She had helped her mother raise her younger sisters. Sometimes she thought she might never want children of her own having already raised her parents' family. Robbie had grown children, so she felt no pressure to give him a baby.

She laughed with Adeline as the baby knocked down the tower they built, scattering blocks far and wide. Watching the sweet child, Althea wondered if she and Robbie would be making a mistake in not having a baby of their own. The war had put all plans on hold indefinitely. What if it lasted so long she was too old to bear children by its end? What a depressing thought. She shoved it from her mind as quickly as it popped up.

A light tread sounded upon the hall runner near the open nursery door. In a moment, the scullery maid appeared and dropped a brief curtsey. The girl was new and still learning who was owed deference and who she could consider an equal. She stood hesitantly in the doorway, casting an imploring look at Althea.

"What is it, Betsy? I won't bite. Spit it out." Althea had become impatient with the girl's inability to fit into the household. Shame prompted her to continue. "Please come in and tell me how I can help you."

The maid scurried over and held out an envelope. "Mr. Ainsworth thought you would want this right away. I'm sorry. I'm the only one he could find to bring it."

"Thank you, Betsy. You don't need to apologize for doing as you are asked."

"Yes, ma'am. Thank you, ma'am."

Althea glanced at the envelope to see who had written. Robbie's hand scrawled across its front. Would the blasted girl never leave? The girl appeared glued in place. Althea tried to keep irritation from her voice. "Is there something else?"

"No, ma'am."

"You are dismissed." Althea would have asked the girl to give Mr. Ainsworth her thanks for sending the letter up, but that would probably have sent Betsy into spasms of anxiety. With another curtsey, the girl fled the room for the safety of the service stairs.

Althea tore open the envelope.

My Dearest Darling,

I hope this finds you well and happy. London is noisy and frantic under threat of air raids. After bombings did so much damage in the central city last September, the public has become much more cautious. Fortunately, there is a shelter just around the corner from my digs. When my neighbors and I huddle together in its dank and gloomy confines, I am eternally grateful that you are tucked away in Yorkshire safe from falling bombs.

By now, you will be aware that Kilnsey Castle has been requisitioned as a hospital for shell-shocked officers. I hope the household will not be too disturbed by their coming. When my superiors inquired about its suitability, I assured them its location, recent renovations, and modern conveniences would make the castle an excellent choice. They then impressed upon me the necessity of keeping our conversations confidential. They also asked that I ensure the household would in no way interfere with the care the convalescents are to receive. The accompanying medical staff will be attempting to ascertain which of several methods of treatment is best.

Major Fraser will inform India of all needed arrangements and requirements, but I felt your being made aware of the terms would help smooth any difficulties. Your influence with India and the staff is far greater than you realize. I know the War Office and I can depend on you to intervene should any contretemps arise.

There goes the blasted air raid siren. I must dash. Give my best to all. I love you and miss you beyond measure.

With deepest devotion,

Robbie

Althea folded the paper and put it in her pocket. While the handwriting was Robbie's, the tone and words did not sound like him. Confidential conversations yet a request she intervene if necessary? Robbie certainly knew India and the Dowager would prevent any interference from the staff in military matters. It was as though someone had stood over Robbie's shoulder dictating what he was to write, but that was ridiculous. He was a clerk in the Ordnance Corps' London office charged with organizing armaments shipments to the front. He was about as far removed from organizing medical facilities as one could get. Perhaps things would be clearer once Major Fraser had given his orders and was installed in the castle.

CHAPTER 29

India, fists on hips, surveyed the transformation of the library to convalescent ward. It would have to do. Thank goodness the major agreed that the carpets should be left to protect the wood flooring. It had taken considerable shifting to clear the room. The leather wingback chairs, sofa, and occasional tables that normally filled the space were stored in the attics for the duration. The patients themselves did the lifting and carrying under the strict supervision of a none-too-pleased Ainsworth.

Surprisingly, only ten cots and a desk sat in the center of the room. These must be very special patients to be treated in such small numbers. India assumed Major Fraser would want the guest rooms and perhaps might commandeer the Great Hall for military use, but he asked for the library and smoking room because they provided unimpeded access to the postern gate.

Within a fortnight of his arrival, Major Fraser had made himself and his patients at home. He was presently ensconced in the smoking room, which he had taken as his personal bedroom and office. His insistence upon the installation of telephone and wireless sent Ainsworth into spasms of envy. The butler had been politicking for such improvements to his pantry without success. Spending money on luxuries seemed imprudent until the war was behind them. The army may have need of lightning-speed communication with the outside world, but Kilnsey Castle and its regular inhabitants did not.

Satisfied with the library's transformation, India glanced at the mantel clock. There was a pile of paperwork awaiting her in the office, but the thought was depressing. Surely she could allow herself a few hours respite. It had been weeks since she started a sketch of Adeline as a birthday gift for Charlie. Babies changed so fast. If she was to capture Adeline at this precise stage, the time to complete the watercolor was now.

Having decided in favor of finishing Charlie's gift, India settled herself at her easel and worked for about an hour. The light pouring through the north-facing window was excellent, allowing her to get Adeline's features set just right. She sat back and admired her work. Yes, that would do nicely. Massaging the kink in her lower back, she rose and drifted to the west windows. The moors were beginning to green under the encouragement of a warm spring sun. She rolled her shoulders and stretched, satisfied with the day and with herself. Finishing a piece of art always lifted her spirits.

Movement in the garden three stories below drew her attention and a smile. Mama, Mrs. Grant, and the babies were enjoying the sunny, mild afternoon. The women sat on the garden bench while the girls played on a blanket spread before it. Such idyllic, domestic scenes made the war seem very far away.

Mama reached down and brushed hair from Adeline's eyes and caressed her cheek. It was touching to see how much Charlie's mother adored the baby. It had become her habit to spend time in the nursery every day. Fortunately, Mary Grant seemed to welcome this intrusion into her nursery. She had commented several times how it "warmed the cockles of her heart to see the Dowager playing with the babes." Envisioning her proper, elegant mother-in-law playing with toddlers took some effort, but it pleased India that Mama took such an interest.

A figure emerging from the tower's corner advanced on the little group. Major Fraser strolled to the quartet, stopping to ruffle the babies' hair before settling on his haunches. Instead of military garb, he wore civilian clothing and had a light rucksack slung over one shoulder. He and the ladies appeared engaged in animated conversation. Mama, despite her usual insistence upon maintaining dignity, laughed several times. At what must have been a question, Mary gestured toward Mastiles Lane, the cart path leading away from the castle to the outlying farms and moors. Major Fraser nodded, then stood, bowed slightly, and marched away in the direction Mary had pointed.

The tall case clock chimed in the Grand Staircase hall. Teatime. India put away her supplies, took one last satisfied look at her work, and set off. Mary and the babies would be on their way back to the nursery and Mama would return indoors as the late afternoons were still too cool for alfresco teas. By the time India descended three flights of stairs, Mama awaited her in the drawing room.

Taking her seat, she received the cup Mama poured. She took several sips before saying, "You and the major seemed to have quite a conversation this afternoon."

Mama gave a small nod. "Yes, he is a charming and amusing young man. If we must have these people thrust upon us, thank goodness the major is entertaining." Mama took a fish paste sandwich made from the last of the tins laid in just after the declaration of war. Placing it on her plate, she continued, "If you saw us, why ever did you not join us?"

"Because I was in my studio. I saw you when I went to the window. Did he happen to mention why he was out of uniform?"

"He did. I asked, and he replied that he wanted his men to deal with their war experiences in as neutral an environment as possible, hence the civilian clothing."

"That seems rather unmilitary, if you ask me."

"It does, but he says he is trying to find better treatments. One must test theories, I suppose."

"Well, I hope he succeeds. It will be wonderful if Kilnsey can play a small part in helping our injured soldiers." India poured herself more tea, adding milk and sugar with a swirl of the spoon. "Why was Mary pointing toward the lane?"

"The major inquired about the public paths and where to access them. He also asked about the tenants and which paths crossed the individual farms. Apparently, physical exercise in the form of long rambles over the moors is to figure large in treating shell shock. I got the impression he intends to use the paths daily. It will be interesting to see if his ideas on treating the mind are successful."

"Indeed it will."

CHAPTER 30

Major Fraser, a nurse, and his patients settled into the community with such speed that their presence was soon taken for granted. They were seen as unusual but welcome neighbors. The increased attendance at Sunday services delighted Charlie's cousin, The Reverend Archibald Howard, though the patients did not sing the hymns or speak the congregational responses of the liturgy. Instead of taking an active part in worship, they followed Major Fraser in an orderly line, filed into the last two rows of pews, and stared blankly during the service. Finding this behavior a little disconcerting, India glanced over her shoulder at them more than was polite. On several occasions, she caught two of the men with their eyes fixed firmly on her tenants instead of Reverend Cousin Archie. It was as though they were scrutinizing those around them and making assessments, but that seemed illogical given their conditions.

On a brighter note, Major Fraser's devotion to physical activity extended to offering his men's services to the locals. The patients impressed the tenants with their willingness to help with spring planting and endeared themselves to the farmers' wives by hauling water and chopping firewood.

While India appreciated what they were doing, she could not shake the feeling something was off in all this activity. She had no experience with shell shock victims, but she certainly had not expected such energetic participation in estate affairs. Although they were withdrawn and uncommunicative when one attempted to engage them in conversation, these men simply did not appear all that ill when one observed them marching away to help on the tenants' farms. Opening her home and giving up some of her privacy to convalescing soldiers was a burden she willingly accepted, but she would be damned if she would put up with subterfuge.

On a Sunday morning in June at service end, India rushed from the family pew. She caught up with Major Fraser at the edge of Mastiles Lane. Breathing harder than she would have liked, she skidded up beside him.

"Good morning, Major. Might I have a word?"

Major Fraser looked at her in surprise. "Good morning. Of course." He turned to his nurse. "Hopgood, please see the men to luncheon. I'll join you presently and we will take our afternoon march as planned."

When the nurse and her charges were out of earshot, India said, "I don't think you've dined with us since your arrival. I apologize for being a poor hostess. Mrs. Bertrand is preparing a leg of spring lamb. Would you care to join us for dinner?"

The major's eyes lit up. "That's very gracious. I would be delighted. And there's no need for an apology. This is an unexpected pleasure."

"Very well, come to the drawing room at seven thirty for drinks. We will dine at eight."

"Thank you for the invitation." A shadow of doubt darkened his eyes. "I'm afraid I don't have my dress uniform or dinner togs with me." He held his hands away from his sides in apology. "I'm afraid what you see is it. I suspect the Dowager Lady Kilnsey might not approve."

India gave him a small smile. "Perhaps, but my mother-in-law will be far too polite to comment upon a guest's manner of dress. In any event, we do not dress for dinner as we did before the war. You will be just fine as you are."

"Until seven thirty, then." The major gave a shallow salute and walked away toward the castle, but at the end of the driveway, he paused and graced her with a dazzling smile, the kind the maids giggled about and tried to elicit at every opportunity.

As disturbing as it was to admit, that smile was difficult to ignore. The major was as good-looking as Charlie while being his visual opposite, black-haired where Charlie was blonde, built like a heavy-weight boxer, while Charlie was on the slender side. Both were beautiful in their own way. Having John Fraser underfoot could become a problem.

The remainder of the day passed quietly with the usual enforced inactivity of the Lord's Day. Reading, walking when the weather permitted, playing with Adeline, and taking meals were about the only options. India looked forward to Sunday afternoons as her islands of calm in her day-to-day sea of stress and chaos.

As India dressed for dinner, she sought Althea's gaze in the cheval mirror. "What do you think of our major?"

Althea paused in buttoning India's dress and shot her a reproving look. "I wasn't aware he is *our* major, or that *we* had opinions where he's concerned."

"Oh, don't be so high-minded. I feel like something isn't right where he and his patients are concerned. I'm not sure exactly why, but these men are just odd and not in the medical sense. Do you think they are really suffering shell shock?"

"I have no idea since I have neither a medical degree nor experience in treating the condition." Althea patted the last button into place. "The gong went some time ago. We need to get going or incur Her Ladyships' wrath. You know how she despises tardiness."

As they headed to the drawing room, India said, "I think these men aren't what they claim, and I intend to find out why they're really here. I invited the major to dinner for that purpose. I have a few questions to put to him that he better be able to answer sensibly or I will be traveling to London to speak with his superiors. I'm all for supporting our soldiers, but I will not be lied to or manipulated."

***

Since receiving Robbie's strange letter, Althea feared something like this might pop up. She, too, noticed Major Fraser and his so-called patients did not fit the descriptions she read of those suffering shell shock. A recent incident had piqued her interest.

Althea had been in the kitchen when the scullery maid, Betsy, scalded her hand while transferring a pot from the range to the sink, splashing her hand with boiling liquid in the process. Nurse Hopgood was called to provide care but seemed unable to help, so Major Fraser was brought into the fray. Neither the supposed nurse nor the purported doctor had any salve, medicine, or advice other than what her mother had always done for burns. Plunge the injury into cold water, dry, smear with butter, and hope for the best.

India was nobody's fool. The War Office should have known she would spot their subterfuge. Of course, being populated by arrogant, mustache twirling, overbearing men, they were in complete ignorance. What a surprise. Robbie had some explaining to do when they were finally together again.

CHAPTER 31

India's plan for the evening seemed to be working. Ainsworth mixed the pre-dinner drinks as instructed, light on the gin for India and heavy for Major Fraser. At dinner, he brought up the best bottles of wine from the cellar and kept it flowing. India observed Major Fraser as he waxed eloquent on the Hun's crimes in Belgium and allowed herself a small, satisfied smile. He was not intoxicated beyond sensibility, but he was feeling no pain. Good. If all went well, his tongue would have reached the desired level of looseness when she asked him to take a turn in the garden. Since the sun would not set until nearly ten, she should have sufficient time to interrogate him before the damp of evening and darkness drove them indoors.

Dinner came to an end with cheese and the last of the dried fruit. Sugar being in short supply, Mrs. Bertram had given up making desserts, or puddings as she called anything sweet served at the end of a meal.

India patted her lips with her napkin and placed it beside her plate. Gesturing toward the windows, she looked at the major. "Sunsets this time of year are spectacular. I fear I forget just how lovely they are. Would you care to accompany me for a turn in the garden?"

Three pairs of eyes looked at her in surprise—Mama's filled with censure, Althea's with conspiracy, and the major's with pleasure. He pushed his chair back. "I would be delighted."

A loud harrumph emanated from Mama's end of the table. "Be sure to take a wrap. Evenings are still cool once the sun begins to set." Her tone communicated far more than her words. There would be an interrogation once their dinner guest had left for his quarters.

"Of course." Wrapped in a shawl that Ainsworth fetched from a wardrobe behind the Grand Staircase, India led the way.

As they proceeded to the garden doors, a stab of anxiety roiled her stomach. What if her imagination had run wild? Was she really on the verge of accusing a British officer of lying with little to no evidence? But then it wasn't just she who had suspicions. Althea had noticed inconsistencies between his purported profession and his actual medical knowledge. Being lied to always made India angry. Tonight she would use anger to stay her course.

As they approached the Chinese Chippendale bench, India gestured toward it. "Shall we sit? I would like a word." Her voice held a brittle note. She took a seat without waiting for his reply.

Major Fraser gave her a curious look, then dropped down beside her. "Tell me, Lady Kilnsey. How may I be of service?"

How might he, indeed. India squared her shoulders and hopped to her feet. Looming over the major, she said, "How about we start with some honest communication?" The major's eyes widened at the fury in her voice. "Who are you? Who are you really? Because I know you're not a doctor. I know more about treating cuts and burns than you seem to. And your men. They are hardly the picture of brain-addled, war-damaged soldiers. Tell me the truth about why you're here."

Major Fraser stood and glared down on her. "Of all the effrontery. We are exactly who I have told you we are."

He turned to storm off, but India grabbed his sleeve. "Oh, no you don't, buster. If you don't tell me who y'all really are and what y'all're doing here, I'm gonna go to the War Office and file an official complaint." Oh, dear. Her southern drawl and colloquial expressions sometimes re-emerged when she was enraged.

The major rounded on her, his face the color of the setting sun. He glared for several seconds, then started laughing. "You know, I believe you would and I can't let that happen. I have a reputation to protect, after all." He tried to tug his sleeve from her grasp, but her fist clenched tighter. He grabbed her wrist. "If you will release me and be seated, I promise not to run away, and I'll tell you as much as I can without jeopardizing our mission."

India kept her grip on the sleeve while she studied him. There. He had said it—their mission. Doctors and shell shock victims did not have missions. She considered what she knew to be true. The material she held had the feel of army issue. The insignias his uniform bore looked authentic. He acted like a British officer and had shown himself to be a gentleman on all other occasions. Most importantly, the Secretary for War, Lord Kitchener, had confirmed his assignment in an official letter. Even though the major had lied from the beginning, maybe he could be trusted to tell the truth now. She let go and dropped onto the bench. The major sat beside her.

He glanced in all directions, then moved closer. India automatically moved away until her back hit the bench's arm.

Major Fraser's mouth became a thin line. "Oh, don't be so dramatic. If I had designs on another man's wife, I would have made a move long before this. You are jolly attractive, you know."

"Major, flattery is most uncalled for. Tell me the truth this instant or this interview is over."

"John."

"What?"

A conspiratorial gleam danced in his eyes. "If we are to be partners in crime, I think we might risk first names, don't you?"

India's anger melted, leaving a residue of humor. "I suppose we may, but you must be truthful."

"Once given, I always keep my word, but where to begin? It's a long story."

"Then start at the beginning. We've plenty of time."

For the next quarter hour, John told her a great deal about himself and his career in the army, ending with his promotion to the Intelligence Corps. "In truth, we are here in Kilnsey to catch spies. You wouldn't happen to know any, would you?"

India sat in stunned silence. Suddenly all the missing pieces fell into place, her questions about her guests answered. It was a relief to know her instincts had been trustworthy, but at the same time, she could not quell a spark of fear. Enemies of England might be found among her friends and neighbors. It was a lot to process.

He asked if she knew any spies. Yes, in fact, she just might know who he should investigate.

India's eyes narrowed. "You have met Mrs. Grant, my daughter's nurse, have you not?"

"Mary? Lovely girl and seems devoted to the children."

"Yes, she's a treasure. Have you met her husband?"

"Yes. We did some planting for him. Wheat, I think. Seems a nice chap. Should I be concerned about him?"

"Far from it. My mother-in-law insisted we bring Mary into the household. Her primary job is to care for Adeline, but her husband, Billy, also sends us information regarding a particularly problematic tenant. Billy and Mary Grant are very reliable and well liked. He is someone to trust. If you ask him to keep an eye out for suspicious activity, he will do it with the greatest discretion. There is someone, however, about whom we have wondered."

The major's face grew solemn. "And this person's name?"

India hesitated. Because she heartily disliked the man, she feared a rush to judgment. Accusations of disloyalty could do lasting harm, even if they were proven false. As a leader of the county, she should not be seen as unfair or a spreader of falsehoods. She valued the respect Charlie and his mother had gained by devotion to their neighbors' well-being. She looked up at the first stars peeping out above the castle crenelations. Maybe she should not name the man. Perhaps the major, John, should speak to the original sources.

She met his gaze once more. "There are people who are closer to the situation than I. I think you should start with Billy Grant and Reverend Howard. Judge for yourself if there is cause for concern."

CHAPTER 32

Althea frowned at the sight in the garden below. The way India laughed and patted the major's arm over some comment he made did not sit right. All summer Althea had sensed something growing between them. With fall upon them, how much longer would their attraction go unnoticed by others? Not that they had acted on it, or at least she was pretty sure they hadn't. That was not her fear. Both India and the major were sensible, ethical people. India would no more betray Charlie than she would embrace the German cause. Althea just did not want to see either of them hurt. Moreover, she could not bear the thought of Charlie picking up on whatever it was between those two seated side-by-side on the Chinese Chippendale bench for all the world to see. He deserved far better than to come home to a wife infatuated with another man. The time had come for a word with India before anyone else drew the same conclusion.

There they went again. This time, both of them practically bent double with laughter. India straightened up and fanned herself, then said something. At that point, they rose and turned toward the house. Good. It looked like they were headed inside. Time to cut India off in the Grand Staircase Hall.

Althea hurried from the master suite and raced down two flights. The door to the dining room clicked shut as she reached the first landing. From the stairway hall, she slipped into the dining room, hoping to catch India before she reached the drawing room, but again a door closed ahead of her.

She tiptoed to the door and pressed her ear against its wood panel. Eavesdropping was unbecoming, but protecting India from herself was too important to allow mere propriety to intervene.

Rats. The Dowager's voice rumbled on the other side of the door. Her tone indicated she would not welcome intrusion.

***

India sat on the settee across from her mother-in-law, trying to figure out what she had done to upset the old lady. Mama's tone communicated far more than her words.

"India, you are being irritatingly obtuse. I am speaking of appearances."

Puzzled, India replied, "I really don't understand." She searched her memory for anything she could have done that violated propriety. Nothing came to mind.

Mama sighed in exasperation. "Have you considered the time you are spending with Major Fraser?"

Heat surged through India. "Whatever do you mean? What are you implying?"

"I am not implying anything, but rather asking if you understand what I, and certainly others, have observed?"

"I have no idea what you are talking about."

Mama's eyes narrowed. "Then allow me to elucidate. It is unseemly for a married woman to devote so much time to a man not her husband. You have just spent a half hour in deep conversation with Major Fraser in full view of the household. If the servants are not already gossiping, they soon will be. You appear to find any excuse to touch him. This undue attention must stop."

India's face burned. "How dare you? If John and I had any objectives other than friendship, we would not conduct our conversations in the open."

"Married women do not have friendships with unmarried men. It simply is not done."

India's pulse raced. "Perhaps in your day, but times have changed. The war has changed everything."

"In some ways it has, I admit, but the rules of extramarital relationships between the sexes have not. If you will not listen to reason for your own sake, I beg you to think of Charles. Imagine what he will feel upon returning home to hear his wife had formed an inappropriate liaison."

India's fists clenched until the skin over her knuckles blanched. It was beyond humiliating that she must defend her actions, but Mama had touched a tender spot. She and John talked of nothing that could ever be construed as intimate, but in all honesty, a growing attraction between them existed. She had felt it and pushed it into the darkest corner of her heart. In unguarded moments, it was clear John felt it, too. It was in the way he looked at her and in the quality of his voice.

When India failed to respond, Mama continued in a more conciliatory tone. "I have long realized you are a young woman with independent ideas. Your work with the suffragists certainly demonstrated it. You will recall I applauded the effort, but surely you can understand my position regarding the present situation. I admit my first concern is for Charles and the Kilnsey name, but I also care for you. You are the daughter of my heart and I cherish you.

You and my son are my world. I do not wish to see either of you hurt."

India stared at her hands and forced them to relax. Despite John's request for complete confidentiality, the time had come to break that promise. Mama could not be allowed to continue her assumptions. "I'm truly sorry. I didn't realize we had given the wrong impression. I thought by conducting our conversations in the open rather than surreptitiously, we were protecting a great secret. I now see how wrong we are. It's true John and I have had prolonged conversations, but not for the reasons you think." India leaned forward and lowered her voice. "If I reveal our purpose, you must pledge your silence. Lives will be at stake should the truth become known."

"My compliance will depend upon the secret."

"I repeat," India hissed. "Lives depend upon no one knowing. You must swear you will not speak of what I tell you."

"Very well. I see you are in earnest. You have my promise."

India rose and sat beside Mama. In a whisper, she continued, "First, John and his men are not doctor and patients and Hopgood is not a nurse."

"I had come to that conclusion on my own. So what is their purpose in invading our home?"

"They have come to catch Irish republican spies working against the crown and the war effort."

Mama's expression did not change. In fact, she looked as though nothing India had said surprised her. "I see. And whom do they suspect? Is it someone on the estate?"

"Yes, but why would you think that?"

Mama's brow rose in question. "Do you recall a conversation we had the day Charles left for war?"

India searched her memory. "Not really. That day was so stressful it's become a blur."

"I warned you then that a certain tenant might be disloyal."

India's hand flew to her mouth, muffling a gasp. "Yes. Yes, I remember now. And I must say your concern may have become reality."

CHAPTER 33

India wrapped Adeline in a towel and nuzzled her little neck. Babies smelled lovely and sweet after a bath. Participating in the nursery's routine was her favorite part of the day. India adjusted the baby's position on her hip. At two years and four months, Adeline was getting to be quite a load. Adeline giggled and patted her mother's cheek in turn.

India watched Mary Grant for a moment. "Would you mind if I stay a little longer? She's growing up so fast. I feel like managing the estate is robbing me of her big moments." Mary had heard Adeline's first complete sentence, and it still chafed.

Mary called over her shoulder as she folded the last of the nursery laundry, "You stay as long as you can. I like to see babes with their mams."

India carried Adeline to the windows overlooking the courtyard to birdwatch. With the nursery on the third floor, one could almost reach out and touch the swifts, sparrows, and the solitary peregrine falcon that swooped and flitted around the crenelations. Adeline's laughter filled the room as she pointed and giggled at the avian antics. Such joy in simple things made one long for bygone days—the innocence of childhood, the safety of Papa's arms, the security of the familiar, a world without war.

It would not be long before the songbirds and other migrating fowl began their journey south. These last mild days would soon be replaced by the chill of winter. India swayed absentmindedly, losing herself for a few minutes in the ordinariness of her child's delight. Life in the nursery was blessedly far above the cares of the estate or a war-torn world.

Shifting her daughter's weight to her other hip, India's gaze wandered to the courtyard below where a figure in military uniform emerged from the portcullis's shadow. The visor of the man's peaked cap hid his face, but it must be John Fraser returning from one of his reconnaissance outings. He and his men came and went so often and at such odd hours, it was difficult to know when one might see them next.

On nights when Adeline was restless, she had seen parties of two or three leaving the castle. They departed by a door that led directly from the library to the postern gate then disappeared over the moors. The nursery windows allowed a clear view of the courtyard and surrounding moorland. After observing their movements for some time, she had a pretty good idea of where they went.

John was proving relentless in his pursuit of the spies hiding in the area. He refused to tell her more than that the persons he sought were British, not German. With Mama's encouragement, she mentioned her concerns regarding a particular tenant family, but begged him to not act against them until he was certain they were guilty. The backlash brought about by false accusations would be swift and fierce. The man was not popular among his neighbors, but Yorkshire folk would band together against someone they still sometimes perceived as an outsider if her actions harmed one of their own.

The nursery clock chimed the hour. She would soon need to change for dinner. She was on the verge of turning away from the window when something about the man made her stop. She put Adeline down and leaned closer to the glass. The figure in khaki removed his cap and let his gaze sweep over the castle. His expression was that of a starving man seeing the stones around him as manna from heaven. Without a word to Mary, India dashed from the room and down three flights of stairs.

She passed Ainsworth at the bottom of the Grand Staircase. "Tell Mama to come at once." Under normal circumstances, she would never have referred to her mother-in-law in an informal manner when speaking to a servant, but this was not going to be a normal day.

She flew through the front door and into Charlie's arms. He cupped her face in his hands and searched her as though he was a man dying of thirst and she was life-giving water. Charlie drew her into a hard kiss filled with yearning. Her passion and longing matched his in every beat of their pounding hearts.

When he finally allowed them to come up for air, she traced his jaw with the backs of her fingers. Dark circles smudged the skin beneath his eyes. Gone were the rosy English schoolboy patches on his cheeks, replaced by sallow hollows. He had clearly been through hell. Her heart swelled with love and anxiety, but she would be damned if she would give in to tears. He needed rest, calm, and peace.

She dropped her head onto his chest as he drew her into a closer embrace. "My darling, why didn't you let us know you were coming? I would have met you at the station."

"There wasn't time. My leave came through without advance notice. We arrived in London in the wee hours." Charlie kissed the top of her head. "It was either catch the first Yorkshire-bound train or send a telegram. I thought getting home as quickly as possible the better choice. Fortunately, I was able to catch a ride from the depot."

The sound of a cane thumping on the cobblestones announced Mama's arrival. India stepped aside to allow Charlie to greet his mother. Mama leaned forward so he could place a kiss on her cheek, then pulled back and studied him. "Oh, my dearest boy. You are home." She took his arm and drew him toward the entry. "Come. You look as though a bath and bed would be welcome. I'm sure Ainsworth will be happy to act as valet."

India followed in their wake, her lips twitching with suppressed humor. Ainsworth would be most affronted being pressed into service as valet, but too bad. Charlie needed all the care they could give him for as long as the army let them have him home.

***

India eased down on the edge of the bed, trying not to disturb Charlie. Just looking at him set her heart dancing. In sleep, he looked more like a little boy than the warrior who had arrived yesterday. The dark circles under his eyes had dissipated somewhat, but the hollows in his cheeks remained. The temptation was too great. She leaned in and brushed away the forelock from his eyes.

Before she could move away, his arms grabbed her and pulled her to his chest. His mouth nuzzled her ear. "How long have I been out?"

"Nearly twenty-four hours. It's midafternoon. You must be starving."

"I am, but for more than food." His hands began caressing her breasts. "God, I have missed you." His lips sought hers and they were consumed. Nearly two years' separation created a firestorm neither of them could nor wanted to deny.

Later, relaxed and sated, India lay on the pillows for several minutes before rising to gather her clothing. "Shall we request an early tea or would you prefer breakfast food sent up on a tray? You surely must be famished."

"What's for dinner?"

"Beef rib roast with fall vegetables. Mrs. Bertrand took one look at you and said she knew where her duty lay. She's run the scullery maid ragged. She sent the girl to the Home Farm demanding a roast and Smith apparently slaughtered the fatted calf. It should be quite a feast, lack of sugar for a proper pudding notwithstanding."

Charlie thought for a moment. "Then let's have an early tea in the drawing room, shall we? I suspect Mama needs some attention." He paused and cast a speculative glance over India. "And perhaps you can ask Major Fraser to drop in for an introduction and a word, as well. I want to get the measure of the man living under my roof in such proximity to my beautiful wife."

In the end, John was nowhere to be found, so India left an invitation with Hopgood for him to join them for dinner. Tea with Mama was filled with talk of Kilnsey doings and news of friends and neighbors. Adeline and Mary joined them, as well. It hurt to see Adeline shy around her father, but it could not be helped. He had been nothing more than a photograph to the baby for many long months, a situation that must be corrected while he was home.

Tea ended with just enough time to bathe before dressing for dinner. India ran her hand along Charlie's thigh as they soaked together in the large tub in their ensuite.

He grabbed her fingers and brought them to his lips. "Are you trying to start something, young lady?"

She giggled. "Maybe."

He tickled her foot, causing her to splash about. When she managed to push his hand away, she continued, "If your mother could see us now, she would be quite shocked."

Charlie leaned back against the tub's porcelain wall and grinned. "Mama has more sense than to enter unbidden. As a young debutante, she learned to never open closed doors without first knocking. I forget who hosted the ball, but it was in a sizeable house and Mama became lost during the evening. She flung open what she thought was the loo door to find her host, father of a great friend, *in flagrante* with one of the other debs. She had stumbled into his private study. Mama cried out. Others came running. It caused something of a stir, I believe."

The sound of the suite door opening and closing drifted to the bath. India stepped out and wrapped herself in a towel. "Althea's arrived. I can hear her at the wardrobe. Ainsworth will be in your dressing room shortly. Better dry off and be ready to dress."

Instead of getting out of the tub, Charlie tugged the edge of India's towel, sending it floating to the floor. Before she could pick it up, he grabbed her wrist. "Wait. Please don't cover yourself just yet. I want an image to carry with me when my leave is over." He made a circling motion with his hand and India complied, turning so that he saw every inch of her. "You are beautiful. I am one lucky man. Looking at you reminds me what we are fighting for."

India rewrapped herself, slapping his hand away when he tried to dislodge the towel again. "I'm freezing. I'm going to get dressed now and you should do the same."

As she turned to leave, he slapped her bottom, making her gasp. His chuckle followed her to the bedroom.

***

The major did not join them for pre-dinner drinks and India began to think he had not gotten her message. She would have words with Hopgood if that was the case. He finally arrived just as they were sitting down.

He appeared to have dressed hurriedly. His tie, usually impeccably arranged, was slightly crooked, and his shoes could have used a polish. As he took his place at the table, India wondered where he had been so late in the day. After introductions, they fell into stilted, banal dinner conversation. At the end of the meal, Mama gave India a look indicating it was time to leave the men to their port and cigars, but she remained seated.

She glanced at the staff present. Only Ainsworth remained in the dining room, but one could not be too cautious. "John..." Her cheeks burned at Charlie's startled reaction to the familiar form of address. "Major Fraser, I believe my husband would like to see how you and your patients are making use of our home."

"Of course, Lady Kilnsey." John looked at Charlie. "We are most grateful for the accommodation, My Lord."

Charlie's mouth curved in a tight smile. "We're only too happy to do our patriotic duty. As a battlefield officer, I've dealt with men suffering shell shock. It is a debilitating condition. I understand some men may never recover their wits. Perhaps you can give me some tips on helping my men avoid it."

India winced inwardly at the hint of sarcasm in Charlie's voice. He seemed resentful. Perhaps he sensed John was not what he claimed, or maybe Charlie disliked strangers living in the comfort of his home while he endured life at the front.

Whatever the reason for Charlie's tone, John looked taken aback. "Of course, I will offer what advice I am able. You must understand my efforts are experimental." John rose and bowed to Mama. "If you will excuse us, My Lady?"

Mama gave him a stern look. "Indeed, I will not. I intend to accompany you."

As they moved from the dining room toward the library, India tried to gauge the others' moods. Charlie appeared stiff and disgruntled, Mama haughty, John reserved and cautious. And what of her own mood? Something akin to fear knocked around her midsection. At John's request, her letters to Charlie had shared only the barest details.

Moreover, she had not asked Charlie to tell her about his experiences at the front. His letters had been detailed enough. Her only desire was to wrap him in a cocoon of domestic normalcy while he was home.

Although she didn't want their time together marred by worry about things over which he had little control, his attitude deemed it unavoidable. It was time he knew what was at stake.

CHAPTER 34

Once they reached the smoking room, John gestured toward the chairs set before his makeshift desk. India allowed Mama to make her selection then sat in the one remaining.

Charlie stood behind India and placed a possessive hand on her shoulder. "If you will be so kind, please tell me why you are here in Kilnsey, Major. Our butler says it has nothing to do with medicine and that you and your men are not what you claim."

John shrugged and gave Charlie a tight smile. "Ainsworth is no one's fool. I suspected he was on to us, but being well-trained, he has been much too polite to ask questions. I briefly feared he could not be trusted, but I soon realized my mistake. Nonetheless, it is distressing that he seems to know so much."

India could not let this continue. "Major Fraser, I have a confession. Ainsworth has been in my confidence for some time. As you said, he is no fool. He sees everything, but only mentions what he believes of concern. It was he who first saw you and your men leaving the house in the dead of night. When he approached me about the odd behavior, it confirmed my own doubts were not simply the product of an overactive imagination. I assure you he is the most trustworthy, patriotic of men. You can count on his discretion and support."

Charlie squeezed India's shoulder and stepped toward the desk. His eyes were dark with anger. "Major, your admiration of our butler is all well and good, but you have yet to divulge your true purpose. I demand to know what the hell is going on under my roof. And it is still my roof, despite what the War Office might think. If my family is being put in danger by your presence, then by God, Kitchener will hear of it. I will not have my wife, child, and mother suffer negative consequences of whatever has you skulking about."

Charlie moved to go around the desk toward John, the crease between his eyes deepening with each step. India placed a hand on his arm. She didn't trust him to get any closer. John, bless him, showed no signs of anger or umbrage. Instead, he went to a small, portable safe he had brought with him from London. The tumblers of the combination lock clicked as he spun the dial. When the door was released, he withdrew a file.

Returning to the desk, he opened the file and arranged three pages so everyone could see them. The pages were police reports from Dublin with pictures attached.

India looked at the reports. One name jumped off the page. Picking it up, she skimmed the document, then handed it to Charlie. "This is Annie's husband." Looking at John, she asked, "Why do you have this?" She feared she already knew the answer, but she needed him to say it aloud. She needed Charlie to hear, as well, so there would be no doubt on his part.

Without meeting her eyes, John put a hand in his pocket. When he spoke, his tone was casual. "Do you know this Kennedy fellow?"

Charlie frowned and handed the report back to John. "In a manner of speaking, yes, we do."

“And what form does the acquaintance take?”

“We have never met, but he is married to my tenant’s daughter.”

“Would that be Horace Holden of Mid-Mastiles Farm?”

“Yes. He’s the best farmer of all our tenants. Why are you interested in him? His daughter and son-in-law are in Ireland. They haven’t been in England since the war began.”

Instead of losing patience with Charlie’s stubborn reluctance to see the obvious, John placed the report on the desk and dropped onto a chair. “That may not be entirely true, at least where the son-in-law Kennedy is concerned. What I am about to tell you is highly confidential. Lives depend upon secrecy.”

He fixed Charlie and then Mama with a stern look. “I have your assurance this will go no further?”

Charlie strolled to the window. Without turning to face the others, he said, “I suppose I should be insulted that you feel the need to ask. But yes, you have my assurance neither my mother nor I will break your confidence.”

“Very well. Thank you, My Lord.” John rested his elbows on the desk and made a bridge of his fingers. “We have known for some time that Irish republicans are working with the Germans. Certain people here in England are helping Irish spies and saboteurs by providing safe houses and other forms of support. I believe your tenant, Holden is one of them.”

Mama stirred, picked up the Kennedy report, and handed it to Charlie. “Good farmer he may be, but Holden has shown his true colors in the past. If anyone in Kilnsey is aiding Irish spies, it would be him. Major Fraser, have you spoken with Reverend Howard?” John nodded. “Then you know about his attack on a Kilnsey man who spoke against the Irish cause. He is also suspected of burning a barn and causing damage to the property of those with whom he disagrees. He creates unrest and fear among his neighbors. Horace Holden is a poisonous thorn that needs removing." She looked directly at Charlie. "You should have turned him out years ago."

India's heart jerked. No doubt the reasons for not breaking Holden's tenancy had as much to do with Charlie's pre-marriage relationship with Annie Holden Kennedy as it did with her father's farming ability. Charlie placed loyalty and honor at the top of his list of manly virtues. While Holden had neither, Charlie possessed both in good measure. Out of some warped sense of obligation, Charlie felt he owed Holden for having had an affair with Annie before either of them was married.

Charlie did not meet his mother's eye. Instead, he returned to the desk and crossed his arms over his chest. "I've experienced enough at the front to know the Germans will not give up easily. If we are to win this war, we must root out traitors. Tell me how I can help. I'll do whatever you ask if it doesn't endanger my family."

John cast a speculative gaze upon India and then Charlie. "I need something you may not be willing to provide."

"Which is?"

"Within the week, I need someone to ensure that Holden and his wife do not raise the alarm before my men and I have made arrests. Holden has created a bunker beneath his barn where his Irish associates hide and store weapons and explosives. Our sources tell us they will be there on Tuesday night making bombs. They plan to destroy enough bridges and rail lines to disrupt the flow of farm goods to market. Not only will the British public suffer, but with sufficient success, they can damage the entire war effort."

Charlie looked grim. "And an army marches on its stomach." He looked at India. "What would you say to a little social call on Mr. and Mrs. Holden on Tuesday evening next?"

India thought for a moment. "Wouldn't it seem odd? We haven't made social calls in the past." She gave him a look that silently said unless we count the visit after our honeymoon when you assured yourself Annie's baby was not your child.

Charlie's cheeks flamed. He had clearly gotten her message. "I suppose you're right. Could we have them here?"

India leaned toward the desk. "Yes. That's the answer, but it can't be just the Holdens." Her eyes narrowed as she cast a speculative gaze over Charlie. "You haven't met with your tenants in over two years. The annual tenants' meeting is long overdue. We can include the wives as well. It will be a new tradition. You will have your meeting with the men over drinks while I entertain the ladies. We will then all sit down to dinner later than usual, say at nine thirty or ten. Ainsworth will be instructed to allow our dinner guests to linger over each course as business might still be discussed. Will that give enough time to trap the saboteurs?"

John looked pensive. "It just might, but how can you ensure they will attend?"

India smiled at his lack of understanding. "The tenants' meetings are command performances. They would not dare refuse, especially since they are being asked to dinner. They will all be overwhelmed and greatly honored. These meetings traditionally only include the men at luncheon."

"Well then, it looks like we have a plan." John extended his hand to Charlie. "You are doing your country a great service. I'm sure I don't have to tell you what a remarkable person Lady Kilnsey is."

"Indeed, you do not." Irony colored Charlie's words as he took the major's hand. "I will do whatever is necessary to protect her and my family."

India spent the time leading up to the tenants' dinner planning a meal that would be memorable but also included only what was available locally. Despite Mama's reservations, she instructed Ainsworth to bring out the best china, sterling, and crystal. She wanted the tenants awed by the display and feeling grateful to be treated as honored guests. Her plan was to lull them into a companionable stupor with food and drink. By the time Holden realized what John had accomplished, it would be too late for him to do anything about it.

Capturing the saboteurs would most likely mean arrests for the Holdens, as well. Compassion for her long-ago rival accompanied India's sense of relief that the danger would soon be eliminated. Within one brief evening, Annie stood to lose her husband and her parents to the darkest holes in the English judicial system, if they were simply imprisoned. There was a real possibility all three would hang. Such was the fate of traitors during wartime.

Tuesday evening arrived blustery and cold—a sure sign autumn was ebbing into winter. At the appointed hour, Ainsworth admitted the dinner guests. John, India, and Mama formed a receiving line in the Great Hall where each tenant couple was greeted with warmth and a brief chat. As they moved on, Ainsworth directed the men to take seats around a table set up by the fireplace, while Mrs. Wilson directed the ladies to the drawing room.

With the last guest welcomed, India went to the Grand Staircase hall with the intention of joining the ladies, but Ainsworth and Mrs. Wilson waylaid her at the foot of the stairs.

The butler and housekeeper glanced at each other, then looked at India. Ainsworth cleared his throat. "My Lady, Mrs. Wilson overheard Mrs. Holden speaking to another lady. We feel you should be aware of her intentions."

"Go on."

"It seems she and Mr. Holden are planning to leave as soon as the tenants' meeting is concluded. She is encouraging others to do the same."

A tremor passed through India. "I see. That will never do. We must let His Lordship know. Together, he and I will avert disaster." India considered her housekeeper. "Mrs. Wilson, why do I get the impression you realize the importance of tonight's dinner?"

The housekeeper looked at her feet then back at India. "Please do not blame Mr. Ainsworth. I have long believed the major and his patients are not what they claim. When I approached Mr. Ainsworth, he had no choice but to explain the situation. I assure you the information has gone no further."

"I see. Are you two the only ones who were suspicious?"

"Yes. The maids are young, simple farm girls at heart. They are too taken with Major Fraser to see beyond his appealing aspects, if you will pardon my saying."

India looked upon her staff with admiration and gratitude. "Both of you are treasures. His Lordship and I are most grateful for your loyalty and discretion. Ainsworth, how best might we get word to His Lordship? I fear it will seem odd if I interrupt."

"Perhaps you might write a note. I will deliver it at once."

"Please make sure His Lordship understands he must read the note immediately and not react to its contents."

"Indeed. We must not let our side down."

India gave Ainsworth a grateful smile. "No, too much depends on tonight going as planned."

CHAPTER 35

Althea breathed deeply of the chilly night air. Spending the evening with Adeline in the overly warm nursery left her wanting fresh air, if only for a few minutes. The housemaid, Betsy, had kindly agreed to sit with the sleeping toddler to give Althea a much-needed break. As much as she loved living in the castle and being treated like a member of the family, she sometimes longed for her little cottage and the solitude it provided. If only Robbie would come home, but it seemed the War Office could not spare him. Getting supplies to the front was vital. Of course it was, but still, on nights like this, his absence was like a deep, black hole from which there was no escape.

Althea pulled her shawl closer about her shoulders and glanced toward the postern gate. The simple wooden structure represented great happiness. Just beyond its panels on the first hill Robbie had asked her to marry him. When she felt his absence most profoundly, she passed through it and walked the moors where they had often sought privacy during their courtship. Tonight, despite the growing cold and moonless sky, the call of the moors was too great to resist. Robbie was out there on those undulating hills, at least he was for her.

She passed through the gate and started up the familiar path leading to the northern expanse of the estate. Atop the first hill, she stopped and looked up at the wide sky. Stars twinkled more sharply, owing their brilliance to the moon hiding her face and the crispness of the air. When she left her beloved Appalachian home, she believed she would never care for another place with the depth of feeling she did for those far-away, misty, craggy peaks and hollows. The moors of Yorkshire had proven her wrong. They now felt as much like home as the Blue Ridge Mountains of her past. As the moors were the place that had born and bred Robbie, they were all the dearer.

The hushed landscape was without a breath of wind. No doubt they would find frost when they arose in the morning. Winter was closing in quickly, bringing with it the enforced quarantine of isolated estates. Perhaps she would make one last trip to London before winter completely gripped the moors, making travel difficult. Like Mohammed and his mountain, Robbie was her mountain to whom she went at every opportunity. Unfortunately, those trips south would be scarce now that ice and snow drew nigh.

Althea glanced back toward the castle. All looked quiet and secure. Perhaps she might be forgiven for walking a little farther—maybe the next hill. When the major returned to the castle, all hell would no doubt break loose. The Holdens would not go quietly and she would be needed to safeguard the nursery.

She started on the downhill path, but a movement to her right brought her up short. She stared into the darkness. It must have been a hare seeking shelter from the cold or perhaps a weasel or stoat seeking his evening meal. She walked on for a few more steps. Stones rolled behind her. She whipped around and stared into the muzzle of a pistol.

The hand that held the gun trembled. “Don’t scream. No one will hear you.” The man’s Irish accent was strong. He winced and grunted as he limped closer. “Get me into the castle and get me the key to a motorcar. Do as I say and no one will be harmed. All I want is to get as far away from here as possible.” He gestured with the gun. “Let’s go. Now.”

At the postern gate, the man put a hand on Althea’s shoulder. “Open the gate and make sure no one is around.” When she had done as he ordered, he nudged her back with the pistol. “How can we get into the castle unnoticed?”

Althea stifled a gasp. Should she risk lying to him? If a man was willing to betray his king and country, he would be capable of killing. She made her decision.

“The door directly across the courtyard is the service entry to the old kitchen. That part of the castle is no longer used for anything except storage. No one will have any reason to go in there tonight.”

“Okay. Get going. Keep to the shadows in case someone looks out a window.” He grabbed her shoulder and shoved her against the castle wall.

They entered the house and made it to the old larder, where the man slumped down on a long-discarded wooden crate. Althea glanced at his pant leg. Blood soaked the fabric from a wound in the thigh.

He gestured toward the stain. “It looks worse than it is. I need to rest for a minute, then take me to my relatives.” Althea suspected who he was, but she didn’t respond. “You don’t know who I am, do you?” A bitter chuckle floated on the stale air of the unused space. “Jamie Kennedy at your service, milady.” He struggled to his feet. “My wife will never forgive me if I leave her parents to face the coppers alone.” He gestured toward the door. “Take me to wherever His High and Mighty Lordship is holding court.”

She led the way through the abandoned kitchen, arriving at the door giving access to the Great Hall. She grabbed the knob, turned, and yanked. Nothing.

"Give it another try." Impatience and anger radiated from her captor.

She pulled harder. After a third try, the ancient hinges creaked and the heavy oak door swung inward. A hard shove in the back propelled her into the Great Hall.

"Where are they? Horace and Fanny's pony cart is still in the courtyard."

Althea swallowed hard. "They must still be at dinner."

"Lead the way then."

As she led him through the house toward the dining room, she prayed they would not encounter any other members of staff. There was no telling what her assailant might do if he felt cornered by too many witnesses. They arrived at the dining room door and she stopped.

"Who's in there?"

"All of the tenants, His Lordship, my lady..." Her voice trailed off.

"How many staff? The nobility can't eat without someone holding the fork for them."

"I assume the butler and perhaps a housemaid."

"Open the door and get one of them to come over."

"That will seem very odd."

"Do it anyway."

Althea opened the door a crack and sought Mr. Ainsworth. Catching his eye, she jerked her head. His eyebrows rose to his hairline, and he gave her a look that asked if she had completely taken leave of her senses. She jerked her head again and rolled her eyes to communicate there was a problem in the stairway hall. Looking aggrieved, the butler stepped away from the sideboard.

He stopped short of the opening and whispered, "What is the meaning of this, Mrs. James?"

Kennedy stepped from behind Althea and brandished his gun at Ainsworth. "I'm the meaning, you puffed up jackass. Go get the Holdens. And don't try putting up the alarm or this lady will pay the price."

Ainsworth drew back, then looked at Althea, who nodded. "Please do as he says." Her whisper came on a ragged breath.

From the far end of the dining room, Charlie called, "Ainsworth, is there a problem?"

Looking as flustered as Althea felt, the butler turned to address his master. "No, My Lord."

"Then pass the mutton again. I believe some would appreciate another serving. I know I certainly would. Mrs. Bertrand has outdone herself." Several calls of "hear, hear" went around the table.

Althea eased the door forward so only a small crack remained. Ainsworth disappeared, then reappeared, serving tray in hand. He approached Charlie's right side, putting his back to the staircase hall door. Charlie opened his mouth but closed it quickly as his eyes widened, then narrowed. Althea's breathing slowed to a steadier pace. Good man, Ainsworth. Smart. Breaking several rules of dining etiquette gave the butler the opportunity to raise the alarm unnoticed by the diners.

Ainsworth backed away and began his circumnavigation of the dining table, serving the guests from the left as a well-trained servant should do. Charlie leaned over to Billy Grant on his right and said something to him that apparently no one else heard. Another rule of gracious dining biting the dust. When Billy nodded, Charlie rose and waited until he had the attention of all his guests.

"Friends and honored guests, it seems we have a small matter at the service entrance requiring my attention and that of Mr. Grant." When Mary Grant started to rise, Charlie continued, "Nothing to alarm you, Mrs. Grant, I assure you. Please excuse us. We will only be a moment."

A murmur passed around the table. Even simple country folk knew it was unusual for an earl to attend to backdoor business during dinner. Althea focused on the Holdens. Their expressions were strained and anxious. Pray Charlie made it through the dining room's service door and around to the Grand Staircase hall before the Holdens bolted or Kennedy caught on.

Kennedy's breathing grew heavy. "What the hell are they up to?"

Althea searched for a plausible explanation. She said a silent prayer that Kennedy was ignorant of local goings-on. "Mr. Grant's missing sheep must have been found. Gypsies camped in his far pasture without permission. When he made them leave, they left a gate open out of spite. Half the flock wandered away. His Lordship was most displeased. I'm sure he wants to reward the person who found them."

Kennedy shoved the pistol's muzzle into Althea's back. "Open the door and go in."

With hammering heart, Althea stepped into the room. When the butler moved toward them, she said, "No. Please do nothing, Mr. Ainsworth."

India, her back to the door, turned to face them and gasped. She started to rise, but Kennedy gripped Althea's arm and stepped forward. He aimed the pistol at India. A shocked murmur circulated among the tenants. "Stay where you are. All of you keep your yaps shut." He then gestured toward the table. "Time to go, Horace, Fanny." He jerked his head in Althea's direction. "We're taking this one as our pass to freedom."

India cried out, "No. Please. She has done you no harm."

He smirked at India, then looked at Ainsworth. "You. Butler. Get me the key to a car." Addressing the tenants, he jerked Althea close. "Anyone follows us signs this woman's death warrant."

Ainsworth glanced at India, who shook her head. "Keys are kept in my pantry. Will you accompany me there?" The butler spoke in carefully enunciated, measured tones, a sure sign of distress.

Kennedy was quiet for a moment. "Yeah. Horace, Fanny, come on."

In the Grand Staircase hall, Kennedy stopped and faced Ainsworth. "Where do they keep the autos?"

"In the former stable block. Left side of the castle's main gate."

"How many?"

"Only the two, the Rolls Royce and a Vauxhall sporting motor."

Kennedy looked at the Holdens. "Go to the Rolls. We'll be along with the key." Pointing the pistol, Kennedy growled through gritted teeth, "Get it."

Ainsworth led Kennedy, still gripping Althea's arm, toward the service hall accessed beyond the Grand Staircase. She swallowed a gasp as a shadow moved beneath the stairs, saying a silent prayer Kennedy had not noticed.

When they reached the green baize door, Ainsworth stopped. "Perhaps I should ascertain whether we will be alone in the hall?"

"Get the damned key. Be quick. Anyone asking questions and the girl here will pay."

"Very well. It will only take a moment."

Instead of pushing the door inward, Ainsworth looked over Althea's head to the spot beneath the stairs and nodded.

The shadow materialized in the form of Charlie brandishing his officer's sidearm. "You will let Mrs. James go unharmed."

Kennedy whipped around, an artery throbbing in his throat, his eyes bulging with rage. "Why should I?"

Charlie gave him a tight smile. "Mrs. James will be released unharmed because Annie will not want her husband and her parents hanged for murder."

"Keep my wife's name out of your filthy mouth. The way you treated her, I should kill you where you stand."

Charlie stepped fully into the light. "Let Mrs. James go now and your in-laws may avoid the hangman. If you care for Annie, and I believe you do, at least ensure her parents live. Your son deserves to have his grandparents."

"If we're caught, we're dead men anyway. I'll take my chances in your Rolls. I'll free the maid once we're clear of this place."

"Then at least let me exchange places with her." He held his weapon out. "Let her go. Take my sidearm. We'll leave together. An earl and active-duty officer will have more value as your hostage than a mere maid."

Before Kennedy could respond, a male voice called from beyond the staircase. "Let His Lordship and Mrs. James go. We will stand back and let you pass unharmed."

Althea twisted in Kennedy's grasp, straining to look over her shoulder. To her horror, she saw the male tenants with India at their head. All were armed with hunting rifles and shotguns from the gunroom. India had no business trying to intervene. Adeline was now in danger of losing both her parents to a criminal. But India's face said all anyone needed to know. Her mouth was set in a firm line and her eyes glittered. It was clear she had come prepared for a war of her own.

CHAPTER 36

India prayed the terror she felt did not show. Hands that shook while aiming a rifle would not inspire confidence in her allies nor fear in her enemy. She drew a deep breath, swallowed hard, and squared her shoulders. Kennedy was at least a foot taller than Althea, who shielded his body. Luckily, he was exposed from the collarbone up.

His head was in sight and in range. Raising her rifle, she took aim. It had been years since she had done any target shooting. She was once quite proficient, but the skills of her Appalachian youth had been untested for a long time.

Willing her voice to be steady and calm, she growled, "You heard him. Let my husband and my friend go and you leave unharmed and unimpeded. Otherwise, you leave in a box."

Charlie stared at India, his mouth agape, his eyes filled with horror. "My dear, please. Let the men handle this."

India shook her head. "Major Fraser and his men will be here any moment. He knows Kennedy is here." She knew nothing of the sort. She could only pray the tenant tasked with raising the alarm had made it to the Holdens' barn in time. If John and his men were successful in capturing the other traitors, they could well be on their way to the nearest military goal.

India watched as Kennedy's dilemma played out across his face. He reached a decision. "I'll take the earl with me. Let us get away safely and I will release him in the village."

India opened her mouth, but Charlie cut her off. "Agreed." He placed his sidearm on the floor and kicked it toward Kennedy. "Release Mrs. James. I'm ready to go with you."

Kennedy jerked his head. "Then get over here." When Charlie reached his side, Kennedy shoved Althea into Billy Grant's arms. He grabbed Charlie by the collar and placed the barrel of the gun against his temple. "Get out of my way." The sea of tenants parted as though Moses held out his staff.

Turning to face the group, Kennedy dragged Charlie backward. At the edge of the stairs, he shouted, "Remember. I got nothing to lose." He pushed on through the Great Hall and out the front entrance.

India flew through the front door, her heart hammering harder with every step. She could not lose Charlie now. He had survived battles, hunger, living in a trench for months on end. His life could not end like this, not at the hands of a traitor and terrorist. She raised her rifle and took aim for the second time. The barrel wavered like it had a mind of its own. She lowered the weapon, took a couple of deep breaths, and took aim for the third, and it was hoped, last time.

Her thoughts raced as fast as her pulse. Just squeeze the trigger. Don't breathe. Concentrate. Look down the sight and ease back on the trigger. It's a perfect shot. Take it now. She adjusted the rifle's placement on her shoulder and prepared to pull back on the trigger.

From the shadows near the garage, a single shot flashed, but no sound followed. Kennedy spun around, sending Charlie staggering off to one side. Shock filled the traitor's face, but his expression melted into a humorless grin as he stumbled and fell to his knees. A hole gaped in his chest where blood bubbled out with every breath. He stared at India for a couple of seconds before his eyes closed and he crumpled face-first onto the cobblestones.

He had apparently thought the shot came from India, but her weapon remained unfired. She strained to see who emerged from the shadows. It was one of John's "patients." The man was dressed all in black and carried a rifle with an unusually long barrel.

Sobs racked India as she flew to Charlie. He was safe and unharmed. He pulled her to his chest in an embrace that said his emotions matched her own. Their heartbeats raced in rhythm.

High-pitched screams mixed with male cries of fury came from the garage. John and several of his men emerged with the Holdens struggling against their captors, handcuffs around their wrists. John broke away from the group and started across the courtyard.

India and Charlie waited, their arms still wrapped around one another, each afraid to let go. Even the arrival in the courtyard of the other tenants, Mama, and Althea did not ease their inner turmoil. India started trembling. The events of the last half hour were taking a toll. Charlie pulled her back against his chest and tightened his grip. The pressure of his embrace eased the shaking she was unable to control. She had come close to losing two of the people she loved most. Althea was her touchstone with her American self and her past. Charlie was the rock upon which she built her life and her future. When she first met Charlie, she couldn't imagine life with him. Now, she couldn't imagine it without him. He had survived so much already. His time at home was so short and had been consumed by the search for spies and terrorists.

John came to them looking more at ease than India had seen him since his arrival at Castle Kilnsey. Charlie released India and stepped forward. "Where do we stand with the saboteurs?"

"Thanks to you, My Lord, we have them all. I'm only sorry you and Her Ladyship were forced to deal with Kennedy here. He slipped the net and ran."

Charlie nodded. "Missions like this carry no guarantees. I'm glad he came here and you followed. How did you know?"

"Her Ladyship dispatched your tenant, Joseph Bennett. He waylaid us in the lane as we were dividing into search parties. Thank goodness he has a swift mount."

"Indeed. What will become of the Holdens, do you think?"

John glanced at the group of tenants before answering. "They'll be fortunate to receive life sentences. From all appearances, they were deeply involved in the saboteurs' activities. Even if all they did was provide the safe house, they're still guilty of high treason which, as you know, is a hanging offense, especially in wartime."

Charlie's expression was grim. "It gives me no pleasure for Mrs. Kennedy's sake, but her parents knew what they were doing. It's not as if they're naïve innocents or were being coerced." He turned to India. "It seems we'll need to find a new tenant for Mid-Mastiles Farm. I'm sorry I must leave the task to you, my dear, but I'm due back at the front within the week."

Mama stepped forward from the edge of the crowd gathered around India and Charlie. She wore a dressing gown and slippers. Having declared dining with tenants too big a break with tradition, she had kept to her apartment for the evening. "If you will pardon the intrusion of an old woman, I believe I may be able to help with that task. I have long had someone in mind for the circumstance in which we now find ourselves. He already has family on the estate."

Three days later, India stood on the Grassington Depot platform awaiting the train that would begin Charlie's return to France. So much had happened during the week that their time together was something of a blur. For his part, Charlie seemed distracted, as though he were already back at the front. She looked at his handsome head craning toward the bend in the tracks and wanted to dissolve in tears.

To distract herself, she said, "Billy and Mary Grant seem delighted to take over Mid-Mastiles Farm."

"As well they should be. Other than the Home Farm, it is the largest holding and the most productive."

"When did Billy's brother say he would be ready to take over their old place?"

"As soon as Billy and Mary have moved out. He should be in residence by late next week."

"And there is no Mrs. Grant?"

"No. He's a bachelor. His name is Robert."

"Did I hear correctly that Robert had a medical discharge from the army? Will he be able to do the work?"

"He's recovered from shell shock enough to work. That's all I care about. Our returning wounded deserve every chance we can give them. I'm surprised you would question giving him the job." The edge in his voice pierced India.

"I was not questioning, only concerned." Her nerves jangled as she sought to explain herself. "You and Mama made the offer without even talking to me about it. When you're back in France, I'm the one who will have to deal with any problems. I just think you could have consulted with me before making the offer."

"Well, I did not," he snapped. "Mama is very fond of the Grant family. They have held a tenancy for generations. We know them to be honest and hardworking. Furthermore, I think you might be grateful you were not required to find a new tenant on your own." Exasperation colored his voice.

"Charlie, I don't want to argue." Her voice trembled with emotion. "You and Robbie left me to run the estate, which I have done to the best of my ability. I'm hurt you didn't take that into account."

Charlie whipped around, a frown creasing his brow, but when he saw her tears, he pulled her into an embrace so fierce it took her breath away. "My dearest darling, I'm a thoughtless cad. I'm afraid returning to the front is more disquieting than I cared to admit." Releasing her so he could look into her eyes, he cupped her face in his palms and kissed her wet cheeks then wiped them with his thumbs. "My only excuse regarding the vacant tenancy is that I wanted to help Robert. He and I played together as children. He is a friend as well as the member of a long-term tenant family. You have every right to feel hurt. Please say you forgive me. I cannot bear for us to part with ill feeling between us. Leaving you seems to have made me a terrible grouch."

She couldn't stop herself. She buried her face in his chest and sobbed. All the stress of years of war, the pain of separation, and the burdens of running a large estate poured onto the khaki wool of his tunic.

He kissed the top of her head and held her at arm's length. "Hold on. I can't show up at headquarters with my uniform a sodden mess." The crack in his voice belied the intended humor of his words. India forced a watery smile.

As she wiped her face, a whistle sounded, and the train chugged to the halt. Clinging to one another, they kissed until the whistle sounded again. Charlie grabbed a carriage door and swung into the compartment as the wheels started rolling.

He lowered the compartment window and stuck his head out. "I love you, my darling. Deeply, always, forever."

The train rounded the bend and he was gone, taking her heart with him. She stared after the train until it disappeared. She loved him so. He had been in the thick of the fighting at the front since the beginning. By some miracle, he had escaped with only bruises and scrapes. How much longer would his luck hold? Too many families of their acquaintance would never see a son, father, brother, grandson, or nephew again. A shiver ran down her spine.

CHAPTER 37

October 1917

My Dearest Darling,

I am pleased to write that your countrymen are finally proving useful six months into the fray. They are a rugged, sometimes undisciplined lot, but their hearts are in the fight. These Americans are eager to prove themselves, which I believe they will as they gain more battlefield experience. Their youthful energy, enthusiasm, and confidence are refreshing. I fear we battle-hardened troops have forgotten how to be young.

Speaking of the Americans, I had an interesting conversation not long ago. I ran across a chap from your part of North Carolina, a Lt. Barnes. No one can mistake that mountain twang once one has heard it. He was complaining rather vociferously to a quartermaster about missing supplies—hardly a good idea at the best of times. I stepped in to help. The Yank was most appreciative and offered me a drink in his mess.

Barnes knew of your family. His grandfather and your Grandfather Ledbetter attended the same mountain school as boys. He said it was to no one's surprise that "the ole fox" prospered. Apparently, Grandfather T.J. was wily and sly even as a boy. I asked if the man's grandfather had ever mentioned your Grandmother Jane. He said everyone knew T.J. married a beautiful woman from somewhere in New York. They also knew about the divorce, but once Jane left Pisgah, no one ever saw or heard of her again. Barnes added that your grandfather's business dealings and the divorce were quite the scandals, but of course we already knew that.

After this is over, we must visit New York. Your mother has not met Adeline and I long to see Clarissa. I haven't seen my sister since before war was declared. Perhaps we can persuade Mama to go with us. If you are still interested in tracing Jane, we can pursue it then. Try one last time to put the ghosts to rest, if you will. Perhaps a more intensive search will yield better results.

I'm glad you finally have Adeline's nurse situation settled. It sounds as if everything has worked out for the best. I'm also grateful you did not dismiss Mary Grant. She will work well as a part-time maid. From what you wrote, it seems that little Ruth Grant and Adeline are inseparable. Having Ruth in the nursery while Mary attends to her new duties works well for everyone.

I almost forgot. I have good news. I received a promotion to major.

Gas alarm. Must run. Kiss the baby for me.

All my love,

Charlie

With her finger, India traced a line of wayward ink that blurred his closing comments. He had clearly been in a rush. Her heart filled to near bursting for him and for herself.

The paragraphs above the smudge, however, engendered an entirely different emotion. She read them a second time. In the weeks prior to their wedding, Charlie's brother-in-law and sister had hired Pinkertons to chase down rumors that occasionally circulated in New York. Sightings of the presumedly deceased Jane Ledbetter had murmured on the lips of those who mattered, ultimately helping to ruin her debut into society. Mother and Grandmama, the port from which she was to be launched, had raged against former friends, but their threats in the end had proven impotent. For India, the rumors had ignited a burning desire to know more of her history.

The detectives claimed to have found no evidence Jane was alive or dead. She had seemingly disappeared from the face of the earth. Grandfather T.J. always claimed she was dead and forbade all mention of her. He wanted all memories of her erased as though she had never existed. Consequently, Papa knew very little about his mother and rarely spoke of her, meaning India knew next to nothing.

And yet Charlie wrote as though the Pinkertons might not have done a complete search. She sighed. If she allowed it, that tidbit would gnaw at her and destroy her hard-won peace. It had the potential of becoming an obsession, something she really didn't have time for. The mystery of Grandmother Jane was best pushed from her mind and left for a better time.

India scanned the letter again, then laid it aside. That single sheet of paper had produced conflicting emotions, as nearly every letter from Charlie did. Knowing he was well and that he believed there would be an end to this wretched business of war gladdened her heart and lifted her spirits. On the other hand, she dreaded his descriptions of life in the trenches. Gas left men with terrible injuries—blind, ruined lungs, horrible burns. His letters were too often a reminder of the daily dangers he faced.

In the year since they had last been together, managing the estate had grown easier. The ever-disgruntled Holdens had been a heavy burden, the extent of which she had not fully realized until they were gone. She felt sorry for Annie and the baby, she really did, but she could not deny tremendous relief in not having to deal with any of the Holden-Kennedy clan ever again.

She flipped through the remaining envelopes from the day's mail and pulled one with a London return from the stack—the barrister's final invoice. Despite the Holdens' treachery, Charlie, Robbie, and Mama had all advised that the estate provide legal representation for Horace and Fanny. It was galling, but India agreed. Hiring a Queen's Counsel defense demonstrated to their remaining tenants that Kilnsey took care of its own, regardless of the circumstances. It had also saved the couple's lives. After appeals, they received life sentences. In their positions, hanging might have been preferable, at least to India it would have been. As it was, Annie could visit when she chose, if she chose.

At the bottom of the stack, another envelope with a London postmark made India's heart contract. She relaxed a little when she saw the Quartermaster General's return address. Robbie was a sporadic correspondent, but he was far away from the fighting in his corner of the War Office. Althea would be happy for days now. India left the estate office with a smile and went in search of her friend. She found Althea attending to some laundry in the master suite.

With the letter between her finger and thumb, India dangled it aloft. She waggled her brows and used a singsong voice. "Guess what I have."

Althea flew across the room and grabbed the envelope. For a moment, India watched in gentle amusement. Althea appeared to have forgotten India's presence. Robbie's letter was all-consuming. Warmed by Althea's joy, India gave herself a mental hug as she ascended to the third-floor nursery. Having broken with her morning routine, she might as well spend time with Adeline before returning to the grind.

***

A blustery afternoon in early December found Althea shivering on the Grassington Depot platform. Whether her body's reaction was due to cold or excitement was open to debate, probably both.

Uncharacteristically, Ainsworth had offered to drive her in the Rolls rather than leaving her to take the pony cart. He did not, however, offer to stand with her in the freezing air.

She glanced over her shoulder at him sitting behind the wheel reading the castle's daily copy of the Times and grinned. Beneath the straitlaced, formal manner beat a kind, sentimental heart. It was he who insisted no bride should walk to the altar alone and offered himself as substitute father-of-the-bride. He had been so endearing and earnest that she did not have the heart to tell him she could manage alone. And so, the castle butler had escorted the lady's maid and given her away to the estate agent. It had been a perfect wedding and the happiest day of her life, but today just might top it. Robbie was coming home at last, even if it was only for a few days.

With a blast of its whistle, the locomotive's nose appeared around the bend in the tracks. Although she could not yet see Robbie, Althea waved with an energy intended to quell an urge to jump up and down like a child at Christmas. The train slowed, and Robbie's head popped out of a carriage window, his face alight with joy. The carriage door swung open, and he jumped from the still-moving train onto the platform. Althea squealed and ran into his arms. The long-awaited kiss warmed them both.

Robbie lifted his lips from hers and eased her away to arm's length. "Just look at you, my dearest darling girl. You take my breath away. More beautiful than the day we married." Glancing toward the parking area, he continued, "I see Ainsworth did not let his favorite adopted daughter down. Let's get going. It's freezing and I want to put my feet on the fender of my own hearth."

Nestled under rugs in the auto, everyone and everything disappeared for them. Alone in their own world, nothing existed beyond being together at last.

Althea drew a long breath, wanting to ask her question, yet fearing the answer. "How long is the wretched War Office going to let me have you?"

Robbie chuckled. "I doubt my superiors would appreciate your description. I'm afraid I only have the three days, so let's make the best of them, shall we?" Without waiting for her answer, he covered her lips with his own.

***

India stood in the courtyard, her coat collar pulled up around her ears. Blast, it was cold. She stamped her feet. Could one get frostbite in just a few moments' exposure? The Rolls engine sprang to life and Ainsworth settled himself behind the wheel. In a moment, it would feel as though Robbie had never come home, or at least that was how she felt when Charlie left after his leave was over.

Tires crunched on the icy cobbles. She lifted a hand and waved at the Rolls back window where Althea's and Robbie's faces were visible in profile. They gazed into one another's eyes, Althea dabbing her cheeks with a handkerchief. India knew exactly how they felt.

She had hardly seen either of them during his brief time home, but she felt no aggravation, only joy in their happiness. She could hardly blame them for wanting the seclusion and privacy of their cottage. Robbie had taken a cursory look at the accounts and declared India an excellent agent. That pretty much summed up his time spent at the castle, but it was all she had expected.

A shiver shook her whole body. Time to get inside before her feet froze. Despite her fur-lined boots, she could not feel her toes.

As she reached the front entrance, a voice called from just beyond the portcullis. "Lady Kilnsey. Please wait." A messenger urged his pony into the courtyard then jumped down from his mount. He rushed toward India, pulling a scrap of paper from his breast pocket as he ran. Her heart lurched.

"Wire came for you this morning. It took me longer than usual because the roads are bad between here and Kilnsey Village. I got it here as fast as I could." The boy did not meet her eyes as he extended the telegram.

India unfolded the scrap of paper with trembling hands. The words that stared back at her made the blood rush from her head.

Post Office Telegraphs

10 Dec.

War Office, London

Deeply regret to inform you Maj. Charles Westmorland, Lord Kilnsey, missing in action presumed dead 6 Dec. Lord Kitchener extends his sympathy.

The words on telegram blurred then the world disappeared.

CHAPTER 38

India awoke in the arms of the messenger, who looked desperately at the castle entrance willing someone—anyone—to come to his rescue.

She struggled to sit up then rose to her feet on wobbly legs. "Thank you. I apologize. I don't know what came over me. I must look a fright. I'm sure you have other messages to deliver. It's cold. Would you like a warm beverage before you leave? Go to the kitchen. Mrs. Bertrand always has a kettle on the hob." The more she babbled, the higher the pitch of her voice rose. "Please come with me. I will show you the way to..." She never finished the sentence. A scream tore from her like the sound of a dying animal.

The messenger put his arm around India's shoulders and supported her elbow with his free hand. "Come, Milady. Let's get you inside."

India could not speak. She became an automaton doing the bidding of another. Together, they shuffled to the castle entrance. Ainsworth must have heard the commotion because the door flew open at their approach.

Relieving the boy of his burden, the butler said, "Go on through to the kitchen. A maid will show you the way." To India he whispered, "Let's get you inside to the warmth. Would you like to go to your apartment?"

India gazed up at him, but her eyes refused to fully focus. He was fuzzy around the edges. He had spoken. She knew he had, but his words seemed foreign. Or maybe she no longer understood the English language. Perhaps her mind had given up all sensible thought.

Betsy appeared in the Great Hall, her eyes large with fright. Ainsworth nodded at the girl. "Send word to Mrs. Wilson and the Dowager to come to the drawing room. Make sure the fire there burns high, then bring hot tea and honey." When Betsy didn't move, he shouted, "Do as I say. Now." His words echoed in the large chamber.

Someone rubbed India's hand and held a vile odor beneath her nose. She opened her eyes. She reclined on a sofa. She had no memory of how she had gotten to the drawing room. Mama, Mrs. Wilson, and Ainsworth all stared down at her. They appeared worried. She searched her muddled brain for a possible reason.

Oh, God. Charlie. It was about Charlie. Willing herself upright, she looked at Mama. "Please sit. I have bad news."

Mama held up the telegram. All color had drained from her face. "I have already read it, my dear. We must be brave. We must not lose hope. Missing is not the same as dead."

They were meant as words of hope. India knew this, but the word "dead" cut through her as though she had been impaled on a lance.

Mrs. Wilson offered a cup. "Drink this. It will warm you. It has plenty of honey for energy."

India gulped the drink, and with each sip, felt marginally better. Mama was correct. She could not, she must not lose hope. If she did, she might lose her mind, as well. There must be a plan. At the moment, she didn't have the resources to formulate it, but she would not let Charlie just disappear. That way spelled disaster. He was not dead. He was not. She would not allow it. He was alive, and she would find him.

Mama cleared her throat, her face a mask of concern. "You have had a terrible shock, my dear. Perhaps you should rest for the remainder of the day. Whatever tasks await can surely be put off for a little while."

India drew a deep breath and exhaled slowly. The combination of strong tea and measured breathing helped dispel the suffocating confusion that had consumed her since the telegram's arrival. She swallowed the remaining tea and straightened her posture. "You're right, Mama. We cannot let despair overtake us."

She sucked on her lower lip as she thought. Finally, she looked up at Ainsworth. "Send one of the maids to the telegraph office with a message for Robbins at Kilnsey House. Tell him Mrs. James and I will arrive on the noon train tomorrow. He should prepare the house for an indefinite stay. Send two additional telegrams, one to Mr. James at his London office and the other to the solicitor, Mr. Savage. Apprise them of my imminent arrival and that I will call upon them at their earliest convenience. Impress upon them the urgent nature of my visit."

The butler looked confused. "The urgent nature, My Lady? Might you elucidate?"

India surveyed the three faces staring down at her, their brows creased in anxiety. They might be forgiven for believing her mind unbalanced, but they need not worry. She had never been clearer in her life.

Rising from the sofa, she fixed each of them with a steady gaze. "I intend to locate His Lordship and bring him home."

***

At precisely four o'clock the next day, Robbins greeted them at the door of Number 34 Grosvenor Street and ushered them into the two-story foyer. India took in her surroundings with a sense of security. Nothing had changed. No German bomb had marred its lovely facade or shaken the plaster from the walls. The cantilevered stone staircase stood sturdy as ever. The white cornices of acanthus-leaf scrolls and rosettes shone above the oak-paneled walls. The house exemplified the cozy formality often found in early 18th century London townhouses. It was home, and she cherished it.

Robbins directed the cabbie to the mews entrance for the offloading of luggage, then returned his attention to India. "I trust your journey was pleasant and Her Ladyship, the Dowager, is well?"

"Her Ladyship is in good health, but travel is a nightmare these days. The train was late departing Grassington. Once we finally reached King's Cross, I feared we might sit in traffic forever. Nothing seems to move in London any more."

"Quite so, I fear." He signaled to a maid hovering beneath the arched entry to the main hall. "See that Her Ladyship's and Mrs. James's cases are delivered to their rooms and unpacked." The girl curtsied and disappeared to the back of the house. To India, he said, "Mrs. Thorn ordered tea served upon your arrival. May I bring it to the drawing room?"

"That would be most welcome. Give us time to clean away the grime of travel, say fifteen minutes."

As they made their way upstairs, India slowed her pace to study Althea. "It's too bad Robbie is at Southampton on War Office business. Thank goodness my telegram to him arrived before he left. He must have dashed off his reply as he boarded the train. Will he be back tomorrow in time for luncheon, do you think?"

"I certainly hope so." A wistful expression played across Althea's face. "Thank you for inviting him to stay at the house while we are here in London. It will be a little like a second honeymoon for us."

India shot her an affectionate grin. "Did you really think I would do any less? Making you happy makes me happy. He is to spend as much time at Kilnsey House as his superiors allow. Friends are the family we choose, and I choose you both." While her words were spoken in a jovial, teasing manner, they were truer than anyone could possibly know. In more ways than she could count, Althea had become the sister she had always longed for. As for Robbie, he had given Charlie what the Fourteenth Earl did not—a father figure to look up to, to learn from, and to emulate. India loved Althea and Robbie both. They were the rocks in her and Charlie's lives.

After a fitful night's sleep, India swallowed breakfast nearly whole and rushed to the offices of Smythe, Britton, Savage, and Gray with Althea in tow. Mr. Savage had agreed to meet before business began for the day, which meant arrival before nine.

The solicitor greeted them in the outer office. "Welcome, ladies. Please follow me."

A sense of relief washed through India as they accompanied him to his office. The solicitor's appearance had always made her think of him as a kindly, wise, fierce little gnome, one she was glad was on her side.

He gestured to chairs facing his desk then settled himself behind it, his expression a study in sympathy. "I was most distressed to hear of His Lordship's, er . . . situation. How may I be of assistance?"

India stared blankly at the window behind the solicitor. She took a moment to gather herself. She needed every ounce of determination she possessed to get through the next few days. Men tended to feel superior to any woman, no matter her position. Mr. Savage was easy. Robbie would only be as difficult as his superiors demanded. It was an interview with the Secretary of State for War, Lord Derby, himself that she dreaded. Thus far, she had not been able to secure an appointment. Maybe the lawyer could help with that, as well.

She focused on Mr. Savage. "I need to know where I stand now that His Lordship is officially declared missing."

"I see. It was my impression that he might be presumed deceased. Forgive my asking, but have you received official notice of his passing?"

"No, and I don't believe for one minute he is dead. I will have no peace until my husband is found. With the bulk of my inheritance tied up in the entail, I need to know what funds I have access to."

The lawyer placed his elbows on the arms of his chair. Making a bridge of his hands, he tapped his index fingers together. "With no official death notice, your status does not change, nor will it until His Lordship's passing is made official." His eyes scanned a document in a thick file open on his desk. He poked at an item of interest and nodded. "Am I correct in assuming you anticipate interference from Lord Hawik?"

"You have placed your finger precisely on the problem."

Savage drew himself up to his full height. "I feared as much. It is unfortunate His Grace is your husband's heir. But rest assured, should it become necessary, I will act on your behalf, not his. Your husband is, and shall remain, the Kilnsey incumbent until circumstances dictate he is not."

"Thank you, Mr. Savage. You have eliminated a serious worry." India did not rise or in any other way indicate the interview had concluded. Instead, she dithered. Should she ask the solicitor's assistance with the matter weighing most heavily?

Mr. Savage observed her with keen attention. "I sense there is something more, Lady Kilnsey. Please do not hesitate. Speak that which is on your mind."

India glanced at Althea, who gave her a determined look and jerked her head, her silent way of saying, "Get on with it."

"Yes, Mr. Savage, there is another issue. If you have any influence in this matter, your help would be greatly appreciated." The words stuck in her throat. If she uttered them, they banished all doubt that Charlie was in real peril. Her nails dug into her clasped hands until pain radiated to her wrists. She looked down and loosened her grip then met the solicitor's eyes. "I have been unable to secure an appointment with the Secretary of War. I mean to determine what efforts are being made to find my husband."

Savage stroked his chin. "Indeed? That *is* a tall order." His tone was emphatic. "Given his responsibilities, it is little wonder his staff guard his time closely. Nevertheless, I will endeavor on your behalf. Are you at Kilnsey House?" When India nodded, he continued, "Very well. I will do what I can to secure an interview. I hope to send a message within the week informing you of the outcome of my efforts."

Having concluded the business with the lawyer, India and Althea exited the building, which sat directly across from Berkeley Square. India paused to take in the park's beauty. It always seemed a place of peace and solitude, even more now that winter had emptied its benches and paths. She needed some peace in her life at present, but circumstances guaranteed it was not to be.

Althea placed a hand on India's arm. "We have a couple of hours before luncheon with Robbie. Shall we return to the house? I can hail a taxi."

India scrunched her lips into a pout and narrowed her eyes. "Not appealing. I love Kilnsey House, but I'm too wound up to simply sit and wait." Tapping her finger against her chin, she searched for better amusement. "I know. Let's go shopping. Neither of us has had a new frock in . . . Gosh, I can't remember how long. It must have been before the war. I need distraction. My treat. What do you say?"

"You shouldn't spend your money on me. I don't really need anything, but I'll happily watch you placing orders."

"Pshaw. Every woman needs a new dress. I want to make you a present. You really have no choice. I will brook no refusals."

India grabbed Althea's hand and rushed her along to the corner, where they flagged down a taxi. India gave the driver the Bond Street address, and they soon found themselves passing through the entrance of one of the most elegant shops in all of London. The owner, also the designer, created gowns and costumes for the gentry, aristocracy, and even royalty on occasion. Her claim to fame was the originality of her designs, her exquisite taste, and her ability to produce garments with lightning speed. India had often wondered how many seamstresses slaved away in the dark recesses of the establishment where no customer ever ventured. Their number must be legion.

The shop owner made her way toward them with mincing steps and an obsequious smile. "Lady Kilnsey, how delightful. It has been ever so long since we have seen you. You are well, I hope?"

"I am. The war has created new responsibilities which have kept me from Town. We are finally up for a few days and thought we might take advantage of this opportunity to order a new frock or two."

The owner's smile broadened, then she cast her eye over Althea and the smile faded somewhat. "Of course. We would be delighted to create something special for you." The woman paused, seeming to search for the right words. "By 'we', did you mean the Dowager Lady Kilnsey? Unless she has changed in weight, we have her measurements, and I believe I have just the fabric to compliment her coloring."

India blinked, then a crease formed between her eyes. The woman apparently felt serving Althea was beneath her. Supercilious old biddy. India drew upon examples set by her aristocratic friends and family.

Raising her chin so she looked down her nose with an implied hint of irritation, she said, "No, my mother-in-law has her clothes made in York by an excellent seamstress who comes to the castle. She prefers to patronize local establishments." She let the implication sink in for a moment, then flashed her most gracious smile and drew Althea forward. "My friend shall have two frocks in the latest style and best fabrics. I know you will not disappoint. I remember how lovely my wedding dress was and made on such short notice, too." She clapped her hands in girlish delight. "Let's get started, shall we?"

At the end of two hours, India had ordered two complete outfits for herself and two for Althea. The selection of styles, fabrics, and taking of measurements had consumed the time leading to their luncheon.

At the shop door, the owner bowed to both India and Althea. "Thank you, Lady Kilnsey. It has been a great pleasure serving you and . . . Mrs. James. I hope we will see you more often. You have made excellent selections."

India gave her a serene smile colored with a hint of condescension. "Perhaps. Much depends on this awful war. Pray it ends soon." India extended her hand, which the owner grabbed.

"Of course. Of course." The woman seemed reluctant to let India leave, but finally released her.

As they climbed into the taxi hailed for them by the shop's receptionist, India giggled. The giggles became laughter which grew into guffaws. She wiped her eyes with one hand while holding her side with the other. "Did you see her face when I mentioned patronizing local designers? She turned a lovely shade of green. Perhaps she will be more open to new clientele in the future." India doubled over, seized once more by mirth. When it finally passed, she sighed. "That felt good. I haven't laughed like that in a long time."

Althea smirked beneath raised brows. "As long as you don't dissolve into full-blown hysterics, I think you've earned a chuckle or two." After a moment, she took India's hand in hers. "You are a generous and kind friend. I feel very lucky you chose me when there were plenty of others better qualified for the position. I will be forever grateful that you brought me with you to England. If not for you, I would not have met the love of my life." Her voice broke with a quiver, then a big grin spread across her face. "And those new outfits are pretty great, too."

"You're welcome. It was my pleasure."

India settled against the taxi seat and watched London chug by, satisfied to simply sit in silence with a good companion. It was comforting to have someone with whom one could be quiet, who did not judge, did not complain, always took one's side. Althea thought herself the lucky one, but India knew the truth. It was she upon whom luck had smiled all those years ago when Althea agreed to become her lady's maid.

Claridge's was at capacity when they arrived. Thank goodness she had instructed Robbins to make a reservation. The maître d' escorted them to a corner table where they sipped tea and looked over the menu while they waited for Robbie. He arrived much later than planned, but at least he made it. Bright sun shining through the ceiling-high windows shed a harsh spotlight on new silver strands at his temples and deep lines around his eyes. As he made his way toward them, India took one look and decided he was in desperate need of a vacation. He was still a very handsome man, but his grave responsibilities had clearly worn on him.

If a desk job could create such changes, God only knew how Charlie would look once he was finally home. India's stomach tightened while the muscles at the base of her skull knotted into steel cables.

By all that was holy, he would come home. She would not allow any other notion. He was alive, and they would find him no matter what it took, no matter who she had to harass, no matter what it cost. Life without him was unimaginable.

CHAPTER 39

Despite the scarcities created by war, Claridge's meal was tasty and filling. India delayed discussion of Charlie while they ate. They spoke only of things one expected in social situations. Broaching the question would bring hope or despair. Until asked, she could pretend this was just an ordinary meal taken with good friends simply for the pleasure of their company. A few more moments of ignorance helped maintain her sanity. When coffee was served, the topic could wait no longer.

She patted her lips with her napkin and returned it to her lap. "Robbie, have you been able to find any information regarding Charlie's whereabouts?" She could not bring herself to utter the words "what happened to Charlie."

Robbie did not look at her but continued swirling a spoon in his already well-stirred coffee. "I have patchy information, but I'm unsure how useful it is."

India leaned forward. "Please. Just tell me."

Robbie took a sip of coffee and returned the cup to its saucer. "Charlie's unit took part in the battle at Cambrai in northern France. His command post took a direct hit from mortar shells. They found Charlie's identity disks at the top of the trench, but not his body. Fragments of his presumed tunic and trousers were caught in the debris for several feet beyond, as though he had crawled away from the site of the explosion. After that, nothing more was found."

He paused, no doubt gauging India's reaction. She met his eyes with a steady gaze. Apparently satisfied, he continued, "Only one man from the post has been found alive. He was evacuated to a hospital here in London. The doctors say he is in bad shape, but conscious. He will see you if you wish, or if you would rather, I can speak with him."

India's stomach churned. Her pulse quickened. She held up a hand. "Wait. Are you saying Charlie has officially been declared dead?"

"No. He is still classified MIA. Since no body has been found, it is impossible to say exactly what happened to him. It can only be surmised."

"Then take me to the injured man. I want to hear for myself what he can tell us."

The taxi deposited them at the door of the Third London General Hospital, housed in the former Royal Victoria Patriotic School in Wandsworth. An orderly directed them to a ward where junior officers were housed. As they passed through the long hall, India fought back tears summoned by what she saw. She was hit by the realization that Charlie could be in the terrible condition of some of these pitiful souls. The room seemed endless.

Row upon row of iron bedsteads draped in white linens held the broken, torn bodies of young men who were in what should have been the prime of their lives. As it was, the lucky ones would eventually return to full strength and lead normal lives, maybe even be able to put the things they had experienced behind them. For the unlucky, they would be blind, crippled, scarred, broken, helpless for what remained of their difficult existence.

The smell of antiseptic assaulted the senses and something else, a faint sickly sweet odor permeated the very fabric of the screens separating some of the beds. Behind those screens, the most critically ill moaned, thrashed in pain, or lay deathly still, unable to lift their heads or even a finger. The men with gas scarred lungs coughed ceaselessly, dabbing at their mouths with blood-soaked cloths. Most distressing were the men who had lost parts of their faces. Once handsome, young, vital men were now reduced to what the cruel would call monsters.

The sheer enormity of the damage overwhelmed India, making her lightheaded. She paused by a table and placed a hand on it for support. She'd be damned if she would make a fool of herself by fainting. These poor men should be everyone's focus, instead of a well-fed matron who lived in a comfortable home in no more danger than having to decide how to keep farms producing at maximum capacity.

Robbie stopped beside her. "Are you all right? Do you need to sit?"

She shook her head. "No. I just need a moment to gather myself. Our Lieutenant Spencer can't be much farther along." She stood very still until her breathing steadied and the dizziness abated.

They found their quarry six beds from the end of the hall. He was swathed in bandages, both legs immobilized and suspended by a contraption of ropes and pulleys. He might have been twenty-five or forty-five. It was hard to tell with much of his face covered by gauze. His eyes held the expression of a man weary with the world and its demands.

Robbie stepped forward and made introductions. When he smiled, Lt. Spencer looked more like the boy he must have been. India watched him in awe. He was so damaged and yet he could still muster a smile for visitors.

Lt. Spencer looked at India. "I was in your husband's unit, Lady Kilnsey. He is a good man and a fine officer. I was with him when our command post was hit. How is Major Westmorland doing?"

India blinked and fought a gasp. This young officer clearly thought Charlie had survived the attack. "I'm afraid we don't know. He is reported missing in action. We are hoping you might tell us when you last saw him, perhaps even what happened to him."

Lt. Spencer looked confused, then understanding dawned. "That's too bad. I'm very sorry. When I saw him crawling out of the trench, I figured he was all right and going for help. That's the last I saw of him before I blacked out. The next thing I remember is waking up in the field hospital. Later, they said no one else survived, but I thought they must be mistaken. Major Westmorland was alive when last I saw him."

India knelt beside the bed. "You've given me great hope and confirmed what my heart has always known. When the time comes for your release from hospital, if you have need of a place to convalesce, please come to us. You will be most welcome and well cared for. Here is my card and that of our solicitor. Please do not hesitate to ask for our help should you be in need."

"That's very kind. Thank you." He tried to raise his hand, but his eyes screwed up in a wince. When he opened them again, they held a peace not previously in evidence. "I'll keep your card. I wish you the greatest good luck in locating the major."

On the drive back to Kilnsey House, India mulled over what she had learned thus far. Charlie's identity tags had been torn from him, but he was nowhere to be found. That left two possibilities—he was either dead or was not able to identify himself to whoever found him. She would not, could not accept the former, so that left him alive but either unconscious or suffering amnesia. He must be lying unidentified in some hospital somewhere. She now knew what she would demand of Lord Derby when they met. And they would meet, even if she had to show up at his office and refuse to leave until he agreed to see her.

CHAPTER 40

India read the note from Mr. Savage, then passed it to Althea. "The man is an absolute miracle worker, a precious gem. I'll ask Robbins to arrange a thank you gift. Maybe a bottle of good port or box of cigars? Does he even smoke cigars? It's hard to know what's available these days."

Althea nodded. "Yes, he's pulled off something I never thought would happen. And I'm sure whatever you send will be unexpected and appreciated." She consulted her brooch watch. "We need to get going. Better too early than late."

Within the hour, they sat in the main reception area of the War Office. Robbie came down to greet them but made it clear his presence in the interview would be unwelcome and probably do more harm than good. Unfortunately, the solicitor was unable to accompany them, so everything rested on India's ability to persuade. As a young officer approached, she rewarded him with what she hoped was a confident, winning smile.

The subaltern made a shallow bow. "Lady Kilnsey, Lord Derby will see you now. Please follow me."

They were escorted up a flight of stairs and through a maze of halls. Open office doors revealed men and women in uniform clattering away on typewriters, grabbing ringing telephones, and scurrying to-and-fro. Frantic busyness seemed the order of the day. India concentrated on her mission. Letting her surroundings intimidate or overwhelm her could not be allowed. They were here to demand information about Charlie. Nothing else mattered.

The subaltern led them past rows of secretaries before stopping at a set of double mahogany doors. Opening one, he stepped aside and announced, "Lady Kilnsey and Mrs. James, My Lord."

As India stepped into the office, a thousand tiny butterflies fluttered in her midsection. She had rehearsed the words many times in her head. Pray to God she would be able to effectively articulate them now that the time had arrived.

Lord Derby looked up from the papers spread before him on his desk. "Ladies, please be seated. I can spare ten minutes, no more."

India swallowed and breathed deeply. It was now or never. "Thank you for seeing me, Lord Derby. I assume my solicitor apprised you of the facts?"

"Yes, yes. I don't know how I can be of service, but do go on."

"I wish a list and the locations of all unidentified injured men evacuated from the battlefield at Cambrai. I believe my husband is among them. I mean to find him and bring him home to Kilnsey."

Lord Derby's eyes widened. "My dear lady, that is an absurd request. There are thousands who were injured at Cambrai. You can't possibly wish to see them all."

"No, not all. Only the ones who have yet to be identified. Surely that is a much shorter list."

"Perhaps." Lord Derby's lips thinned. He clearly thought she was on a fool's errand.

"Please, Lord Derby." India's voice cracked with desperation. "Please. Can't someone compile such a list for me?"

"I'm afraid not. Men are not classified by their injuries or states of mind." As he studied her, sympathy and compassion peeked out from behind his otherwise stern demeanor.

"While I cannot spare the manhours to search the injury lists, I see no harm in allowing you to do so. If you wait in the outer office, I will arrange it."

"Thank you. I'm grateful beyond words."

Lord Derby harrumphed. "You may not thank me when you see the task ahead of you."

India raised her chin so she could pretend to look down upon him. "I have never been afraid of hard work. I look forward to the challenge because it will bring me to my husband."

"Indeed. I admire your faith and determination." He called for his secretary. "See that these ladies are given access to the records they require." To India, he said, "I wish you good luck in your search." His tone implied the search would prove fruitless. He could be forgiven his doubt. He did not carry Charlie in his heart as she did.

India and Althea rose and followed the secretary. At the office door, India turned back. "Lord Derby, I *will* find my husband and bring him home. You will have played an important role. You have my undying gratitude."

Over the course of the next two days, India and Althea compiled a list of all unidentified men who had been involved in the Cambrai battle. It was fairly short when compared with the full lists of the injured. Her back ached from bending over stacks of files and her hand cramped from writing. Most of the men were in London, but a few were scattered about the nation. They made quick work of visiting those in London.

***

India removed her hat and gloves as soon as she and Althea entered Kilnsey House. Home had never felt quite this good. It seemed months since they had departed Yorkshire instead of a mere week.

Robbins greeted them with an anxious smile. "Did you have any luck today, My Lady?"

"No, I'm afraid not. This was the last of the London hospitals, but there are others beyond Town to be searched. We will find him." Robbins and Althea exchanged a look that held both sympathy and doubt. Well, they could believe what they wanted. India refused to abandon her faith that Charlie would be found. They would simply have to search farther afield.

To divert them all from depressing thoughts, she said, "The weather is getting harsher by the minute. We need tea and a warm fire." She glanced at herself in the mirror hanging above a Chippendale credenza. The girl who looked back had dark circles under her eyes and hollows in her cheeks. She made a note to get more rest. She wouldn't have Charlie think her ill when they finally found him.

To Robbins, she continued, "I want to see Mr. Savage again before we leave for Yorkshire. I have an early-morning appointment two days hence. Mrs. James and I will depart by the noon train on the same day. I don't want to miss Christmas with Lady Adeline. Please send a telegram to Ainsworth notifying him of my plans."

Robbins gave a single nod. "Of course, My Lady. Tea will be brought to the drawing room when you are ready. The fire is laid."

After changing into ensembles better suited to an afternoon at home, India and Althea settled on the sofa by a roaring fire.

Althea grinned and gestured toward the teapot. "Shall I be mother?"

The quaint English expression had become a standing joke between them. India smirked and donned her best imitation of British aristocrats. "By all means, please do."

For the millionth time, India thanked Providence for bringing Althea into her life. All of this would have been much, much harder without her help and support.

At the front of the house, a bell sounded followed by the front door being opened. Voices murmured in the foyer, then the door closed once more. Robbins came into the drawing room, his face pale and his breathing quick. He held out an envelope to India.

"This has just arrived by messenger."

India removed the contents of the envelope and unfolded a telegram with shaking hands.

Post Office Telegraphs
Kilnsey Village, Yorkshire
Urgent. Return Kilnsey at once.
Ainsworth.

CHAPTER 41

Ainsworth agreed to meet them in the Rolls. Unlike his past trips fetching and carrying to and from Grassington Depot, India spied him on the platform as the train pulled to a stop. He paced up and down while peering at each passing carriage, craning his neck at each door that swung open. His expression was a cross between frantic and desperate. Something was terribly wrong. Ainsworth never showed emotion, no matter the circumstance.

India stepped from the carriage and waved, catching the butler's notice. He rushed to her. "Oh, thank goodness. I have done what I am able, but I'm only the butler. He simply will not listen to reason."

"Slow down. You aren't making sense. About whom are you speaking?"

"His Lordship's cousin, Lord Hawik. The man has moved in and is ordering the staff about as though it is he who owns Kilnsey. He has even established himself in your apartment, but I drew the line at removing your and His Lordship's things to another part of the castle. The staff are more afraid of me than they are of him."

India glanced at Althea, who raised her brows.

"Your Ladyship, perhaps we should send for Billy Grant and some of the younger tenants as soon as we arrive home."

India sucked on her lower lip while she considered the situation. "No, not yet. Let me get the feel of things before we resort to physical action."

On the way from the depot, India was quiet, lost in thoughts about how best to deal with Bumpy. As they approached Kilnsey Village, she made a decision. Leaning forward, she rapped on the communicating window separating passengers and driver.

"Stop at the telegraph office. I'm sending a message to York for Mr. Mitchell."

Althea cast India a sidewise glance. "Planning on lawyering your husband's cousin, are you?"

"If I must. Mr. Savage and Mr. Mitchell are in constant communication regarding our legal needs. Perhaps Mr. Mitchell can impress upon His Grace that until Charlie is declared . . . ." She could not bring herself to say the word. "Until it is clear Charlie will not return, nothing regarding the title or the estate has changed."

"Too bad John Fraser is no longer with us. He would never have let the blighter trespass in the first place. Because it *is* trespassing. You do know that, don't you?"

India sighed. "Of course I do, but I would rather evict Bumpy with as little fuss as possible. God forbid the gossip rags get hold of the story. Mama would have a coronary."

With the decision to contact the York lawyer made, an unseen hand chipped away a few pieces of the boulder crowding India's chest. She had taken a positive step toward getting rid of the odious Bumpy, but that left another dilemma. Having to deal with him meant delaying the search for Charlie . . . unless. Perhaps there was another way.

She turned to face Althea. "I can't be in two places at once. I must be at the castle while Bumpy remains there, but I must continue the search for Charlie, too. What do you think about hiring a private detective to narrow the possibilities?"

Althea was quiet for a long time. Perhaps India's question had shocked her, but that made no sense. India placed her hand on her friend's arm. "Please. Tell me what you think. I'm going to go mad if we must delay the search."

Althea placed her hand over India's. "How can you be sure a stranger, even a good detective, will do a complete job looking for a man he has never met?"

"I would give him pictures."

Pained sympathy filled Althea's eyes. Almost in a whisper, she said, "All of them were taken before Charlie had been to war. His appearance may have changed."

India's heart dropped. What Althea had not said aloud was that Charlie could be so scarred as to be unrecognizable when compared with a picture taken years ago. India shook her head as tears rolled. "I don't suppose I can."

Althea pressed a fist against her mouth as she focused on something outside the auto. Again, she was quiet for several moments. "What if I went with the detective? He would provide the male connection that is often needed with all things military and I would be the memory of Charlie that he will need to do the job. He and I could at least narrow the field until you can join us."

India threw her arms around Althea and hugged her hard. "Oh, my goodness. You are brilliant. You have saved my sanity." She broke the embrace and drew back, searching Althea. "But only if you feel safe doing this. The detective would be a strange man and these are dangerous times."

"Perhaps, but if he is recommended and hired by Mr. Mitchell, I think we can assume he will be dependable."

India alighted from the Rolls and stretched her back. The frozen road had been rough. Each bounce of the wheels jarred every bone to the breaking point, or at least it felt that way. The damp cold probably contributed as well to making her bones feel brittle. She looked at the darkening sky. Low clouds portended snow either tonight or tomorrow. They were too heavy to hold their contents much longer. A shiver ran through her and she pulled her coat closer. A nice hot bath was in order before retiring for the evening, but that lovely escape was still several hours hence. At present, she must go to Mama.

India mulled over their hastily concocted plan as she and Althea made their way into the castle. Althea would need to go straight to her room to repack for a very quick turnaround to the telegraph office in Kilnsey Village, then on to the depot. Ainsworth was headed across the driveway to Cragfast Mastiles where he would secure a man to do the driving. Desperate times called for desperate measures. Putting the Rolls in the hands of a neighbor certainly fit the description, but it had to be done. Ainsworth was needed at the castle. Knowing Mr. Mitchell's efficiency, he would have the services of a private investigator secured by the time Althea reached York, or at the latest, by the following day. It was expecting a great deal of a friend, but there seemed to be no other choice.

India stopped Althea at the bottom of the Grand Staircase. "You know you can withdraw your offer. It seems a great deal to ask."

Althea's face shifted into her best older sister look. "You did not ask. I offered. Remember? You are needed here and we all want to find Charlie. As you said, you cannot be in two places at once."

India threw her arms around Althea. "No one could ever have a better friend. If at any time you do not feel comfortable or safe, you must come home." Althea's body shuddered beneath India's arms.

Althea broke the embrace and said, "I'm going to say goodbye now because you have a big task ahead of you. You be safe also, and do not let that blighter bully you."

The sound of the front door closing drifted from the Great Hall, followed by boots trodding upon the stone floor. Ainsworth came through with the Reverend Archibald Howard in tow. Cousin Archibald wore a disgruntled expression.

Althea waggled her brows and whispered, "It looks like Reverend Howard is to drive me to the depot. The good Lord protect us and give me strength. He is already tapping his foot in impatience. I must hurry if I'm to catch my train."

India found Mama in her apartment ensconced on a sofa by a roaring fire. Even in the soft glow of lamps and firelight, the toll of the war years was written on her once-unlined face. Deep lines now etched her forehead and circled her eyes. The flesh of her cheeks lay in folds and sagged below the jaw. The room was overly warm, but she was wrapped in two shawls and a rug lay over her legs and feet. The cold she had come down with earlier in the month had worsened. She now coughed with every few breaths. She had thus far refused to allow India to send for the doctor, but that decision no longer lay with Mama. After bringing her up to speed on the Bumpy situation, India would announce that the doctor would be summoned first thing tomorrow.

Mama smiled and held out her hand. "Thank God you are home. He has been unbearable. Surely he cannot take over at this juncture." A coughing fit shook her, leaving her gray with the effort to breathe.

India placed an arm around Mama's shoulders. "Bumpy has no right to be here, and no, he cannot make any claims. If we are unable to convince him to leave, Mr. Mitchell will be summoned. We have the law on our side. Do not fear. I'm going to confront him now. There's no reason to wait."

She found His Grace lounging in the drawing room, his feet propped across a silk damask sofa. His shirt collar was open and his belly protruded over his pants. How anyone could have gained weight during this war was hard to comprehend, but he had managed. Perhaps he dealt in the black market. She would not put anything past him at this point.

He did not rise when she entered. The smell of alcohol reached her as she approached. "Cousin-in-law. Welcome. I expect you, the Dowager, and your child to vacate the premises by Christmas Eve. I have friends coming for a Christmas week house party. You may stay in a guest room."

India spread her feet and crossed her arms over her bosom. "You and your friends are not welcome here. You are trespassing. You will leave in the morning or I will have you bodily thrown out. Your choice. And you are lucky I am allowing you to stay the night."

"You allow me nothing. It is I who am allowing you to shelter in my castle. Perhaps you would prefer to leave now?"

A throat cleared behind India. She did not need to look over her shoulder to know who had entered. Ainsworth had come to stand guard.

"This is not your castle. You have no right to be here uninvited."

"I have every right since your husband is dead. I am his heir. Not what you prefer, I realize, but such is the way of the entail. Too bad your child is a girl, but there you have it."

India fixed him with a glacial stare and spoke through gritted teeth. "You will stay the night in a guest room and depart at first light." Her blood turned to ice, generating an unexpected calm. "Ainsworth, escort His Grace to the red room and lock the door. He will take his evening meal there. The door will not be unlocked until Billy Grant has arrived in the morning. His Grace will be taken to the depot and put on the first train to York." To Bumpy she said, "After that, you are on your own to get home. What you fail to comprehend is that missing is not the same as deceased. Charlie is still the Earl of Kilnsey and will remain so until further information becomes available. Mr. Savage has the situation well in hand."

As Ainsworth's six-feet-two-inch frame loomed over Bumpy, India fought a snigger. For the first time since she had known him, His Grace displayed a touch of fear. He struggled to his feet and left with the butler as instructed. India waited until the pair were out of sight, then fell onto the sofa and melted into the upholstery. It took several seconds for her heart rate to return to normal.

Instead of eating alone in the dining room, India took a light supper with Mama in her apartment. After the meal, she insisted that Mama take two aspirin and get into bed. India left her snoring peacefully.

Alone in her own suite at last, India bathed and crawled into bed. It had been a long, exhausting day. By now, Althea would have arrived in York. She had promised to send word once the search resumed. India tried to bury thoughts of Charlie lying injured, alone, and unidentified, but images from the London hospitals haunted her. She drifted between light slumber and wakefulness, tossing and turning until the bed linens were a tangled mess.

She straightened the sheets and blankets and finally drifted back into a fitful sleep until howling wind and soft knocking against the windows brought her upright and fully awake. She shoved her feet into her slippers and went to the window closest to her bed. When she parted the drapes and looked through the glass, her spirit sank.

CHAPTER 42

The next day Althea found herself shaking hands with the York solicitor. She stayed the night at a little inn near the depot and took a taxi to the lawyer's office just before noon. Snow had fallen much of the night, but the streets were still passable. Reports from the Dales indicated the snowfall was much heavier. Pray India was not snowbound with her uninvited guest.

Mr. Mitchell greeted her as a kindly old friend. "Please sit, Mrs. James. I was most concerned when I received Her Ladyship's telegrams, but I believe I have just the man for you." He took a card from his desk and handed it to Althea. "You can place your trust in him. I know how reliable you are from our previous collaboration. Together, you and Mr. Sykes will be a formidable team." He removed his watch from its pocket and opened the engraved gold cover. "I have asked him to meet us at The Guy Fawkes Inn for luncheon. We will have an excellent meal in a private dining room where we will not be disturbed." He glanced at Althea's valise sitting on the floor beside her. "I will instruct the office boy to bring your things to the restaurant in an hour."

The inn, located in the building on Petergate, where the infamous Guy Fawkes had been born, was within the shadow of the Minster. It was a lovely old place with many windows looking out on the church. India preferred to take rooms there when they had to overnight in the city.

Mr. Mitchell guided Althea to the promised private room, where a gentleman was already seated at the table. He rose at their entrance. The winter sun coming through the window highlighted his white hair, creating a halo effect around his large head. A mustache curled upward on either side of his mouth and stretched nearly to his ears. His deep blue eyes held a twinkle. His three-piece suit was clearly bespoke. The total picture was of a kindly grandfather who might have been a judge or a member of the gentry. His very appearance inspired confidence, which no doubt it was intended to do.

They all ordered the sole with roasted potatoes and green peas. York's being on the coast had its advantages when it came to access to fresh seafood. As the meal drew toward conclusion, the conversation turned to business.

Mr. Sykes patted his lips and mustache with his napkin. "I believe you have a list of locations we are to search. May I see it?" Althea reached into her handbag and passed the list to him.

He glanced over it and nodded. "This should not be difficult. We will start with the hospital at the greatest distance." To Mr. Mitchell, he said, "If you will send telegrams to these hospital administrators describing our purpose, that will speed our work."

He returned the list to Althea and glanced at his pocket watch. "I believe we should begin our search immediately. We can take the train to our first destination this afternoon. Mrs. James, are you prepared to travel to Norfolk? With luck, we should be able to confirm or eliminate one gentleman by this evening. From Norfolk, we will work our way north until we have exhausted all possibilities."

***

India sat bolt upright in the bed, awakened by shouting coming from the vicinity of the guest rooms. Bumpy must be awake. After rubbing her eyes, she peered at the mantel clock. Dawn should be breaking. Slipping from the bed, she padded over to a window and opened the drapes. The world had become one big snowdrift overnight. Snow piled on the Chinese Chippendale garden bench nearly to the top of its seat back. She shook her head in dismay. No doubt the roads would be impassable today—maybe for several days to come. This was all she needed right now. What on earth was she to do about their trespasser?

There seemed only one solution. They could hardly keep him locked up for the duration of the freeze. Donning a robe, she ventured to the suite door and peeked out.

A red-faced Ainsworth marched toward her. "My Lady, I do believe His Grace will pull the door from its hinges if he is not released. He is threatening legal action."

"Thank you, Ainsworth. Give me the key. I will see to him." She stopped and thought. "On second thought, go with me."

With the butler hovering behind her, India trudged to the red room and knocked.

"Let me out immediately. You will hear from my solicitor and the constable. This is unlawful detention. It is tantamount to kidnapping." The knob rattled sharply. "Open the damned door."

The sound of an object shattering came from the room. Bumpy must be having a tantrum. Okay. Act like a child . . . be treated like a child.

"This door will remain locked until you demonstrate appropriate behavior. Will you be calm? I will not countenance temper tantrums. You will not throw things, nor will you shout. We are stuck with one another until the roads are passable. Truce?" Silence reigned on the other side of the door. "Bumpy? Did you hear me? You will behave yourself or spend the rest of your unauthorized stay behind a locked door. Which will it be?" It was like scolding a toddler for bad behavior. "Bumpy? I will not open this door until I have your promise to act like an adult and a gentleman."

Disgruntled grumbling came from the other side of the door. "Okay. You win. Now, open the door."

"I still do not have your promise to behave. Well?"

"All right, all right. I promise."

"Promise what?"

"To act like a gentleman."

"Very well." India put the key in the lock and turned. "I have unlocked the door. I am returning to my apartment. Breakfast will be served presently. When it is laid, Ainsworth will help you to the dining room."

To the butler, she said, "Stay here until he comes out. Do not allow him to roam. He is to go straight to the dining room and nowhere else. If you have not sent for Billy Grant, please do so. In addition, please ask Cousin Archibald to come to the castle. We may need reinforcements and a reliable witness."

***

Althea and Mr. Sykes went straight to the hospital from the depot. She alighted from the taxi and stopped to look up at the gray stones of the former municipal building. A shiver ran through her. The hospital was as gray as the clouds that hung above it. It was a dreary place for wounded men to heal and try to regain some normalcy in their lives. It was selfish to be glad Robbie was safe in a London office instead of fighting in the mud of France, but she rejoiced in the knowledge all the same. They were very lucky. Pray the search for Charlie ended in swift success.

Mr. Sykes gave her a concerned look, perhaps wondering if she was up to the task that lay before them. He motioned for her to go through the door he held open, then followed her into a large reception area where a middle-aged man in a white coat watched their approach with interest. Mr. Mitchell had worked telegraphic magic because the hospital administrator was expecting them.

The administrator offered his hand. "Always happy to help family identify a loved one." He gestured toward double doors leading to a long hall. "We are, as I'm sure you are, in great hopes you will know this young man. His injuries are of the mental variety. He has no physical ailments as far as we can determine. He does not seem to be in pain, but neither does he seem to recognize his surroundings. We aren't sure what he feels or knows, for he either cannot or will not speak."

They were led to a ward where the patients lay or sat staring into emptiness as though they looked but could not see. The silence was frightening and deafening, broken only by the occasional moan or cry. The sounds were worse than the silence because they bore little resemblance to human speech. Althea braced herself and tried not to look at the men. Instead, she kept her eyes trained on the administrator's back.

He stopped by a screen that blocked a patient from general view. Swinging it back, he stepped to the bed and placed a hand on the occupant's shoulder. The face looking up at them was not Charlie. Althea shook her head and they returned to the reception area.

As they shook hands with the administrator, he said, "I'm sorry this was not your man and I wish you good luck in your search."

In the taxi taking them to their night's accommodation, Mr. Sykes pulled a pipe from his pocket. "Do you mind if I smoke?"

"No. I've always liked the smell of a pipe. If it were a cigarette or cigar, that would be different." She wrinkled her nose and he laughed.

The glow of his match illuminated his bushy, white eyebrows. After several puffs, he took the pipe from his mouth. "I hope you are not too disappointed. I didn't suppose we should expect to find him on the first try out of the box. We'll leave for Lincoln in the morning, shall we?"

***

India looked across the dining table at her unwanted guest. For a solid week, he had eaten like a gluttonous hog and now sat wiping his mouth with the damask napkin while his eyes darted toward the sideboard where a single chop remained in the serving dish. If smacking his face would have accomplished anything, she would gladly have done it. She had avoided him as much as possible during their weather-enforced confinement, barring him from the estate office and the nursery. Poor Ainsworth had shadowed him like a hound. She would try reason, but that failing, they would resort to physically evicting him. First, however, she signaled to Ainsworth to start clearing. She'd be damned if Bumpy would get the last chop.

She placed her elbows on the table, leaned over her plate, and fixed him with a hard stare. "It looks like the roads will be passable in another day or two. You are to leave as soon as they are open. You are not to return without an invitation. You are family, so after a period of adjustment and if you do not offer further offence, you may be allowed to visit, but not until my husband returns home. Until that time, you are to stay away." It was surprising how calm she sounded and how in control she felt. These years of managing everything and everyone had built a strength she had not realized she possessed.

Bumpy's face went from pasty white to an ugly shade of pink. He struck the table with his open palm. "We will see about that. My solicitor has already begun researching what it will take to have Charles declared dead. He assures me we have an excellent case."

"You may think what you like, but I have the War Office and the law on my side. Mr. Savage has everything well in hand. It is not as easy as one might think to have a war hero declared dead." She nodded to Ainsworth, who pulled her chair back as she rose. "This is the last we shall speak of these matters. You may take your meals in your room or here in the dining room when I am not present. I do not wish to see you again. Go to your room now and do not come out until you are summoned to breakfast."

If there were to be legal repercussions from having locked Bumpy in his room each night, so be it. She would counter those charges with one of unlawful trespass exacerbated by foul weather and impassable roads.

Whatever the upshot of their week together, she would soon return her focus to finding Charlie. She had received no updates since the blizzard, but that would change. She would join Althea and the private detective as quickly as possible. Maybe then she would be able to sleep at night.

***

The week of constant traveling and searching had left Althea tired and depressed. She and Mr. Sykes visited as many as three hospitals in a day with no results. The thought that Charlie might be dead after all constantly tried to intrude. She pushed it away with all she had, but she did not have India's faith. With every failed attempt, with every bed or wheelchair filled by someone other than Charlie, it had begun to feel like their efforts would prove worthless in the end.

She looked at Mr. Sykes sitting in the opposite carriage seat. He was reading the Times and puffing away on his pipe as though he didn't have a care in the world. This was just a job to him, so she should not expect him to be as emotionally invested as she and India. He had been very professional and helpful, but she still had to fight feelings of resentment that he could relax when she was keyed up all the time. Knowing her telegrams to India were probably not getting through didn't help her mood either.

Mr. Sykes must have felt her eyes on him, because he glanced at her over his paper and did a quick double take. Lowering the Times, he gave her a sympathetic smile. "If these last two are not His Lordship, would Lady Kilnsey agree for me to begin a search abroad?"

"I can't speak for her. Would the War Office allow a civilian near the field hospitals? They're close to the trenches and battlefields."

"Oh, I think that can be arranged. My chief concern is the possibility of Lord Kilnsey's having been taken prisoner by the Germans. Without identity tags and if he is unable to identify himself, then we have a truly serious problem."

Althea's hand flew to her mouth. "I had not considered that. If he is an unidentified POW, that could spell disaster."

"Let's not create problems where none may exist. We still have these final two men to see." The train whistled and the depot platform came into view. Mr. Sykes folded his paper, opened a window, and tapped the contents of his pipe onto the concrete below. “Leeds. Jolly good. If unsuccessful, from here we go on to Ripon Camp. His Lordship was with his Leeds Pals unit, so perhaps he is here. In any event, we shall all be home for Christmas. Once the holidays are behind us, we can discuss searches farther afield, if necessary.”

Althea shot him a grateful smile. Thank goodness he had used the present tense and not the past in reference to Charlie.

CHAPTER 43

India read Althea's telegram with shaking hands, then called for Ainsworth. "Please get the Rolls out. I'm driving to Leeds. There's a soldier in hospital there who might be His Lordship."

Ainsworth cleared his throat, his face filled with doubt. "My Lady, might I make a suggestion?"

"Of course."

"Would you permit me to drive for you? You should not be traveling alone at a time like this, if you will forgive my saying."

The butler hated driving. In the past, he had silently communicated he felt it beneath his dignity. What he refused to admit was that it also made him nervous, a fact India and Althea had privately joked about. India only pressed him into service when necessary. Overwhelmed by his offer, she replied, "I would be most grateful for your company and support. Thank you."

He made a small bow, perhaps hoping to hide the mist brightening his eyes. "Always, My Lady. It is an honor and a privilege to serve you and His Lordship."

The thirty-five-mile journey between the castle and Leeds took longer than usual. Had it been summer, they would have arrived within an hour and a half, but the roads still showed the effects of the week-long blizzard, adding another hour. It was going on three p.m. when Ainsworth guided the Rolls to a stop under the hospital portico.

He came around and opened the door for India. As she stepped onto the driveway's stone pavers, it felt as though hundreds of butterflies had been released in her midsection. She held out her hand to the butler without thinking. He looked somewhat taken aback, but took it nonetheless. "Thank you for driving. I don't think I could have made it alone."

Ainsworth nodded. "I am gratified to be of service, but I suspect Her Ladyship is capable of accomplishing anything to which she sets her mind."

"Yes . . . well . . . " Dread, fear, excitement, anxiety battled for dominance. Spying Althea through the entrance glass, she said, "I guess I'd better go in."

Ainsworth smiled encouragingly and patted her hand. "And I will await you in the auto." He hesitated, then added, "You are braver than you know, My Lady."

India greeted Althea with a hug. "I will never be able to thank you enough for all you have done this week." She hiccupped with a stifled sob. "I'm so afraid."

Althea whispered, "You would have done the same for me." Giving India a tight hug, she drew back to look at her. "Mr. Sykes has been invaluable. We are nearing the end of our search. Are you ready to see this officer?"

India swallowed hard and nodded.

They made their way to a common room that was deserted save for a single chair facing a western window. The setting sun cast a weak glow over the chair's occupant, highlighting his blonde hair. His body, visible above the chair back, indicated he was Charlie's height and build. India's heart leapt into her throat and she rushed to face the unidentified man.

When he looked up, it was clear he shared her hope. His expression brightened, and he straightened up. He searched her face, trying to find some connection with who he once was.

India stammered, "I . . . I'm sorry."

The light in his eyes faded as hope died. He slumped against the chair back once more and returned to staring at the vista beyond his window. Before she completely lost control, India turned and fled the room.

India stopped when she reached the reception area. She sank onto the nearest chair and stuffed a fist into her mouth.

Althea knelt and placed an arm around India. "I know you're disappointed. I am, too. We have one more man to see in Ripon. Let's go home and get a good night's sleep. May Mr. Sykes come with us? He has been very kind and helpful. I hate to leave him to fend for himself."

A handkerchief appeared, held by the private investigator. India took it and wiped her tears. "Thank you. Please forgive the emotional display."

"No need for apologies, dear lady. This is surely a very trying time for you."

"Perhaps more than you know." Taking Althea's hand, India continued, "Mrs. James is right. We should return to the castle. Mr. Sykes, please be our guest tonight. We will have a fortifying meal and rest. Maybe tomorrow will be a better day." She did not say good sleep because for her that would be impossible.

***

India awoke with first light but did not get up. Rolling onto her back, she threw her arms over her head and studied the ceiling medallion above the bed. Today felt like the most important of her life. Funny that her wedding day and

Adeline's birth could suddenly take a back seat. She did not love the baby less. Of course, she didn't, but both of their lives would be immeasurably worse if Charlie was never found. She had not asked Mr. Savage the unimaginable question that now haunted her. How many years must a person be missing before they could be legally declared dead? It was a possibility she must now entertain if today's visit ended in disappointment. Bumpy had already contacted his attorney. She covered her face with a pillow and muffled a scream. Oh, God. Please. Let the man in Ripon be my Charlie.

With her stomach in open rebellion, India had only dry toast and plain tea at breakfast. As she waited for the others to come to the Great Hall, she could not stop pacing. Her hands had minds of their own. They wrung themselves and twisted her flesh until her wrists were burning and red. She locked her fingers behind her back but could do nothing about her tapping feet.

Althea and the private investigator arrived in the Great Hall dressed for the journey upon which all their hopes hung.

Mr. Sykes smiled reassuringly. "Ready, My Lady?"

India's mouth was as dry as the cotton that grew in her native North Carolina's coastal counties. She could not manage speech, so she nodded. Ainsworth awaited them by the Rolls in the courtyard and they were soon headed to Ripon.

The twenty-six miles went by faster than India expected. She was torn. Seeing the unidentified soldier was all she could think about, and yet she dreaded the end of the journey. This man was her last hope that Charlie had been found.

When they pulled up to the front gates, a vast military encampment spread before them, created on the Marquess of

Ripon's former agricultural acres. The guard standing watch directed them to the North Camp where a hospital had been erected along the Pateley Road opposite the turning to Studley Roger. As they approached the concrete block building roofed with gray Welsh slate, India started trembling, unable to control the movement in her hands or sit calmly. The Rolls slowed, and she jumped from the still moving vehicle.

Althea called out, her voice as sharp as an irate schoolmarm. "Good God, be careful. You do no one any good if you get yourself injured."

India stopped at the front entrance. Now that she was about to see this man, terror froze her. It would all be over within a matter of minutes.

They were conducted between rows of beds in a long ward. The patients who were able to sit up or were ambulatory wore blue uniforms with red trim and ties. The naked shoulders of those unable to rise protruded above sheets and blankets covering their lower bodies. The doctor leading the way slowed near a bed secluded behind screens. Only the foot was visible. A frame of some sort lifted the bed coverings over one leg.

The doctor noticed India had fallen behind and was staring at the frame. Sympathy played in his eyes before he regained his stern, professional manner. "I'm afraid this man has lost his right leg. By the time he reached us, the infection was too far gone, and we had to amputate below the knee. He lay in a muddy shell hole for a day or two before medics discovered he was alive. They searched for his identity discs but found nothing. He has been in a coma since he arrived. His mind has shut down so that his body can heal, I believe." He gestured toward the bed. "Are we ready?"

India closed her eyes and stepped to the other side of the screen. She said a quick prayer, then opened them and looked upon Charlie's battered, bruised, beautiful face.

Her knees buckled. She grabbed the top of the iron footboard as she choked back a cry. The room spun for a moment and then righted itself. She raced to the side of the bed and dropped to her knees.

Taking his hand, she said, "Charlie, it's me, India. Can you hear me? Please come back to us." No response came from the bed other than the measured breathing of an unconscious man. "Please, Charlie." Her voice was a sob-filled plea.

The doctor put his hand on her shoulder. "I am very glad you've found your husband. You may come to see him whenever you wish. Your presence may help him come back from the depths."

"No."

"No? But surely you wish to visit your husband now that you have found him."

"No, I am going to take him home. He will recover faster in familiar surroundings."

"But we have the latest treatments here. You cannot possibly give him proper care."

"I can give him something you never will."

"Which is?"

"Love. He will be surrounded by people who care about him in a place that is his whole life. How soon can I engage one of your ambulances?"

CHAPTER 44

"Lady Kilnsey, we cannot simply loan out government property. We need all our ambulances on site. We take in wounded men every week. We simply cannot spare one."

"It's only twenty-six miles. Vehicles can come and go in a few hours, four at most. Surely you don't need every ambulance every single afternoon of every single day." Her tone was imperious and rude. She didn't care. She would have Charlie home no matter who she had to harass or bully. She would use her position and the estate's wealth to ride roughshod over every obstacle all the way to the Prime Minister, if needs be. "I saw two sitting idle as we arrived." Looking out the window, she pointed. "There they are, still performing no service whatsoever."

"Madame, surely you can understand that we must be prepared for all eventualities. Just because the ambulances are not in constant use does not mean we can loan them out to anyone who asks."

India stepped closer to the doctor and drew herself up to her full height. She was several inches shorter than he, but he looked intimidated as she glared at him through narrowed eyes. "I am not anyone. I am Lady Kilnsey, wife of the Fifteenth Earl Kilnsey. You will either transport my husband to our home or Lord Derby shall hear of it. It was he who assisted me in my search." Turning to the private detective, she continued, "Our solicitor should be informed that these people are holding His Lordship hostage."

The doctor held up his hands palms out in self-defense. "Please. There's no need to involve the Secretary for War or your legal advisor. I'm sure we can work something out."

"I want His Lordship in an ambulance headed to Kilnsey Castle within the hour."

"But his medical condition .... How can you possibly provide the care he needs?"

"And exactly how are you caring for him here? I see no progress being made in ending his coma. He will be far better off in familiar surroundings."

The doctor's mouth became a thin line. When he spoke, irritation colored his words. "And care of the amputation site?"

"We have a very competent doctor in Kilnsey Village. He has treated serious injury throughout his career. In case you are unaware, farming has its own set of dangers." India crossed her arms over her bosom. "Well?"

The doctor placed an arm on his stomach and rested his other elbow on it then supported his chin with the extended hand. He searched India for what felt an eternity. Finally, he laughed. "I see you are a woman with whom to be reckoned. Are you positive my ambulance will be away from camp for no more than two hours at most?"

"I do."

The doctor snapped his fingers, and an orderly appeared. "Prepare this patient for transport." He picked up Charlie's chart and studied it. "Yes, that will do nicely." He handed the chart to the orderly. "Tell Sister Fitzpatrick to see me at once."

The orderly's eyes widened. "But she . . . "

The doctor gave the young man a stern look. "Do as I say and do it now."

"Yes, sir." The orderly chuckled as he walked away toward the nurses' offices.

India extended her hand, which the doctor took. "Thank you. I appreciate the care you've given His Lordship. You no doubt saved his life. I will write to Lord Derby praising you and your staff. If you will excuse me now, I must alert my driver and prepare for the trip home."

As she walked away, she could have sworn the doctor muttered something about praise for his staff perhaps being a bit premature. To Althea, she said, "Did you hear that?"

"Uh-huh. I guess we'll find out what he means pretty soon."

When they reached the Rolls, India said, "I want you all to go on ahead. Please tell Mrs. Wilson we will put His Lordship in the library and will need a bed placed there immediately. Mrs. Bertrand is to have a plain, nourishing evening meal prepared. I will travel in the ambulance with His Lordship."

Althea gave her an astonished look. "Surely not. They'll never allow it."

"With you three and the auto gone, they will have no choice. Now, get on with it."

Althea and Mr. Sykes climbed into the vehicle while Ainsworth turned the crank. The engine roared and within a minute they were trundling toward the camp entrance. The last India saw of them was Althea's unhappy face looking back at her through the rear window.

Tires crunching signaled the arrival of the ambulance. Presently, two orderlies bearing a stretcher exited the hospital. Charlie lay calm and oblivious. Following on their heels was a large, red-faced woman in nurse's uniform.

Sister Fitzpatrick gave India a quick once-over. "You must be the wife." She then turned her attention to the orderlies. "Hey, you two. Get that stretcher clamped down tight and the patient well strapped in. I will box your ears if we have flying bodies on this wretched trip." To India, she said, "How're you getting home? I thought you arrived in a fancy auto." Her tone was derisive.

"I'm riding in the ambulance with my husband."

"You will do no such thing. I can't have a civilian mucking about with my patient." Her voice rang in the crisp air.

Heat crept from India's throat onto her cheeks. "He may be your patient for the next hour, but he is my husband now and forever."

"The next hour? I'm being dispatched to care for this man until further notice."

India placed a fist on each hip. "And just who invited you into my home?"

For the first time, the nurse looked a little unsure. "The doctor told me to go with him and care for him until he recovers. I have my orders right here."

She held out a paper embossed with a military crest. As India read the document, she began to get the picture. The doctor apparently disliked Sister Fitzpatrick and she, India, had given him the excuse he needed to be rid of her, at least for a while. As much as she disliked being used, India had to admit she could use the help. After all, she had no medical training.

Folding the paper and returning it to the nurse, she said, "I see. Let's start over, shall we?" India held out her hand. "I am Lady Kilnsey. My husband is Fifteenth Earl Kilnsey. We live at Kilnsey Castle. You will be made comfortable during your stay."

Sister Fitzpatrick looked at India's hand, then at her face. Finally, she grasped the hand. "Thank you. I will ride with the driver. You may sit in the van with His Lordship. If you need me, rap on the window."

India climbed into the ambulance and sat on the floor beside Charlie. She stroked his forehead and caressed his cheek. Leaning in, she kissed his lips, hoping intimate contact would stir some deep memory in him and bring him to the surface. Because she could think of nothing else, she chattered as they traveled.

Her view of the road was limited to what she could see through the small windows at the front of the van. She knew the route well, so narrated their journey mostly from memory. They rounded a distinctive curved in the road.

India fell back against the wall, then righted herself. "We're passing Ripon Cathedral, Darling. We haven't been there since the Bartlett's daughter married that bounder, against her parents' wishes, of course. Her father gave the new husband a job managing the breeding program. It was said they preferred having him where they could keep an eye on him. The girl was pregnant or the parents would never have agreed to the marriage. By all accounts, he made good with the horses before he joined the army." She stopped there. What she did not want to say was that the bounder had been killed at the Somme.

She talked until her throat was dry and a touch sore. They bumped over the River Wharfe. "Darling, we're almost home. I can just see Kilnsey Crag."

"Old..."

The sound was faint. She was not sure she had heard it or whether it was her profound desire playing havoc with her imagination. She leaned close to Charlie's mouth. "Darling, I can see the crag fully now. You remember Kilnsey Crag, don't you? We have picnicked atop it."

"Old Nan." That time the words were distinct. While his eyes remained closed, Charlie had spoken.

“Yes, yes. Old Nan, the witch who lived under the crag long ago. Your father used to frighten you with tales of her when you were little. Old Nan. You do remember, don’t you, Darling?”

“Yes.” It was soft, a mere whisper, but he had spoken.

He would come back to them. That was the most wonderful Christmas present she could ever wish for. India buried her face in the blankets covering his chest and wept. All the tension of the war years and fear for Charlie seeped into the coarse wool. It didn’t matter that he had lost a leg. It meant he would never have to go to war again. People managed with missing limbs every day. He would, too.

CHAPTER 45

Christmas was once again a quiet affair with not one, but two patients in Kilnsey Castle. Charlie drifted between moments of partial lucidity and unconsciousness. Sister Fitzpatrick said he was healing from the inside out, but it was hard to see it. Mama had been confined to bed since the day India went to Leeds. She wanted to visit Charlie in the library, but the nurse forbade it.

In early January, India placed her hand against Mama's forehead. "You're burning up. I'm sending for the doctor. He will attend both Charlie and you. I will brook no refusals. In the meantime, I shall ask Sister Fitzpatrick to look at you."

As she rang for a maid, India glanced back at the bed. Mama was positively gray, with eyes sunken back in her skull. Her breathing was labored. Each breath rattled. The maid came and went, then the nurse arrived.

She placed a thermometer in Mama's mouth and felt her pulse. "We must get her temperature down. It is dangerously high. Send for the doctor at once."

"It's already been done. I'll get cold water."

India went to Mama's bathroom and filled the porcelain bowl once used for washing face and hands before the castle was plumbed for running water. She grabbed a washcloth and towel. Returning to the bed, she placed the basin on the bedside table, dampened the cloth, and handed it to the nurse.

Watching the care with which Sister Fitzpatrick bathed Mama's face, India said, "I haven't said how much I appreciate what you're doing for my family. You are an excellent nurse. I'm surprised the hospital can function without you."

The sister stopped swabbing and fixed India with a stern look. "Oh, I think we both know why the doctor sent me here."

Heat played across India's cheeks. "I've guessed you two don't get along, but you are such an asset. Whatever he has against you, he's wrong. You are a godsend."

Fitzpatrick's mouth lifted in an ironic smile. "He and I have different ideas about how a hospital ward should be run. I believe patient care comes first. He thinks doctors' convenience is paramount. We've nearly come to blows on more than one occasion."

India chuckled. "Why do I think you would win a bout of fisticuffs?"

The sister gave her a wry smile in return. "In truth, we needed a break from one another. When I return to camp, perhaps we will have more patience with each other." Her demeanor softened. "If I'm honest, I must say I've enjoyed my time here. You have been most gracious. I haven't felt this at ease since before the war. It isn't only soldiers who suffer trauma at the front."

"Were you in France long?"

"Long enough to have seen too much."

India nodded. "I'm happy we've returned the care you've given my family."

She would have said more, but the maid, Betsy, burst into the room. "Milady, come quick. His Lordship is awake and calling for you."

India met Dr. Millhouse coming through the Grand Staircase hall. "You made very good time. The sister is with Mama. Her fever is quite high. His Lordship is asking for me."

The doctor nodded. "I'll meet you in the library presently."

India flew to Charlie's bedside and dropped to her knees. He appeared fully awake and aware. She ran a hand over his hair, then trailed her fingers along his jaw. "Oh, my darling. You have come back to us."

He gave her a puzzled smile. "Have I been gone long?"

She laughed and kissed him. "Yes, for a long time, but you are home now."

He looked at the frame over his right leg. "What's that thing?"

India swallowed hard and forced her voice into as normal a tone as she could manage. "It's nothing to worry about. For now, you must regain your strength."

He closed his eyes. "I'm tired. I think I'll sleep for a while."

"Yes, darling. You do that."

India sat by his side holding his hand until Dr. Millhouse arrived. "He has awakened. He spoke and knew where he is, and he knew me. He's just resting right now."

"That's wonderful, my dear. I am not surprised. The story of your ride home in the ambulance was a very good sign." The doctor came to the end of the bed and lifted the bedcovers. "Has he realized his situation?"

"He did ask, but I thought it best to delay the news until he's stronger."

"Yes, yes, probably best." He unwrapped the bandages from around the amputation site. "This is healing nicely. Soon we will dispense with the wrappings other than to keep the site comfortable. These places can be very tender for quite a while. Wouldn't want it to become irritated."

India turned away while the wound was completely exposed. It hurt to see what the war had done to Charlie's beautiful body. "How is Mama? She looks terrible."

"I fear she is not doing as well as I would hope. I've left medicine. How long is that nurse going to stay? She's the best I've worked with. Would love to have her in charge of the nursing staff in our little hospital once this dustup in France is over."

"I didn't know you were planning a hospital for Kilnsey."

He rewrapped Charlie's leg. "Oh, yes. Didn't I say? We will have many injured local boys returning from war who would rather receive care close to home. They shouldn't have to travel to Leeds or York for it. I'm hoping His Lordship will be our patron. What do you think?"

"Well, I can't speak for him, but I suspect he will agree. Would you like for me to speak with His Lordship on your behalf?"

"That would be most kind. Please do."

Right before bedtime, India looked in on Mama and administered a dose of Dr. Millhouse's medicine. Mama made a face. "Awful, simply awful. Tastes like turpentine, but it seems to be helping. I haven't coughed as much."

India smiled at Mama's simile. An English countess could not possibly know how turpentine tasted. She picked up the bottle and took a whiff. Her eyes watered. Mama might be right about the turpentine. "It does have a distinct odor. I'm glad it's helping. Dr. Millhouse is a good physician."

Mama nodded. "Old sawbones that he is. He's delivered every baby in the county, I believe, including Charlie." A crease formed between eyes that were dark with worry. "How is my son?"

"He was fully awake and completely aware. The doctor thinks he will be sitting up in another day or two."

"Does he know about his leg?"

"No. He will soon enough."

"To think he will be a cripple for the rest of his life is unbearable. My beautiful boy." Mama placed her hand over her mouth.

India embraced Mama. "It will be all right. At least he's alive. At least we have him home. We should be grateful. So many families' boys will never come home."

"Of course, you are right. I worry about how he will manage. The thought of him hobbling around on crutches for the rest of his life is appalling."

"Charlie is young, strong, and intelligent. He will find a way to cope. What he needs from us is our love, support, and confidence in his abilities."

"Correct again." Mama pulled away and turned to face India. "You have grown into the perfect countess, my dear, albeit an American one. Luck was with us the day Charlie chose you."

India kissed Mama's cheek. "I learned from the best. Now, go to sleep as the doctor ordered."

By the time India reached the bedroom door, Mama snored softly. It was not only Charlie for whom she was grateful. With each chest cold, India feared the worst for Mama. They had received a reprieve with this one. Pray that would be the case for many years to come. Castle Kilnsey would not be the same without its matriarch.

The door clicked shut, but India's progress toward her own bed was cut short.

"Bloody hell." Charlie's cry rang through the castle.

CHAPTER 46

India flew to the library, where Charlie sat upright with the bed covers thrown off the frame over his stump. He was completely alert for the first time since they brought him home. The combination of rest, medicine, and constant care had worked, but now the real work would begin. He must learn to live with this new reality.

"What the hell happened to my leg?" India tried to wrap him in her arms, but he shoved her away. "Why didn't you tell me? Did you think I would somehow not notice that I'm missing half of my goddamned leg?"

India took both of his hands in hers and fixed him with a firm look. "I did not tell you because you needed to use your strength to recover your senses, which you obviously have done." She then recounted what she learned from the Leeds Camp doctor.

At the end of her explanation, his body relaxed a little. He looked absolutely miserable. Shaking his head, he said, "I remember crawling out of the trench to try to find help. I thought some of the boys might still be alive. I remember falling into a shell hole. After that, everything is a blank."

India took his face in her hands and forced him to look her in the eye. "That squares up with what little we know. The camp doctor thinks you must have hit your head when you fell into the shell hole. It took a day or more for the medics to realize you were alive. They tried to save your leg. They really did, but by the time you got to Leeds, the infection was out of control. If they hadn't taken it, you would have died of sepsis."

He broke free and looked away. "Maybe it would have been better that way."

Shocked at the bitterness in his voice, India slapped the headboard. "Stop it. Don't you dare say that. You have people who love you and need you. Other men and families are dealing with situations like this, and we will too."

"But how can you want a life with a cripple, one with an ugly stump where a leg should be? How can you want to be a wife to me or for me to be a husband to you?"

India stood and shook her fist in his face. "How little you know me. Do you really think I have stopped loving you, wanting you?" Her voice rolled around the room. "I am proud of the man you are. You did your duty when you could well have shirked it. We will adjust as people do, as they must. Be grateful you are alive and have people who will take care of you."

Charlie picked up the frame and threw it across the room. It clattered into a broken heap in the corner. "Can't you understand? I don't want to be taken care of. I want my old life back."

India boiled. "Well, guess what? Everyone would like the life we had before the damned war, but we aren't going to get it. Wish with one hand and spit in the other. See which one fills up first."

Charlie looked startled, then a grin crawled across his face. He snickered, then chuckled, then howled. When the hysterics passed, he wiped away tears and asked, "And just where did you pick up that vulgar expression?"

Smacking him would feel good. India locked her fingers behind her back to forestall temptation. "Nanny Gordon. It was a favorite of hers."

"I wish I could have known your old nursemaid. She must have been a fount of homespun wisdom."

"She was the rock foundation in my otherwise confusing childhood."

"Now you're claiming to have been a poor little rich girl?"

"No, but you don't have a corner on the market when it comes to difficult parents. Surely your time with my mother in New York and London taught you that. Your father may have been hard to live with, but would you want to live with Mother?"

He stroked his chin. "You have a point." He paused, and his expression became solemn. "But what are we going to do? How will I be able to function?"

"We will do what we must."

***

Charlie's crutches thumped on the Grand Staircase. India looked toward the dining room door and sighed. That thumping was a bittersweet sound. He had survived war, but he believed himself to be a lesser man. Almost a year had passed since she brought him home from Leeds Camp hospital. He had worked hard to regain his former life. He had joined her in the estate office and acquainted himself with the years of her management. He had rejoiced with her when Parliament passed the Representation of the People Act, enabling her to cast her vote once she attained the age of thirty, only two years off. He made the rounds of the tenant farms and was greeted as a friend, but he would never again be able to do the physical labor he had loved. There were days when despair seemed as if it would completely overtake him, but he soldiered on. She and Mama would not let it be otherwise.

Taking up the newspaper, India read the Times front page again, then shoved it aside and drifted in memory. Life had changed so much since June 1914. Adeline had only been a month old and India had looked forward to a peaceful life with Charlie and the hope of more children arriving quickly. Surely one of them would have been a son and heir. But then, Archduke Franz Ferdinand was assassinated and the world exploded into war. The Bolsheviks now ruled Russia, their power grab destroying the royal family and ending the Romanov line. America finally abandoned her policy of isolation and joined the fight. This war to end all wars had been very costly in terms of human suffering. It had cost Charlie his leg. His life would never be the same. Maybe today's headlines would improve his spirit and outlook. In a moment, he would join her for breakfast.

The dining room door opened, and he made his way to the table's head. India passed the Times to him. He read the headline and eagerly scanned the front page, then looked at India. "Thank God." He hit the table with the flat of his hand. "Thank God it's finally over."

For the next few minutes, he read aloud, describing how the Kaiser had abdicated and fled to Holland, how the German generals had signed the armistice in a rail car outside Paris, how the total cost in terms of men and resources were staggering. When he finished, he wilted against his chair.

"I feel limp, like a wet rag that has been wrung dry. That's an odd feeling in the face of such wonderful news, don't you think?"

India took his hand and ran her thumb over his knuckles. "No, not particularly, but I would describe it as a spring suddenly being released after having been wound tightly for far too long."

He raised her hand to his lips and kissed it. "You're right. I have forgotten what it feels like to be completely relaxed, without tension and stress." He turned to Ainsworth. "Do we have any of the Pol Roger left?"

"Yes, My Lord. There are several bottles in the cellar."

"Good, good. Bring all of them up, then have the staff assemble here. Today we have cause for celebration. I want everyone to join in. Please send word to my mother, also."

After the butler left, India laughed. "Champagne at this time of day? Mama will be scandalized."

Charlie grinned, then the smile faded and he became solemn. "If the end of this godawful war is not reason to celebrate, there will never be one good enough."

***

March 17, 1919

My dearest India,

As you might imagine, New York is alight with St. Patrick's Day celebrations and the streets are clogged due to the parade. Jonathan and I went out to watch it for the first time in years. Somehow, it seemed our patriotic duty. I suppose the feeling was created by having a newly returned military unit marching alongside the usual participants. It was very invigorating.

As a follow up to my last letter, I have now completed my investigations into prosthetics and have discovered something quite astonishing. I could not wait a moment longer to write. It seems the US is far advanced in the field due to the ravages of last century's Civil War. I implore you to convince my stubborn, foolish brother to cross the pond and take advantage of our doctors' knowledge. Use all means of persuasion. Kidnap him if needs be. He must come here for the best care.

I am glad Mama's health has been restored. Give her my love and tell her I will write tomorrow.

I must close now. We are off to a dinner hosted by one of Jonathan's business associates. It is wonderful life is returning to pre-war normalcy!

Your devoted sister-in-law,

Clarissa

India tapped her pen against the blotter on her little desk in the bedroom suite parlor. With Robbie soon to be demobilized and to retake the reins of estate management, it might be possible to convince Charlie to go to New York. She dropped her pen and went in search of her husband.

***

Althea paced impatiently. The train should have arrived by now, but then nothing seemed to run on time these days. She cupped her hand over her eyes to guard against the July sun's glare and stared into the distance. Robbie was coming home for good. After almost five years of separation, they would once again live in their little Cragfast Mastiles cottage and be a normal old married couple. Her heart was full. If a person could explode with joy, then no one near her was safe.

Her vigil was at last rewarded. The faint sound of a train whistle drifted toward the depot. Soon, smoke from the engine stack would appear at the bend. She glanced at the edge of the depot yard to see if India had heard the whistle. India waved and smiled encouragingly. That girl was closer and dearer to her than her sisters were now. Althea thanked God every day that she had agreed to take a chance on a new life in England. India had her Charlie, and she had her adored Robbie. Life was full and wonderful.

Thinking of Charlie, she eyed him waiting patiently by the Rolls, the recently demobilized Barton at his side. India's plans to take him across the Atlantic could now be set in motion. The man had no idea there would soon be four people, including his mother, who were prepared to drag him onto a New York bound ocean liner, if necessary.

The whistle sounded again and the engine came into view. Althea started waving with such vigor that she might have dislocated her shoulder, but it was worth the risk. Robbie had raised the carriage window and was waving in return. Her life would soon be complete.

***

India leaned on RMS Adriatic's railing and breathed in the salty air of the September morning. The Statue of Liberty's upraised arm grew closer with every ripple created by the ship's bow and brought with it both excitement and anxiety. She had not seen Mother in over five years. The war had prevented her returning for Grandmama Van de Berg's funeral. She faced the return to her native land with mixed emotions.

Charlie settled beside her and placed one crutch against the railing. He slipped an arm around her shoulders. "Do you remember the first time we passed Lady Liberty together?"

India tilted her head. "Hmmm. I believe you compared yourself to members of the huddled masses yearning to breathe free or something like that."

"What I said was that I found her promise alluring and the lady herself magnificent. I still do."

"Should I be jealous?"

"Only if you think you might turn into a metal statue. Otherwise, you have first place in my heart now and forever."

He kissed her temple. “I want to send a cable to Mama as soon as we go ashore. She is ever anxious for our safety. I think having had friends on the Titanic and the Lusitania left a mark.”

“How could it not?” India laid her head on his shoulder. “I love your mother. She said the sweetest thing to me while you were ill.”

“Well, don’t stop there. What did she say?”

“She said I have made a good countess and that you both were lucky the day you chose me.”

“She’s right, you know. You are my wonderful American countess. I am the luckiest man alive.”

India’s heart leapt. Maybe the veil of self-doubt and despair was lifting from him. He had been more at ease on this voyage than he had in months. “And being your countess is the greatest privilege and joy any woman could have. Surely that makes me the luckiest woman alive.”

He hugged her closer. “Do you think you will regret not having Althea come with us? I know you look on her as more than a companion.”

“No. She and Robbie will see that things run smoothly at home. They deserve the time together. They were separated for as many years as we were, you know. Besides, Mama has come to depend on her quite as much as I do. She was rather cross when Althea moved from the castle back to their cottage.”

India and Charlie slipped into a companionable silence and stood with their arms around one another until the ship reached Ellis Island. India searched the crowded dock for Charlie’s sister, Clarissa, and her husband, Jonathan Rivers, the prominent New York banker. She found them waving madly in front of the baggage area.

A ship’s steward approached. “Lord and Lady Kilnsey?” When they nodded, he continued, “The captain has instructed me to ensure that you disembark comfortably. Please follow me."

As the steward gestured toward the gangway, India said, "Please see that our child and her nurse are escorted to us."

"Of course. Shall we go before the crush begins?"

Within minutes, they hugged Clarissa and Jonathan.

India looked around, then asked Clarissa, "Where are Mother and David?"

"Your mother and stepfather will be joining us for dinner. Your mother may be hurt that you are staying with us. She has mentioned several times that she does not understand why you insisted on staying with us." Clarissa placed her fists on her hips in a position Mother often adopted when provoked. "I am her mother, after all." Clarissa's imitation of Mother was spot on.

Guilt speared India, but she ignored it. "I suspect she is, but you have made the arrangements with the doctors." When Clarissa eyed her with a speculative expression, India continued, "I don't really want to be with Mother for extended periods. She is demanding and can only see her own point of view. I should be ashamed to say it, but it's the truth."

Clarissa gave her a sympathetic look. "There is no shame in knowing what one can tolerate. We all have our limits even where loved ones are concerned." Her attention shifted, and she waved toward a woman and child approaching. "Oh, look. Is that baby Adeline? She's such a big girl. I'd forgotten she's not really a baby anymore." Clarissa held out her arms and five-year-old Adeline went right to her for a hug and a kiss. India was amazed. Usually, Adeline was shy with strangers.

Turning to India, Clarissa said, "The car is waiting. Shall we?"

CHAPTER 47

India watched Charlie struggle with his evening suit trousers. Dressing for dinner, or any other occasion for that matter, had become a contest of wills. His stubborn refusal to hire a new valet was infuriating. There must be hundreds of men discharged from service who would gladly fill the position and do a good job. His prewar valet, Yarboro, had gone with him as his batman and was killed in the same mortar bombardment that cost Charlie his leg. Guilt and loyalty ruled his decision, or rather created his inertia, where the position of valet was concerned.

India edged closer to Charlie. "Please, let me help you."

He frowned and snarled, "I can manage." He swayed to one side. Grunting, he grabbed the bedpost only just preventing a fall to the floor. "Goddammit. This bloody stump keeps me off balance." Defeat radiated from him as he plopped down on the edge of the bed. He studied the pattern in the carpet and muttered, "I apologize for speaking sharply. Please help me with these wretched things."

She helped him stand and pulled his trousers up while he held onto the bedpost. Once she had the waistband secured and the suspenders buttoned in place, she knelt and folded up the trouser leg over his stump and pinned it in place.

She rose and caressed the nape of his neck with both hands. "You really seem to not know how devastatingly attractive you are. Tonight, you will have to fight me off."

He searched her for a moment before giving her a lopsided grin. "I'm not a fool. Fighting you off is the furthest thing from my mind." He ran a finger under her chin. "You, my darling, should be prepared for a night of connubial bliss."

At the appointed time, they descended to the first-floor drawing room for pre-dinner drinks. Everyone else was already assembled. The gentlemen stood at their arrival. India paused in the doorway and met Mother's gaze. She went to her and placed a kiss on Mother's cheek. Next, she went to David, her stepfather, and gave him an awkward hug while he kissed her cheek.

Drinks and dinner presented more opportunities for awkwardness. Mother questioned Clarissa repeatedly about the doctors Charlie was to see. Over dessert, she glared at India. "I see no reason for you and your family to be here with Lady Clarissa and Mr. Rivers instead of with me. Adeline is my granddaughter, after all. By refusing to be my guest you are deliberately keeping me from her."

India wanted to scream, but she kept a grip on her temper. "You may see Adeline whenever you wish. As I have said, it is easier for us here. Clarissa has set up a nursery with an adjoining room for Adeline's nurse, something you are unable to do. Jonathan has arranged all the appointments. It is his chauffeur who will transport us to them." It was time to change the subject. "You have not told me. What have you decided to do with the Washington Square house?"

"We've rented it to a nice young couple. We talked about selling it, but it has been in the family since it was built in 1833. I couldn't bear to part with it."

It was comforting knowing Grandmama's house would remain in the family, but a less pleasant subject must be addressed. India placed her fork on the plate and studied the residue of the Charlotte Russe. Now was as good a time as any. Looking at her stepfather, she said, "David, I have a task I'm hoping you will help me with."

David Havemeyer looked surprised. "As conservator of your father's estate, I've always been happy to help you. What may I do?"

"Do you or your law partners ever use the services of a private detective?"

"I can't say I've personally had the need, but the firm does keep a very reliable man on retainer. Why do you ask?"

"There is someone who should have been part of my life but was not. Rumors of her, among other things, ruined my New York debut. Surely you remember the questions I asked and you so kindly answered on that awful evening. I intend to either find her or put her ghost to rest once and for all time."

Mother's face flamed. "You will do no such thing. Why rake up all of that? No one even speaks of her now. Everyone has forgotten."

India fixed Mother with a determined look. "Everyone but me."

"You are just a silly child. Why can't you leave well enough alone?"

"You say I am a child, but I'm twenty-eight. I have successfully managed an ancient English estate while my husband did his patriotic duty. Because of the work of our suffragists, with whom I played a small part, I'll be able to cast my vote when I turn thirty. I have a right to know what happened to my father's mother."

Clarissa rose and fixed India with a reproving smile. "Surely this can wait for another day. Ladies, shall we leave the gentlemen to their port?"

Charlie studied India, then said, "I think my wife should stay in the dining room long enough to explain to David what she has in mind."

Mother glared at Charlie. "Do you mean to say you approve of this . . . this ridiculous venture?"

Charlie reached across the table, and India placed her hand in his. "My beautiful, kind, accomplished wife should have whatever her heart desires. She has earned it. If she wishes to discover what happened to her Grandmother Ledbetter, then so be it."

Mother puffed up like an angry hen. "You have doctor's appointments. Her place is with you."

"I've lost a leg, not my mind or my ability to make decisions for myself. India will accompany me to the initial appointments where the diagnosis and treatment plans are discussed. After that, she is free to go with me or pursue other interests as she sees fit. In fact, I see no reason for her to attend the therapy sessions, which I hope will be part of my recovery."

"But . . . but our name. My family's reputation. What will people think?"

India could hold back no longer. "I thought you said no one talks about her anymore. If so, then you have nothing to worry about. I'm sure David's law firm would not hire anyone who is indiscreet. The only way the people who count, as you and Grandmama always referred to them, will know is if you tell them."

Mother turned to her husband. "David, I will not countenance your assisting in this absurd search. Jane Ledbetter died long ago. My first husband always believed his mother was deceased, as his father said."

India watched for David's reaction. He was the great love of Mother's life, the man she yearned for all the years of her marriage to Papa. In Mother's defense, she had essentially been sold by her own mother, Grandmama Van de Berg. The nuptials between Mother and Papa had been a merger rather than a wedding. Grandfather Ledbetter had bought some secondhand respectability by marrying his son into one of New York's founding families. Grandmama Van de Berg had received a financial settlement that enabled her to return to her former style of living, although she never returned to the level of respect and esteem in which she was once held. Old, revered family names and connections only went so far in protecting her from scandal.

David didn't answer for several moments. Finally, he rose and went to Mother. Placing an arm around her, he spoke quietly. "Petra, dearest, your daughter has a right to know who her family is or was. I will assist her in this matter because I am her lawyer. You will not object further because you are her mother and you love her. Isn't that right, my dear?"

The man must be a magician because Mother simpered and acquiesced. "Of course, you're right. It's just very upsetting having the ugliness dredged up."

India gripped the edge of the table and glared. "The past was certainly ugly when Grandfather Ledbetter cheated people out of millions, including your father, Grandfather Van de Berg. It was even uglier when Grandfather Van de Berg killed himself over the financial mess and scandal. But all of that is truly in the distant past. Mother, what do you know about Jane that you're not saying?"

Mother fanned herself with her napkin as if she were about to faint. "I know nothing other than what I have always told you."

"I'll bet."

"Don't be vulgar, Daughter."

India looked at Clarissa. "Please take my mother through to the parlor. I'll join you after I have concluded my business with David."

CHAPTER 48

At the end of a month and while Charlie was at a therapy session improving his mobility with his prosthetic leg, India paced Clarissa's parlor, awaiting the arrival of David's private investigator, Mr. Adams. The man called on the telephone to make the appointment. It still felt strange to her, this talking to a disembodied voice traveling over wires linking locations miles apart. Jonathan installed their instrument several years ago, and Charlie was eager for one in the castle.

The front bell rang, and India sank onto a sofa. Mr. Adams asked that someone be with her when he imparted his findings, but India refused. His steps sounded in the foyer and within seconds, the butler announced him.

India extended her hand. "Please sit and tell me what you've learned. I sense you have less than good news about my Grandmother Ledbetter. Is she deceased?"

Mr. Adams looked around the room as if he hoped another person would miraculously appear. When no one materialized, he wet his lips and frowned. "No, she is not deceased. Far from not, in fact. However, what I must reveal is not suitable for a lady's ears. I had very much hoped your husband or brother-in-law would be present."

"It is I who hired you, and I will have the answer to my grandmother's disappearance. Do not keep me in suspense any longer."

Looking pained and defeated, Mr. Adams said, "Well, you see . . . it is . . . she lives here in the city and has for many years." He stared at the floor.

Radiating impatience, India snapped, "Go on. What's the address?"

"Lady Kilnsey, it is a place genteel ladies simply do not visit."

"How intriguing. Tell me the worst and get it over with. I intend to see, no matter the circumstances. Is she in the poorhouse, prison, an insane asylum, what?"

"No, in fact she lives in luxury of a sort."

"Oh, for goodness sake. Spit it out."

Turning a deep shade of crimson, he spluttered, "She lives . . . in a house of ill repute."

India had to admit she had not expected that. She swallowed hard. "Is she a maid? Or perhaps the housekeeper?"

Mr. Adams rolled his eyes. "Hardly. She owns the place." His voice was clear and strong. Probably due to his own rising irritation, Mr. Adams had lost his reluctance. "She is what is referred to as a madam. For a place of its sort, it is of a very high caliber. Your grandmother caters to only the finest quality clientele—wealthy businessmen, legislators, councilmen, foreign dignitaries. I believe she even counts a US senator and a couple of congressmen among her patrons. Her girls are beautiful and clean, if you understand my meaning."

"I see. Please give me the address."

"Please, Lady Kilnsey. You must not go there."

"I want the address. I have paid for it. Now, hand it over."

"I simply do not know what Mr. Rivers or Mr. Havemeyer will say."

"I will deal with my brother-in-law and stepfather. Once, long ago, I asked Mr. Rivers to find my grandmother, and he failed me. Mr. Havemeyer is fully apprised of my intentions." She extended her hand. "I want that address."

Looking aggrieved, he finally placed in her palm an embossed calling card of sorts. Hotel de Jeanne was inscribed in beautiful, flowing script. The address given was at the northern edge of the area known as the Tenderloin. The card bore the motto "For the Discriminating Gentleman."

India needed to be alone to process what she had learned. "Thank you. You have done the job most admirably. Mr. Havemeyer will see to your compensation. You must excuse me now. The butler will show you out."

After Mr. Adams's departure, she waited a few minutes, then went to the front door and stepped onto the sidewalk. Clarissa's house, lovely as it was, suddenly felt like a prison. She needed air and sunshine to help her think. Anger, frustration, and shock made her jumpy and restless. She gazed south along Fifth Avenue. Should she hail a cab or wait for Charlie to arrive from his therapy session? He would no doubt be livid if she went into the Tenderloin unaccompanied, but she had reason to be angry with him, as well.

As she contemplated her next move, Jonathan's auto pulled up to the curb and Charlie, aided by the chauffeur, disembarked.

He took one look at her and said, "What's happened?"

India seethed. "When the Pinkertons were supposed to look for my grandmother before we married, were they ever really contacted?"

He leaned on his cane and fiddled with his prosthesis instead of looking at her. "Why do you ask?"

"Look at me." At her shout, a man passing them increased his pace, no doubt startled by her tone. When Charlie finally met her eye, she jabbed her finger toward the south.

"Because Grandmother Jane lives right here in the city and has for many years. Apparently, she is well known in certain circles."

Charlie's expression cycled between guilt and fear. "Darling, you must understand. We had only your happiness at heart. I could not bear to see you hurt. We felt it best that we not search. If she lived, I wanted to save you from whatever secret she might have been hiding."

"That's no excuse for lying to me."

"You're right. I'm very sorry we deceived you. It seemed best at the time. I did not know you then as I do now. I thought you a fragile, vulnerable young girl. After all, you were still grieving your father's death and had seen very little of the world." He took her hand, which she tried to jerk away. Despite his months of convalescence, he was still much stronger than she. "India, think about it. She clearly did not want to be found or she would have contacted you when your debut or our engagement was announced. Both events were in all the newspapers. Your attendance at balls and dinners was written up for months before either. If she had wanted to meet you, she had plenty of time to let it be known. In all the years you visited your Grandmother Van de Berg did Jane ever once try to contact or see you? For that matter, did she ever contact your father, her own child? There must be reasons she hid from you."

Some of the tension went out of India's body. As angry as she was at being tricked, what Charlie said made sense. Jane did have a secret—a big one. "There is a reason, but let's go inside. I prefer that the neighbors and passersby not know what I've learned."

Once inside, Charlie went to the drinks cart. "I think I'm going to need a drink. Shall I pour one for you, as well?"

"Yes, please."

The parlor door opened and Clarissa entered. "I thought I heard you coming in. How did today's . . . " She did not finish her question. She looked from Charlie to India. "Is this a bad time to join you?"

India shook her head. "No, you'll have to be told eventually. You might as well hear it now."

For the next ten minutes, India recounted all she had learned from the private investigator. Clarissa had the good grace to appear contrite when India described how she felt about being deceived.

When she finished the tale, India said, "I've decided to see Jane before we return to England. I think tomorrow would be as good as any day."

Charlie jerked around to face her. "Please, no, dearest. Please do not put yourself through what can only prove painful. I beg you."

India's lips thinned, and her eyes narrowed. "I've come this far, and I want to know the truth. I will not be deterred."

Charlie looked at Clarissa, who chose to avoid his gaze. Sighing, he said, "Are you going to make an appointment?"

"No, I think I'll simply knock at the door."

"What if she refuses to see you?"

"I'll cross that bridge when I come to it, but I have a strong feeling she will want to see me. After all, I'm the granddaughter she's never met."

Charlie sat forward, his face a study in determination. "Then I'm going with you. I will not have my wife go alone into a brothel, grandmother or no. It's too dangerous. You will oblige me in this, India."

At two o'clock the following day, India dressed in a flattering, conservative ensemble intended to impress, and maybe just a little, to intimidate. It was Worth, of course.

She twirled in front of the mirror. "What do you think? Will this do?"

Charlie gave her a onceover. "You look marvelous, as always. But I have no idea why you are trying so hard. You're not even sure you'll be received."

"She'll see me. I'm confident any woman would be willing to meet her long-lost granddaughter."

"Shall I call for the auto?"

"No, it's a beautiful day. Let's walk to the end of the park, then hail a cab. I need time to screw up my courage." She covered her mouth. "I'm sorry, darling. Let's drive the entire way."

"No, walking is fine. I'm supposed to practice with the prothesis. This will count toward my required daily exercise, if you don't mind being seen with a man using a cane."

India's heart sank. He could go on the turn of a dime from his old, charming, confident self to this man who felt inadequate and insecure. She put her arms around him and gazed into his eyes. "I'm proud to walk or drive or fly or swim or any other form of locomotion you choose. I'm proud of your service and to be your wife. You are the Fifteenth Earl Kilnsey, scion of an ancient and revered line of warriors and nobles and I do love you so."

Walking along Central Park and then hailing a cab gave India the time she needed to plan what she would say when she met Jane. They arrived at the Twenty-fifth Street address David's investigator had provided and ascended the steps of a three-story brownstone. India drew a deep breath, slowly exhaled, and gripped the bell pull.

Presently, a uniformed butler answered. He looked India and Charlie up and down then frowned. "I believe you have the wrong house. If you will give me the address you seek, I will try to be of assistance."

India cleared her throat. "We have the correct address. I wish an interview with Mrs. Jane Ledbetter."

The butler gave her a blank stare. "Whom do you seek?"

Charlie stepped closer to India. "I believe she may go by the name Madame Jeanne now."

The butler's eyes narrowed. "May I ask your business with Madame Jeanne?"

India realized her foot was tapping and stopped it. She must not show impatience or irritation. This man could refuse to deliver her message. Donning her most winning smile, she said, "Please say her granddaughter, Robert's only child, would like to meet her grandmother."

Shock spread over the butler's face. "Please come into the parlor. I will see if Madame is at home."

Upon entering the house, it was India's turn to be shocked. The foyer and parlor were furnished with the most costly and newest decor and amenities. A gallery of oil paintings lined the walls of the entrance and ran along the stairs. The brothel's parlor had rosewood furniture, immense mirrors, and Parisian figures. It was all overdone and somewhat tacky in its opulence, but Jane had clearly done well in her chosen profession.

When they were seated, Charlie grinned and whispered, "Did you notice the bulge under the butler's suit coat?" India shook her head. "I believe our good man is armed with a pistol."

The parlor door clicked open and a woman of about sixty-five entered. She was still beautiful, with only a little gray at her temples. Her complexion glowed with health and artfully applied cosmetics. Her day dress was of the latest fashion and conservative in its cut and design. Had they passed on the street, India would have assumed she was the wife of a successful businessman.

Jane closed the door but did not sit. She studied India with a hard, unsmiling expression. "Yes, you must be Robert's child. You have the look of both your mother and your father about you. And I assume this is Lord Kilnsey? You both made a good match. Congratulations. What do you want?"

India looked at her grandmother in amazement. The woman knew about her marriage to an English earl. Now that the time had finally arrived, the questions stuck in India's throat. She swallowed hard. "For my entire life I was told you were dead. I want to know who you are."

Jane harrumphed. "It may have been best had you not sought me out." Irony colored her words.

"Please. My father, your son, thought you were dead and had very few memories of you. I just want to know what happened. My father would have wanted to know you, if he hadn't been told a lie."

Jane finally sat. "You speak as though my son is dead."

"Then you don't know. He died of dropsy eight years ago. It was in the papers here."

Jane seemed deflated. "I make it a habit to avoid the obituaries. In my line of work, there's nothing to be gained by reading them." Her eyes glittered, and she looked wistful. "Robert was a lovely, sweet child. Did he have a good life?"

"He had a very good life. He loved our home, The Falls, and rarely wanted to leave his horses, gardens, and library. He was a good husband and father. I loved him dearly and still miss him." There was no need to share that Papa's married life had not been exactly happy.

After a moment's silence, Jane's expression hardened again. "I followed your debut and engagement. Some of my most devoted clientele often find their comings and goings written about in the society pages."

"Then why did you never contact me? I'm your granddaughter. Did you just not care?"

"Good God, girl. Do you think your mother or that old battle-axe Elisabeth Van de Berg would have opened their home and arms to me? Do you think their social circle would have welcomed me at the ball? It was far better for you that I stayed away. The women of old New York and the 400 may not deign to know me, but I assure you many of their husbands do."

"I suppose you're right, but would you at least tell me why you never contacted Papa after his father died? He would have welcomed you and provided for you. He would have loved you."

"By the time that bastard T.J. Ledbetter was dead, too much had happened to me. I didn't want to taint my child's life or his marriage with my sordid past. Robert was so little when I was forced to leave him. I thought he wouldn't remember me and that reentering his life would only cause pain and embarrassment."

"What happened with you and T.J.?"

A harsh chuckle filled the parlor. "What happened, indeed. What do you know of him?"

India told all she had learned of his nefarious business dealings, treatment of Grandfather Van de Berg and his resulting suicide, and the divorce, ending with, "I know a lot about him, but very little about why he treated you the way he did. Why did he divorce you?"

"Because T.J. Ledbetter didn't like being a cuckold."

India felt the pieces falling into place. "Who was the other man?"

"It doesn't matter after all this time. What did matter was that T.J. found out about him. My former husband was a hard, mean man. He was a cold, distant husband. I turned to the other man to fill the void in my life and because I was so very lonely. No one would receive us. T.J.'s reputation saw to that. He divorced me for adultery. Part of the decree stipulated I would receive a little money if I gave up all claims to Robert. Otherwise, I would get nothing and still be barred from seeing my child."

India glanced around the room. "But why this . . . life?"

"The divorce settlement was small and soon ran out. I had no education or employable skills thanks to my own father, but I still had my looks and a head for business." She gestured, indicating the room's contents. "I've done very well, as you can see. I plan to retire soon. I have a little cottage on the far end of Long Island. It looks out over the ocean. I have friends there who know nothing about my life here. They believe I am a moderately well-off widow. I'll be happy there. Speaking of houses, what are you planning to do with the monstrosity in North Carolina?"

"I've directed my attorney to see that a school for the mountain children is established in the mews. The terms of T.J.'s will prevent the main house being used for anything other than a memorial to himself, but the outbuildings are large and will be converted. The will made no mention of how the outbuildings were to be used, so we've taken a liberal interpretation."

Jane raised an eyebrow. "Smart *and* a philanthropist. My, my. Maybe Robert wasn't my husband's son after all. No one related to T.J. Ledbetter ever considered the plight of the less fortunate as far as I know." India couldn't stifle a gasp. Jane laughed and said, "Oh, don't look so shocked. I'm joking. Robert was born before my amour with my lover began."

Heat crawled across India's cheeks. To have a female speak of such delicate matters so openly was a bit unnerving. "Thank you for telling me about your life. You didn't have to, but you've helped me understand more about myself. You have a great-granddaughter. When we return to New York in the future, may we visit you on Long Island?"

Jane rested her fingertips against her mouth and considered the request. "No, I don't think so. You remind me too much of what I lost. You seem a sweet child and I'm sure I would have adored being your grandmother if circumstances had been different. As it is, this must be the last time you contact me. I will not receive you if you call again. Now, I must ask you to say goodbye."

Out on the sidewalk again, Charlie put his arm around India's waist and leaned close. "Well, that was an abrupt dismissal. Are you all right, my darling? You look a little bruised around the heart."

"I'm okay. I'll be better when we're home in Kilnsey. I didn't realize how much I would miss Mama, Althea, Robbie, even Cousin Archie. I miss his dreadfully boring sermons. Can you believe it?"

***

Two weeks to the day after the interview with Jane, India and Charlie once again stood with their arms entwined, watching Lady Liberty slip past.

Charlie nuzzled India's ear and said, "I'm glad to be going home. With this new leg, I feel as if I can be useful again. I'll be able to ride instead of using the pony cart. I can't do the physical labor as I once did, so I've decided on a different way to serve our community."

"Oh, I *am* glad. What are you considering?"

"Do you remember before the war I was approached about seeking a seat in Parliament? I'm again being encouraged to do so. What do you think? Could you bear being a political wife?"

"Since I was political long before you, I don't suppose I can object, but I need to know. Lords or Commons?"

"Well, it is the Liberals who are asking."

"Will you mind being in the Commons rather than the Lords?"

"No, I believe the Commons are the future. The Lords' power is waning. We're looking toward a new world with new ideas about the rights of every man."

"And woman."

"Yes, of course. I won't miss any opportunities to advance your cause."

"I'm glad because I may . . . ."

"May what?"

"Have to miss some chances to advance the cause."

"Why would that be?"

"Because I've missed something rather important. I believe I'm going to be rather busy over the next few months.

Charlie cast her a sidewise glance. "Busy doing what?"

India smiled up at the man who had become her life and her world. Charlie would have new opportunities to feel involved and useful, and she had an important job ahead of her, as well. Now was the perfect time to make her announcement. "Darling, my most beloved husband, I shall be busy producing your heir, the Sixteenth Earl Kilnsey."

ABOUT THE AUTHOR

Linda Bennett Pennell has been in love with the past for as long as she can remember. Anything with a history, whether shabby or majestic, recent or ancient, instantly draws her in. It probably comes from being part of a large extended family that spanned several generations. Long summer afternoons on her grandmother's wrap around porch or winter evenings gathered by the fireplace were filled with stories both entertaining and poignant. Of course, being set in the American South, those stories were also peopled by some very interesting characters, some of whom have found their way into Linda's work.

Linda resides in the Houston, Texas area with her sweet husband and an adorable Labradoodle, Lulu, who is quite certain she's a little girl, not a dog.

DON'T MISS WHERE THE STORY BEGAN!

NOTE FROM LINDA BENNETT PENNELL

Word-of-mouth is crucial for any author to succeed. If you enjoyed *The American Countess,* please leave a review online—anywhere you are able. Even if it's just a sentence or two. It would make all the difference and would be very much appreciated.

Thanks!
Linda Bennett Pennell

Made in United States
Orlando, FL
22 November 2023

39296194R00200